"Where did he go?"

Grady shook his head, lifting up to sit. "I don't know."

Skylar sat up, as well. She scooted across the floor toward the driver's side. As she moved she looked around for a toolbox. A knife. Even a sharp piece of metal would help her to break the ties that secured her hands and feet.

Before she could reach for the driver's seat to climb in the front, the van started to move.

"What—"

"He's pushing us."

Skylar lifted up and looked in front of the vehicle. "There's a drop-off, a boat ramp. It goes down to a river." Her stomach bottomed out.

Grady's gaze darkened. "Gravelly Point. He's going to drown us in the river."

She hadn't wanted to say that and wasn't all that glad Grady had voiced it out loud. Skylar had never considered the fact she might die like this.

Lisa Phillips is a British-born, tea-drinking, guitar-playing wife and mom of two. She and her husband lead worship together at their local church. Lisa pens high-stakes stories of mayhem and disaster where you can find made-for-each-other love that always ends in a happily-ever-after. She understands that faith is a work in progress more exciting than any story she can dream up. You can find out more about her books at authorlisaphillips.com.

Books by Lisa Phillips

Love Inspired Suspense

Secret Service Agents

Security Detail
Homefront Defenders
Yuletide Suspect
Witness in Hiding
Defense Breach

Double Agent
Star Witness
Manhunt
Easy Prey
Sudden Recall
Dead End

DEFENSE BREACH

LISA PHILLIPS

⟨H⟩HARLEQUIN® LOVE INSPIRED® SUSPENSE

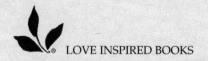 LOVE INSPIRED BOOKS

Recycling programs
for this product may
not exist in your area.

ISBN-13: 978-1-335-54402-5

Defense Breach

Copyright © 2018 by Lisa Phillips

www.Harlequin.com

Printed in U.S.A.

A father of the fatherless, and a judge of the widows,
is God in his holy habitation.
–Psalms 68:5

Thank you, as always, to my wonderful readers
for being so encouraging and inspiring. God bless you!

ONE

Skylar Austin trailed along in a line of veterans and their families waiting for their VIP tour of the White House. As a former army corporal, she'd technically qualified for the tour. However, today she wasn't dressed as herself. Some of the finest deception experts the FBI employed had disguised her as an eighty-two-year-old lady. They were so good she even had wrinkles.

"This way, ma'am."

Skylar nodded to the Secret Service agent, considering whether to call him *son*. No, it was best to stay as quiet as possible. Otherwise she might give herself away. The success of her team—the "hostiles"—meant she had to stay in character. Not let on that she wasn't who her ID said she was. Just the fact that the Secret Service hadn't questioned her fake driver's license said something about the quality of the fabrication.

Did she feel guilty about the fact that she was fooling the Secret Service, breaking into the White House to get up to trouble? No way. They were expecting her team. They would be ready for the exercise. The Secret Service didn't know when it would start, but the hostiles did.

Skylar checked her watch. It was just after six thirty in the morning. Seven minutes until "go" time.

The line of tourists snaked around a security building at the southeast entrance. Skylar had to give them credit. She'd learned a lot in the past few weeks spent at Secret Service training. Security at the White House was good. Almost impenetrable, in fact. She figured *almost* since the Secret Service could never assume a breach of their defenses was impossible.

Soon enough she would be one of them—a real agent. Skylar smiled as she stepped inside the security office. She'd already had the full-body scan. Now she stood by a desk, staffed by a big Secret Service agent. He was sitting, so she couldn't see how tall he was. His dark brown hair was cut short, his eyes denim blue. Brooding.

Sunglasses had been pushed up on top of his head. His bulky vest was covered with pouches, and a dozen things had been clipped to his belt. He pulled a cell phone from the zippered pouch on the left front side of this vest, looked at the screen for a second and then replaced it.

He glanced up at her, caught her staring at him and gave her a perfunctory nod. If she wasn't dressed as an elderly lady she might be offended he hadn't given her more attention than that. Her ex-husband, Earl, had been a flatterer.

Ancient history.

Last month was the second anniversary of their divorce going through. There had been some good times. Early on. Like, really early. Before he'd started cheating on her.

She wasn't going to look at the cute agent again. Skylar was done with relationships. Done like burned toast—throw it in the trash and hit the drive-through on the way to work. Done.

The line inched around the desk, toward the kind of security checkpoint present in basically every building in Washington. Surrender all bags to be scanned, and walk through the metal detector—just like the ones in the airport. At the corner of the desk, she glanced one more time in the direction of the agent. Banks of phones. Computers. The file open in front of him.

Skylar sucked in a breath so fast it got stuck. Forced to cough, she pulled a handkerchief from the sleeve of her blouse and held it in front of her mouth.

"Ma'am?" The agent looked over. "Are you okay?" Concern softened his features. His voice was like the rumble of car tires on a country road. She could listen to that all day.

Skylar nodded even though she was far from okay. The file had her picture on the first page, along with her personal information. Why was the agent looking at her file?

Skylar had to continue. There was nothing else she could do. It was probably part of the exercise. But that didn't negate the surprise at seeing her own face in the folder.

The Secret Service higher-ups knew she'd been sent to the White House, and she just wanted to get on with the day's activities. Did he know she was part of the exercise? Did the file tell him she was currently an agent-in-training?

She'd scored so high, busting through long-held records by an agent named Grady Farrow that they'd offered her this opportunity. The chance to be part of an actual Secret Service exercise.

The event today was real—the White House wanted to honor veterans with a special tour. The first family was at Camp David this week, and the West Wing was undergoing renovations, so a lot of the staff were working from home. As soon as most of the tour people had exited the front door, everything would really begin.

She'd been briefed, and she was going to carry out those instructions to the letter. The Secret

Service, and all their personnel and dogs, were experts. Still, the higher-ups figured there was always opportunity to improve. They were going to test their response time in a live environment.

Skylar was part of a group which consisted of three people on the tour and three currently posing as HVAC repairmen who were supposed to take a couple of on-duty agents as "hostages." Then the plan was to hole up in one of the rooms and make demands. There was a whole script to follow.

Since it was actually really difficult to take over the White House—a good thing, given their job was to protect the president and his family— they also had a "mole" in the Secret Service who was going to help them. The job of the agents on duty was to resolve the situation and figure out which one of them was working with the hostiles. Personnel were far more vulnerable and susceptible to security breaches than any computer system.

After the security checkpoint, the tour headed outside and up a path that wound around a corner to the East Wing entrance. An agent waited outside the door, dog at her side. Skylar gave her a nod and said, "Morning."

They trailed down a long hallway. Rooms had been roped off and carpets rolled up so they didn't mar the fabric with their shoes. Skylar didn't want to feel like a peon, but it kind of did make her feel inferior that she wasn't even allowed to walk on their rugs.

The whole place didn't seem all that dated, like a lot of historic buildings. Maybe it just didn't get used that much, and they cleaned it really well. She'd been in some old castles in Europe, on weekend leave, back in her army days. Those had been visibly old. Crumbling walls, and a stale smell. The White House was pristine, and yet Skylar couldn't even appreciate the splendor of it. Not with the impending exercise.

They meandered past the library. Agents watching over the tour from both ends of the hallway were engaged in conversation with some of the vets.

She checked her watch.

Two minutes until—

"Yes, now!" The words were a brash whisper from a man in front of her. Not a great attempt by him at lowering his voice.

He spoke closely to the guy beside him. Both were dressed in army uniforms, and she recognized them from the briefing but couldn't remember their names.

She was the only other person close to them. The line had thinned out to small groups lingering through the tour route. No one paid any attention to the little old lady.

"The library is coming up," the first said. "It's right here. Thirty seconds. You distract them, and I'll run in and grab it. I'm sure it's there. Wilson will probably pay us double if we do this with no fuss."

Grab it?

Were they going to steal something?

Skylar gasped. The two men turned. She fumbled for a weapon she wasn't carrying, instinct driving her to the crux of her training. But it was no use. The two men grabbed her.

They crowded her against the wall, both standing way too close, but casual. Like they were just talking.

A gun pressed into her ribs.

"Wanna know what happens to eavesdroppers?"

Secret Service agent Grady Farrow shut the file and leaned back in his chair. Most of the veterans had filed through, leaving the office quiet now. How he was supposed to find Skylar Austin, former army corporal and current Secret Service trainee, was anyone's guess. She was part of the exercise, and Grady had been picked to keep an eye on her.

They had no idea when the exercise was going to happen, but he'd kind of hoped she would be on this tour of veterans. Her name hadn't even been on the list, though, so that was out. He flipped the file open again and stared at the photo of her—blond hair, and those blue-gray eyes. He'd stared at it far too much already. She was beautiful, but his assignment was to make sure she had a good experience as part of the exercise.

His job was to protect the president, but it was so much more than that. The Secret Service also protected the White House and all the people who worked here, investigated financial crimes and had offices all over the world. The scope of what they did was huge.

As part of the White House detail, Grady served the *office* of the president rather than the man himself. No matter who held the title, Grady's job was to be on duty. Day to day, it wasn't super exciting. If it was, that meant something had gone wrong. No one looked forward to that. Secret Service agents liked quiet days where they didn't have to deal with attention-seekers trying to run across the south lawn. There wasn't an agent employed here who enjoyed taking down a misguided member of the public.

He swiveled in his chair and rolled his shoulders. The constant vigilance was exhausting. The exercise would be a good distraction from whatever was nagging at him. This unsettled feeling hadn't gone away since he'd left the party for his thirty-second birthday. Four months ago.

He was starting to wonder if he'd have to live with it for the rest of his life. Not that Grady could even put a finger on what was bugging him. His mom said he needed to start dating again, since it'd been more than a year. But after Paula had left him for the friend that was supposed to have been his best man, he didn't feel like he had all that much to give to a woman.

There must have been a reason Paula had cheated on him and then dumped him. The other agents told him to "buck up" and "get back on the horse." Stringer, his closest friend, kept telling him about nice women he met but didn't want to date himself. Like he'd just pass them along. Grady mostly ignored it, considering Stringer wasn't going to explain what *his* deal was.

His radio crackled. The announcement drew his eyebrows up as he realized the scope of what was going on. A full on brawl in the entrance hall? *The exercise.*

Agent Stringer rapped twice on the doorjamb. "Let's go."

Grady rushed after him to the cabinet where the rifles loaded with blanks were kept. They had guns with live rounds on them at all times. No one was going to lay those down, even for an exercise. However, if they had to shoot a so-called hostile it was better to do that with blank bullets when this was only role play.

He and Stringer headed to the east entrance and took the stairs up to the hall where a fight had broken out. The tour had made its way through, and now most of them were outside. The stragglers had apparently walked slowly in order to start the exercise.

Two men were facedown, being cuffed by agents, while others looked on. If this was the exercise, it had failed. Were they simply that good at their jobs, or was this only one part of a larger plan? It could be nothing more than a distraction for a multipronged attack. They'd have to be cautious still.

"The veterans?"

Grady said, "I guess so. Was this their whole plan?"

"If it was," his friend replied, "it wasn't a good one."

Grady grinned. "And we got here too late to help." Not that there wasn't still plenty to do, but they'd missed the bulk of the action. Maybe.

He motioned to the door at the far end of the entrance hall. "I'm going to sweep that side." He gestured at the usher's closet, behind which was the family dining room and a pantry along with a hallway, stairs and an elevator. Plenty of places for hostiles to hide. Plenty of blind corners, and an escape route for any hostile wanting to regroup in order to plan the next phase of their operation.

Stringer nodded. "I'll work on this end."

Grady radioed in to Command and got the go-ahead. Between the two of them, and the other agents no doubt now dispersing through the White House, they'd get the hostiles all cleared out in no time.

There was no way things had begun and ended with a fight in the entrance hall. Some of that was likely veterans not knowing an exercise was taking place. They'd be questioned and then released. The hostiles already arrested would be a point each for the Secret Service. If they scored too low, though, heads would no doubt roll.

No one in the Service wanted that to happen.

Grady twisted the door handle but froze immediately when he heard voices.

"I didn't hear anything," a woman pleaded. "I don't know anything." He could hear the desperation in the woman's voice. An innocent had been caught up in the exercise? Grady's brain spun with what this could meant.

A man snorted. "Won't matter. Either way, you'll be dead. No one will be any wiser until your body is on a slab at the morgue and they realize you lied to everyone." He laughed. "We'll make them think you're behind all this."

Grady wasn't about to let the woman get hurt. He kicked the door open. "Freeze!" Two men started. Both dressed in army uniforms, they had been part of the tour. "Guns on the floor. Hands up."

The woman they had with them wasn't at all what he'd expected. Her voice hadn't made her sound all that advanced in age, but she seemed to be in her wise years. He said, "Drop your weapons, and put—"

One gunman, the one closest to Grady, turned and shoved the other as he fled the room out the back door. The man he'd shoved stumbled to one side, his gun up and pointed at the woman. It went off. The blast was loud in the small room.

The woman's breath escaped in an *oof*, and he heard her go down. Grady was already running at the man before he even registered the move. He slammed into the guy and tackled him to the ground.

The man fought him, waving the gun around.

Grady grasped his wrist and slammed it against the floor until he let go. "You're under arrest." Then he flipped the man to his front and zip-tied him, while the captive grunted and struggled.

Had he killed that poor woman?

TWO

Grady sank to one knee beside her, pulled his radio out with one hand and called in to Command about the man who'd run off. There wasn't any visible blood, and yet her floral print dress had a hole in the front. He laid two fingers of his free hand on her throat. Strong and steady pulse. She was alive? He glanced back at the gunman he'd secured, now lying on his side watching them. Johnson his shirt said. Was that his real name?

Command responded that they would send agents to find the man who'd run off.

Grady said, "See if you can figure out why he has a weapon with real bullets as well." A woman had been caught in the crossfire because someone messed up. None of the hostiles were supposed to have real bullets, just blanks. And how had the man managed to get that past security? "I'll bring in the guy I have here, once I get the woman up and escorted out."

The woman gasped. He looked at her in time to see her eyes were open. She sat halfway up, much faster than an old woman should react. "What—"

He touched her shoulder, keeping half his attention on the man. "Easy."

She shifted her shoulders and hissed in pain. "I can't believe they shot me." The woman felt the area where the bullet had hit her, then pulled aside the hole to reveal the end of a bullet lodged there.

"You have a protective vest on?" If she was fine, he didn't need an ambulance to come. But he did need to get the gunman glaring at him from the floor booked into custody. They would have to figure out who his partner was, and whether this was all part of the exercise. But why involve an old woman?

One wearing a vest.

Okay, so nothing about this made any sense.

The woman sat up fully, frowned and scooted farther from him on the floor. Her gaze was a million miles away. "They were going to shoot me."

"Who are you?" Nothing about her made any sense. "I'm glad you're alive and all, but you need to start talking."

She clasped one wrist with her other and slid her hand down, peeling back the skin.

"Wha—"

The wrinkles fell to the floor and revealed soft skin on her wrist and hand. Young skin. Now that he was closer to her, not behind the security desk, he realized her gray hair looked like it could be a wig. But without the discrepancy between that young skin, and the wrinkles on her face it was hard to tell. It wasn't synthetic hair.

Someone had gone to a great deal of effort to make this woman look nothing like herself. A disguise? Grady shifted while his mind roiled with questions. Was she yet another part of the exercise? "Why did that man shoot at you? Was it part of the exercise?"

"I don't think so."

"He had real bullets."

"I overheard…" She shook her head. "They were actually going to kill me."

She shrugged one shoulder, then pulled the wig off. Removed the stocking and shook out her blond hair. She pulled a hairband from her dress pocket and tied her hair back. Now he could see the edges of where wrinkled skin had been cosmetically added to her face.

A face he'd seen before, but only in a photo.

"That's some costume. But I can see your face showing." Grady stared her down. "Tell me your name."

The corner of her mouth curled up. Before she

could answer, a response came over his radio. He held up one finger and listened to the conversation while she peeled the latex off her face. That was when he realized who she was.

He relayed to her what he'd heard over his earpiece. "Agents downstairs haven't seen the shooter… Skylar Austin."

She gaped at her name but said, "Did Simmons go upstairs?"

"Simmons?" He glanced around, mostly to keep himself from staring at her blue-gray eyes. The tanned skin of someone who enjoyed being outdoors. The only upside was that in saving an old woman, he'd inadvertently completed his priority task: making sure Skylar Austin came through the exercise unscathed.

She said, "That was the name on his jacket." Then motioned to the man still bound on the floor. "That one is Johnson."

"If this Simmons guy went upstairs, they'd have seen him emerge in the hallway." He got back on his radio. "Anything on camera?"

"Negative," was the response back from Command. "Cameras are down."

The command post, set up outside as though the White House really were under siege, would have limited contact now that things were underway. It was up to the agents inside, and how it played out would depend on what angle the hostiles took. How they planned to commandeer the building and everyone inside.

Sometimes an agent would play the commander-in-chief for an exercise, but not this time. Did the hostiles want to destroy the White House itself, a blow to America that would be felt nationwide? Or was their plan something different? Of course, it was only an exercise, but they had to be prepared for any eventuality. For any of the threats made against the office of the president, the man himself and the White House, on a daily basis. The Secret Service could never be over prepared.

He shook his head for Skylar's benefit. "The hostiles must have taken out the cameras."

"So, he's hiding somewhere?" She shifted her feet under her and hopped up to standing, all pretense of being elderly gone now. Though she seemed to still be stiff, and she laid a hand on her sternum.

"Hurts?"

"I didn't think it would be that painful."

He glared at Johnson. Still watching them, a calculating look on his face. What was the guy up to? "He might have broken your sternum if he was close enough."

She exhaled a breath and smiled. "Sure feels like he might've. So you know who I am. You gonna tell me *your* name now?"

"Secret Service Agent Grady Farrow."

Her eyes widened.

Why that intrigued him, he wasn't sure. Something about his name meant something to Skylar Austin.

She covered her reaction fast and said, "I figured out the Secret Service part from the fact that you have a badge, a star *and* the words *SECRET SERVICE* plastered across the front of your vest."

He shrugged. "This way there's no confusion about who is in charge."

She laughed, a low chuckle that almost sounded rusty. "I'll have to remember that."

He got on his radio and called in that he had Skylar Austin with him.

"You've been looking for me? I thought my file you have on your desk was just about the exercise."

"We don't know who the hostiles are beforehand, and considering you're a trainee, everyone is on the lookout. I had your file because Intel sent it over. We take care of our—"

"Grady!"

Johnson slammed into him.

Grady felt the hands wrap around his own a second before his hip hit the floor. Johnson had cut himsef free of the zip ties, and now the man was intent on using that knife on Grady.

He spilled over from the crouch he'd been in to land on the hardwood. Plastic cracked, but he ignored whatever it was and deflected the knife while he grabbed for his weapon. Johnson—if that was his real name—tried to wrestle the gun from Grady.

There was no way he would let this guy get his gun.

Skylar grabbed the pillow of a nearby chair, the only thing within reach from the floor. She swung it around and slammed it into Johnson's head. The knife fell to the floor.

The gunman blinked. Probably more in surprise than anything else. Skylar kicked the knife away.

Grady punched him. Johnson fought back. Grady reached out to grasp the guy, but he got up and raced out the door. Grady jumped up to follow as the gunman ran through the hall. The door began to swing shut right before Grady collided with the solid wood.

He slammed against it, then shoved. The door didn't move. "Hey!"

The resistance was such that there had to be another person on the other side helping Johnson close it in his face.

"Come on, get it shut," he heard from the other side, right before it closed. "We have to tell Wilson. Find out what to do!"

The door shut, and the lock clicked. Grady tried the handle from his side. What on earth? He hadn't even known this door could be locked. How was it these men knew more about the White House than a Secret Service agent?

He tried the handle again but couldn't open the door. "It's locked."

Skylar was at the other door. "This one, too."

"We're locked in?"

"Looks like it." She frowned, the wrinkles in her skin not quite lining up with the frown.

Grady reached for his radio and felt the jagged pieces. Broken? He glanced down. "I guess that's what broke when I fell."

"What did he say, right before the door shut? I heard something."

He hesitated a second, unsure whether to trust information to someone obviously in disguise. Maybe she was part of this, and it was all a ruse—a portion of the exercise where he was rendered trapped and unable to contact Command.

This was an exercise. If she was a hostile, could he trust her?

Skylar could see the question on his face. He was wondering if he should share. If he could trust her. She flipped her ponytail forward and shook out the rest of the pins she'd missed. If they were going to be a team, she wanted to be herself. At least as much as she could in this polyester floral dress.

"You know those men were trying to kill me." She phrased it as a statement, but it was really a question. When he nodded, she said, "I heard them talking about taking something from the library. They didn't know for sure it was in there but seemed convinced it was possible."

Skylar thought back over what had happened. "When they realized I'd overheard them, they decided to kill me." She paused. "They also said someone named Wilson was going to be pleased if they took whatever it was easily."

Grady nodded. "They mentioned Wilson right before the door shut."

"Any idea who he is?"

He shook his head. "Do you?"

"I met everyone on the hostile's team at the briefing, and I don't remember that name."

"Those men trying to kill you, were they hostiles in the exercise?"

"Yes." Skylar paced away, tried the door again—still locked, which wasn't surprising, but she had to do something—and then turned back. "So, what do we do now?"

"They're going to come back soon, which means we can ambush them when they do."

She didn't have a weapon. If they came in,

guns blazing, the vest she wore might not protect her as well a second time.

His eyes narrowed on her. The great Grady Farrow, former Secret Service training record-holder, didn't like the fact that she was nervous? Skylar didn't need another man finding her wanting. That definitely wasn't part of her five-year plan.

It was also why she'd pushed herself so hard in training. She wasn't about to let them pass on her. Not when she knew what she was capable of.

Skylar wandered around the room, pulled open the couple of drawers in the desk and rummaged. The knife had slid under the hutch, but surely there was a decorative letter opener, or… something she could find to defend herself with.

"Is a theft part of the exercise?"

She looked up. "No. There was nothing about a theft in the plan."

"So they're doing this on their own?"

She didn't answer. Grady turned away and scratched his jaw.

"And my radio is broken." He tried the handle of the door that had been shut in his face, and then snatched up the phone. He sighed. "No dial tone. We need to get out of here so I can contact Command and let them know the exercise is being used as a cover for a theft."

Skylar nodded.

The doorknob rattled.

Grady spun around to the exit behind him. Someone knocked. "Farrow, you in there?"

"Stringer." He strode to the door. "We're locked in."

"Let me find a key." The muffled answer came from behind the door.

The relief on Grady's face matched her own feelings. They were going to get out of here. "What happens next?"

She didn't really want to leave, but if those men were still going to try to kill her, then she wasn't about to hang around.

"I take you to Command. We inform them of what's happening, and get to the bottom of this."

"By finding that Wilson guy?"

Maybe they would let her sit in the command post while the agents brought these potential thieves to justice. She'd like to know how it played out. If she could watch the action for herself it would be a great experience. So long as she was safe.

"Okay, I found a key," Stringer—whoever that was—said from behind the door.

Skylar could hear the key in the lock and a click.

"One second and—" A crash rang through the space beyond the door. Echoed off the high ceilings.

Grady pulled the door open. Skylar moved to

the side, out of the line of fire of anyone on the other side ready to shoot at them.

He rushed out to help his friend. She could hear the muffled sounds of fighting. She waited. Would he come back and tell her the coast was clear? The expression *sitting duck* came to mind. If this hadn't been a life-in-danger situation, she might have thought it was amusing. Too bad there was nothing funny about this. She could actually use some humor in her life.

Skylar crept to the door, keeping her back against the wall. She peered out. A hall, then another to her left that ran perpendicular to the one outside this door. This place was a maze.

She heard someone grunt, then a whooshing sound like a quick exhale. The sounds of a fight.

She peered around the door. A takedown, two Secret Service agents against one hostile. Johnson was back.

Movement to her left brought her attention around. Two men, one dressed in HVAC-repairman overalls and the other an agent, crossed the end of the hall. Guns bared. She took an involuntary step back. Not anyone she was going to mess with.

But the HVAC guy she recognized from the briefing. What was his name?

Skylar crept past an elevator to the mouth of the hall and peered around. They were walking fast, not wanting to be caught out in the open of the hallway. What were they doing?

"Skylar!" Grady barked her name in a low tone.

She waved once, behind her back, for him to shush. That wasn't likely to go down well with a man like him—the in-charge type. She tried to hear what the men were saying.

Too far away.

"Skylar." He tugged on her elbow.

She turned back to him. "I saw—"

"It's not safe for you to be exposed like that. You need to stay where there's cover." His eyes were hard, but she thought she detected concern as well as that do-what-I-say authority. "And don't walk off so I don't know where you are."

Behind him, farther down the hall, Stringer— dressed in a uniform that matched Grady's— hauled Johnson to his feet. The agent evidently thought that exchange between her and Grady was immensely funny.

She brushed past Grady and strode over to Stringer and Johnson. She faced-off with Johnson and set one hand on her hip. Yes, she looked ridiculous in this half-disguise, but she wanted answers.

"What does Wilson want to steal?"

Johnson's eyes flashed. "You think I'm just gonna tell you?"

"You tell me…" She waved at the Secret Service agents. "You tell them, and they tell me. What's the difference? Either way, I find out what's so important it's worth you trying to kill me to cover it up."

"Maybe you shouldn't eavesdrop on other people's conversations." Johnson smirked. "Didn't your momma teach you that?"

"Actually, no," Skylar said. "My mom didn't teach me anything." She felt Stringer's and Grady's attention on her but ignored it. "Now tell me what Wilson wants to steal."

"You think this is legit? Like a real theft?" Johnson's gaze had an edge to it. "It's all part of the exercise."

He was going to stick with that line? If it really was part of the exercise, that didn't explain why they'd had real weapons. Or why they'd been so determined to kill her.

"You shot me."

"Accidents happen all the time." He smirked again. "You should be more careful. You never know when you could get hurt. Even dead."

THREE

"I'm gonna take this one out to Command."

Grady nodded to his friend. "We'll be right behind you."

Agent Stringer stepped through the usher's closet to the entrance hall. Skylar glanced at Grady, a question in her eyes.

"You're with me. We're going out to Command, but Johnson's pal is still loose in the White House. Keep your eyes open."

She nodded. "I wish I knew who that Wilson guy was they were talking about. Or what they were planning on stealing."

"Johnson will talk."

"But what if he doesn't?"

"He will." Grady wasn't going to argue it. If a theft was really about to be undertaken in the White House, the Secret Service would find out everything about it. Round up all responsible. That was how their world worked.

He crossed the room and peered out of the far

door of the usher's closet. Only a few steps to the entrance-hall door that led out to the north portico. Stringer had already headed out. Once they were outside, they would be seen by the agents in the command post. They would've set up cameras to get as many angles on the hostiles as they could from outside—whether surveillance was down or not.

Most of the hostiles were Secret Service agents from around the country, or they were with other federal agencies. As long as they didn't personally know those stationed in the White House, they were eligible. And everyone was thoroughly vetted. Occasionally the director threw in a wild card—someone like Skylar who had earned her place on the exercise.

Grady walked out into the entrance hall, Skylar right behind him. Like it had all week, the place almost echoed with a lack of people. It was weird not seeing and hearing that constant bustle of work. Humanity. The lifeblood of the country pumping through the halls.

Behind him, the squeak of Skylar's sneakers on the marble floor was almost a dance. An excited trot, like a horse itching to gallop. She probably wouldn't like being compared to a horse, but he'd always thought they were majestic, beautiful creatures who were both strong and incredibly vulnerable at the same time.

"They're here!"

He spun, gun raised, to see the second man—Johnson's friend, Simmons—was back.

Grady yelled, "Get to the door!"

Skylar ran for the exit. The man fired, and glass shattered. She screamed and lost her footing for a second.

Grady fired. The gunman yelped.

Her momentum carried her away from him. Grady ran to her, grasped her around the waist, and they ran for the door. They were cut off from the exit, but this way could get them to a different door.

When the gunman followed them, he would probably assume they'd head downstairs. Instead, Grady took her into the East Room, which was on this floor. It essentially trapped them, but Grady needed the element of surprise on his side.

He held her back with him, out of sight, and heard footsteps approach their position.

Grady braced for the incoming attack, but as he'd thought, the gunman raced down the stairs.

Instead of going after the man now, he moved Skylar with him through the East Room. Away from that man. This room was huge and looked like a ballroom. The sparkling chandeliers and gorgeous curtains would be completely out of place anywhere other than here or at Buckingham Palace. If they could get through and back into the entrance hall they'd be able to get out.

Grady prayed the coast would be clear and then moved her forward toward the Green Room—the same route she'd have taken with the tour. He halted at the first door. The one before the Green Room and which led back to the entrance hall.

The first door was closed. He didn't see a shadow under the door. No one was moving out in the hall—not close to this door, anyway. Grady led her to the Green Room. It was a maze of rooms in here, which meant there were plenty of places for a gunman to hide.

Where was this guy? He kept disappearing, then reappearing.

Grady glanced back but saw no one following them. He didn't hear the man who had raced past them and gone downstairs either. The gunshots had stopped. Maybe this *Wilson* guy had called him off to get back to what they'd really come here to do.

"…here. I don't know what he's thinking, but you had better fix it." A man's voice drifted to them from somewhere in the rooms beyond.

Grady stopped short. That voice sounded familiar. Skylar must have heard it, too, because she didn't say anything to give away the fact that they were there. Someone was in the Green

Room. Or possibly beyond that. He couldn't tell without looking…and exposing himself to more gunfire.

"You figure it out. And fast."

A second man spoke, a slight English tightness to his words. "If the girl isn't dead and we don't get the clock out of here, then not only do none of us get paid but we'll also be in jail. If she hasn't already told everyone what she overheard you imbeciles say."

Skylar grabbed his vest from behind. He swung around with a look on his face she couldn't fail to decipher, and mouthed, *What?*

She mouthed back, *A clock?*

He nodded, but did that matter? This was probably the guy who had shot at her. But Grady couldn't call it in on his busted radio. They still needed to get outside.

Was it worth the risk to backtrack and try to head out the same door as before? Or go downstairs?

More than one man was there. It would be up to him to capture them, exercise or not. He mouthed to Skylar, *You need to help me.* Two against two would be better.

She nodded, but there wasn't much time for a plan. How was he going to do this?

"What about Johnson?" the first man said. "Your man probably already told them everything."

The one with the slight English accent spoke again. "Johnson isn't your concern. He's my guy, and I'll clean up this disaster."

"You do realize you've messed the whole thing up, right?"

"We can still use her, though," the English guy replied. "Make it look like she's the thief."

Skylar sucked in an audible breath. Grady's chest clenched. Were they talking about her? He didn't want her here if these men were going to blame everything on her. They needed to get to a door, or a radio at the least.

"You'll still have to get rid of Johnson," the first man said. "Think you can do that without messing it up as well as everything else today?"

They were going to infiltrate Command and kill Johnson before he could talk? If Grady could call this in, then he could warn the agents in the command post.

Instead of taking these men down, he needed to get the word out. Keep Skylar safe.

He motioned behind her, and she got the idea. Together they crept back along the East Room to the front. They'd hit the top of the stairs before the door to the entrance hall. The door to outside.

He peered out anyway and saw the gunman talking to a Secret Service agent. Who was that? The angle was all wrong, and he could only see the man's shoulder and one leg from this vantage point.

The gunman who'd shot at them was nowhere to be found. Instead, the agent spoke with a man dressed as an HVAC repairman. The repairman's attention snagged on Grady. He said something to his friend.

The agent ducked out of sight.

"Let's go."

"Where to?" She'd stayed out of sight but could hear someone in the entrance hall headed their way. The gunman?

"Downstairs. Now."

That was where the other guy had gone. Skylar might not be a full-fledged agent yet, but did it make sense that they were heading toward danger? Or were they essentially pinned from both sides? Either way, she didn't have much hope they would be able to get out of the White House without her getting hurt.

Grady tugged her down the stairs she'd ascended as part of the tour. Was he planning on exiting that way, or did he have another idea?

"We should keep going, right?" she whispered.

Grady brushed past her. He stopped at the hall at the base of the stairs and listened.

Skylar glanced back. "He's coming."

She didn't want to be the female who needed saving, but he was the one with a gun.

It wouldn't help her to consider the fact that, yes, she was attracted to him. Grady, with his thick chest and the way he commanded the situation. Definitely not part of her five-year plan. *Remember?* He should probably intimidate her, he had such a formidable presence, but he didn't. Still, it couldn't be denied he was in charge, and he knew it. Which was great for the Secret Service. He was a great agent.

Not so great for Skylar, her sense of self-preservation and her broken heart.

A second later he said, "The hall is clear."

He went first and ducked right. Kept his body close to the wall. Skylar did the same as they trotted away from the east exit.

Had the gunman met up with someone else? Were they lying in wait down here, ready for Skylar and Grady to emerge from their hiding spot so they could pick them off? She shuddered at the thought, tempted to pray they got through this. She felt so exposed with no weapon. She had to rely on Grady. And God.

"You okay?"

She opened her eyes. "Just praying." Or, at least, thinking about it.

"Oh, good idea," he said.

They crept along the hall, their footsteps silent. Focusing on the present helped her not give in to the fear. They had hostiles—real hostiles—running around shooting real bullets, trying to steal from the White House.

Grady glanced both ways, then shoved her into a room on the ground floor. "Quick."

Skylar glanced around and gaped. "What is this place?"

"Secret Service office."

Two desks, on which sat a row of computer monitors, and a valance of TVs that hung from the ceiling. All of them were switched on, but the room was empty. Nothing but blank screens—no signal.

She grasped the first phone. "No dial tone. Just like upstairs."

Grady tried one of the computers. "I've got nothing here. This isn't good. If this office has been cleared out, that means the agents in here were captured. No one is trying to get the feeds restored, and no one's here to take you to Command."

He wanted someone else to get her out?

Why did that bother her? The man was a trained agent. Of course he wanted to get back in there, as it were, and get things fixed.

Skylar saw a radio on one of the desks and grabbed it. Turned the dial. She put the earbud to her ear. "Listen to this." Since the door was shut, she pulled the headphones out of the port in the radio on one of the desks and turned up the volume. Not too loud but enough they could both hear it.

"…surrender immediately." The voice was male. Authoritative. "The White House is now under my control."

Skylar said, "Is that one of the men from upstairs?"

Grady shook his head. "This guy is American, and he doesn't sound like the one we heard talking."

The voice continued. "I know some of you Secret Service agents are skulking around, still trying to play hero. You will not best me. Surrender is your only option. If you do not give yourselves up in the Yellow Oval Room in the next thirty minutes I will begin killing staff members."

The man paused, then a different voice came over the radio. "No, don't." It was a woman, though she wasn't entirely convincing in her desperation. And instead of pleading with the man not to kill her, she said, "Four hostiles! Don't surrend—"

The woman cried out.

"Nice try," the man said over the radio. He chuckled. "This is fun. I know there are more of you out there. We will ferret you out, and you'll be taken down. Then we move on to phase two. Out."

Grady waited a second, but no more came. He turned to her. "Phase two?"

She just smiled. For a minute the excitement that the exercise had promised washed over her. "It was a good plan. Too bad it's ruined now."

Grady said, "He almost sounds like a guy who washed out of Secret Service training and went to work for another agency. Now he's drunk on power, having the time of his life getting back at us."

Skylar decided to leave that whole federal agency rivalry alone. She said, "So what are we going to do?"

He looked at her like she'd surprised him. What? Didn't he think they should work together on this? She'd thought that was what they were doing. After the shock of thinking her dead only minutes earlier, maybe he didn't want her anywhere near this. She couldn't blame him for that. Not really.

"You're the agent." They needed to get out of the White House, right?

Grady used the radio to call Command and update them about their current location. Then he strode to the wall at the far end and pushed. It clicked and then slid backward.

She looked inside and gaped. "Seriously, a secret room?"

He shrugged. "It's more of a closet."

Skylar shifted closer, until she could feel the heat of him in front of her as she practically peered over his shoulder.

He moved inside the room, barely bigger than a walk-in closet, and began gathering up magazines for a rifle. He loaded the weapon. "This is purely precaution, in case we run into any more of these guys. I don't want you vulnerable as we make our way to the secondary command post."

"Where's that?"

"On the street outside. So we load up and roll out. Meet up with Command. The longer we stay here, the greater the risk."

"Okay."

He handed her a rifle that matched his own. "You good with this?"

She took the weapon, checked it was loaded and tucked it against her chest. "Top of my class."

"Good. Bring the radio. I'll let them know we're on the move."

Skylar snapped it up and looked around, trying to consider other options. It wasn't about being scared. She just didn't want to meet any of those gunmen again.

The ache in her chest made her wonder exactly how bad the bruise was going to be. Still, she wasn't dead.

She wondered if she could she stay here and wait instead. He was supposed to get her to Command, but at what cost? Maybe staying here and hiding was the best course of action. When it was over, he could come back for her.

Okay, so maybe she was a little bit scared. Who wouldn't be?

The door from the hall opened, and a flash grenade rolled into the room. The thing sparked to life faster than either of them could react.

The bang rattled her eardrums and eclipsed all thought. The flash of light was so bright she blinked, but it was like staring into the sun. Grady clapped his hands over his ears. Skylar did the same.

Something hard hit the back of her head and she fell to her knees. She was unconscious before she hit the floor.

FOUR

Skylar's shoulders resisted her attempt at moving. She blinked against the lights and her head swam. Yellow walls. The smell of fresh paint wrinkled her nose, and she lifted her head to look around. Her hands had been secured behind her back. Her ankles were zip-tied together as well.

This was the Yellow Oval Room. Instead of rounding up all the agents, as had been the plan for the exercise, she was the one who'd been brought here. Did someone think she was a Secret Service agent they'd taken hostage? Did these people not know she was supposed to be one of them? They would have been in the same briefing as her—one Johnson and his friend had been part of as well. Had the English guy been there? She tried to remember, but her head was too foggy.

Skylar shifted from her right side, her shoulder twisted beneath her. She winced and sat up, even though it hurt. A lot. The aftereffects of the grenade? She didn't realize the disorientation would linger this long. Who had thrown the flash grenade into the Secret Service office?

Where was…

Finally able to look behind her, she saw him on the floor. "Grady."

His eyes were closed, and he didn't respond, still unconscious from the attack on them. Was he hurt? Skylar glanced around again, made eye contact with a couple of other bound agents. Saw guys she recognized from the briefing, Homeland Security agents, dressed as HVAC repairmen. And holding guns.

These guys thought the exercise was still happening. They had no idea about the thieves. Which meant they were likely to follow the script, because they had no idea what was really going on.

Furniture in the room had been shoved to one side. Covered with drop cloths that looked nicer than the sheets she used on her bed. The chandelier had been taken down. Probably in pieces somewhere, being cleaned.

She counted five other suited agents on the floor, tied up and sitting around where she and Grady had been tossed. The gunmen had to have tossed her here, or her hip wouldn't smart like it did. Not defeated, these agents looked ready.

Across the room the two men paced. Both held semiautomatic rifles and carried radios, neither of which she'd been issued. That was not part of the exercise.

Skylar gritted her teeth and tried to quit swaying. It was like her equilibrium didn't know which way was up and which way was down. She racked her brain to try to remember at least one of their names. Phil. *No.* Will. *No, that wasn't right.* Bill? "Billy!"

Gunman Bill jerked his head around. Okay, so she hadn't meant to yell that loud. "Hey." She felt her cheeks flush hot and saw a couple of the agents beside her give her the eye. Whatever for, she didn't know. "It is Bill, right?"

He nodded. "Yeah. But we said no talking."

"I didn't hear that," she said. "I was unconscious. Sorry. Anyway, I'm Skylar. Maybe you remember me, from the briefing?" She barely took a breath and then kept going, motioning at Grady. "I was with Agent Farrow, but only after one of the other hostiles shot me. With a *real gun.*"

One of the agents on the floor snorted.

Skylar shot the guy a look. "The bullet is still embedded in my vest." She looked back at their captors, determined to befriend them into releasing her. But she also had to let them know so much of this had gone wrong. "Some of the hostiles and someone called Wilson are all trying to steal a clock." She waited for them to react but didn't get much in response. "They're thieves, and we have to stop them."

When they still said nothing, Skylar turned to the other agents on the floor with her. "I'm serious. And now that we're all occupied—" more like restrained, but she was trying to downplay it "—they could be doing anything right now. Stealing anything."

One of the bound agents frowned. "No one gets in the White House without being vetted."

She shot him almost the same look back. "I was vetted, but you guys let in an eighty-two-year-old retiree named Agnes Fulford."

It wasn't their fault she'd had expert help. Still, she had a point. They couldn't assume everything was fine.

Assuming security was perfect wasn't going to stop infiltrations from happening. This agent had to know that. Skylar didn't yet understand all the ins and outs of White House security. That was why she wasn't assuming it was foolproof. He probably *did* know all the ins and outs, but what was she supposed to do?

These Homeland agents dressed as repairmen were maintaining security in this room, so they weren't going to leave and help them search for potential hostiles. That meant Skylar had to get free and go herself if the Secret Service guys didn't believe her. Or if they thought this was just another part of the exercise.

She wanted to scream out her frustration. They would believe Grady, wouldn't they? These guys just didn't know her.

Why wasn't he awake yet? Had they hit him hard? She couldn't see any visible injuries. Skylar wanted to pray some more for help but also couldn't help realizing she actually cared about Grady. She needed him, sure. But if he was hurt because he'd been with her…

Skylar didn't like that at all. Whether she was responsible for him being hurt or not.

She didn't need to be thinking this much about a man she'd just met. The Secret Service filled the gaps in her life. Yes, she knew it wasn't healthy to focus so much on work. On being the best she could be, and having the most fulfilling career she could. But only once she'd reached those goals would Skylar think about relationships again.

Skylar prayed as she waited for one of the Homeland agents to look her way. "Can I talk to you?"

He shrugged and wandered over, apparently considering none of them a threat since they were trussed up like Thanksgiving turkeys. "What?"

"I was serious about the live rounds. I think

some men sneaked in with the exercise, and they're up to something. They might even be the ones who brought me and Grady here."

What if they'd been dragged to the Yellow Oval Room purely because they had overheard what they weren't supposed to? Those men wanted to silence her and Grady. They'd succeeded in getting them contained in this room—buying the thieves a period of time to steal whatever they wanted. But Skylar and Grady could tell everyone what they knew, and how would that help Wilson and his agenda?

Her brain was still sluggish from being unconscious, but this still didn't make sense. Why bring them in here? These guys didn't seem to know the exercise was moot at this point. Which begged the question, had they been brought here as part of the exercise or because those thieves wanted them out of the way?

"So what if they were the ones who dropped you off here?" he said. "It's all part of the exercise, right?"

"Please just listen to me." She had an idea, one she hated resorting to, but it just might work. She tried to look helpless. Men always liked to fix a woman's problems, right? Looking like she was distressed was good. Tears would be too much.

He came closer, his gaze softening. "I know you think something's wrong, but it isn't. The guys who brought you in were in overalls like the rest of us." He moved, his boots right beside Grady's legs.

"So were those men. Did one of them have an English accent, even just a little—"

Grady's legs lifted. He swung them into the man's knees.

The Homeland agent tipped forward, right onto Skylar. She shoved at him with her shoulder as he came toward her, purely out of reflex. Self-preservation, that was all.

Breath whooshed out of him as he fell to the side. The guy on the other side of her kicked him in the head with his bound legs and knocked him out.

The other agent ran over.

One of the Secret Service guys grabbed the Homeland agent's gun with his bound hands and held it on the second agent. "Drop it."

The Homeland agent put his hands up.

Grady sat up as admiration filled him for Skylar's quick assessment of the situation. Getting the hostile to come over had been a good move. "Well done, Skylar, distracting him so we could get the drop on him. That was a nice move, too."

Skylar's smile held more surprise than anything else. "You're welcome."

A couple of the agents had guns on the Homeland gunman. They didn't look pleased about how things had played out so far.

Grady said, "You were really trying to ask that man about the English guy?"

"Well...*yeah*."

He shook his head and checked the unconscious gunman's pockets. "Anyone got a knife?" He glanced around. "There are thieves in the White House, and we need to stop them."

No one argued.

"You don't think I should've tried to find out what they know?" Skylar's head tipped to one side and she said, "These guys could be part of it."

One agent twisted and pulled out a multitool from the side pocket of his cargo pants, which he used to cut everyone's bonds. When everyone in the group was free, and the gunmen were secure, they huddled up. One of the men was Grady's team leader. The gray-haired agent lifted both hands. "Okay, people—"

Skylar said, "Wait a second." She wasn't done talking to Grady about this.

The agent shot Skylar a look, and she closed her mouth rather than argue. Which was good. His speech was long-winded considering they needed to get moving. Procedure dictated their next move. First, they needed to retake the White House, and bring in everyone who was inside and not a Secret Service agent. That would take care of Wilson and his gang. Afterward, they could figure out who those men were.

The team leader said, "Does everyone have their—"

A deep-toned, slow clap preceded a man walking into the room.

"That's the third HVAC repairman who's a hostile. From the briefing."

Grady nodded.

This guy and the two Homeland agents. Then Skylar and the two army guys—Simmons and Johnson. Six hostiles.

"What are—" At her outburst, Grady squeezed Skylar's elbow, and she closed her mouth, then shot him a look. "Is that that?"

She was right. This was Wilson, which meant they had to play this carefully. The man could have live rounds in his weapon. And why had he come in now, when he could've come in while the hostiles had them tied up?

Grady braced while Wilson continued his lazy applause. He crossed halfway into the room and faced them like he was some magnanimous leader, used to wearing a mantle of power. Not uncommon in this house, but still. Who was this guy, really?

He glanced at his team, but none of them seemed to recognize Wilson. They just looked quietly cautious—like they weren't sure whether to believe Skylar or simply wait and see what was about to happen. That caution could likely save as many lives as quick action often did, but right now Grady wished he could communicate to them all that they should just rush Wilson and take him down.

"Well done. Well done." The words were smooth, like a concerted effort to downplay the sharpness to his accent. He almost sounded fully American. Almost. "I congratulate you both on figuring it out." Now no trace of the English accent remained.

The guy was good.

"Is the exercise over?" one of the agents said.

Wilson shook his head. "You'll still get your chance to take down all the hostiles, but this part is complete. The next phase will begin soon. I just couldn't pass up the opportunity to congratulate the lady present on her clever deduction."

Grady studied him. The perfect posture under those baggy overalls. The long line of his Roman nose and dark eyes. He almost looked like a Victorian-age villain from a movie. A throwback to a bygone era. The English accent would have fit better.

Grady was probably reading way too much into this. "Great," he said. "Good to know."

He didn't like the idea someone might've

sneaked in under cover of the exercise for an entirely different reason. The Secret Service didn't need any more black marks on their record, when day-to-day their skill—and heroics—went largely unnoticed. They only got mentioned in the media if they did something wrong. Not every other day, when things were normal and everyone remained safe.

If there was something untoward going on in the White House today, they would all go above and beyond to neutralize the threat. It was what they did.

Wilson smiled, though there was no humor in the curl of his lips. "This was no ordinary takeover of the White House, but *so much more*."

Like what? The theft of a clock? Grady couldn't help asking himself that question. More likely this display of theatrics was a further attempt to silence Skylar. And Grady. The two of them were in danger now.

What was Wilson going to do?

"Congratulations." Wilson paused, giving an exaggerated wave toward the door. "If you would come with me, the two of you." He glanced at Grady. "I'll endeavor to make the rest of the exercise a little more…interesting for you."

Skylar went first. More than a little caution in her steps.

"Farrow."

He glanced back at his team leader. Mouthed, *Find the thieves*.

His team leader nodded, playing along so Wilson didn't suspect. If there was even a chance he and Skylar were right about all this, the man couldn't ignore it. "Get yourself a radio. I'll coordinate."

The agents grabbed the weapons that had been confiscated from them as well as the unconscious gunmen's.

Wilson gave him no opportunity to get a gun of his own. "Let's go." The man moved to the door, his motion giving Grady no choice but to be herded to the door.

He followed Skylar, figuring a couple of men as backup would be right behind them. He was going to question this guy and get to the bottom of what was happening here.

Grady shifted his ankle on the next step to feel the holster there. Even his backup weapon was gone. He had no way to protect himself, or Skylar, if Wilson tried to silence them.

He glanced back to see where their backup was at.

"This is so fun," Skylar chattered as they walked the hall. "It's turning out even better than I'd expected." She was playing her part— the rookie agent who believed this was just all part of the exercise. But why did she think that tactic would work with this guy now? Was she still determined to get answers?

The man smiled, but there was no life in it. "I'm so glad."

Grady caught an edge in the man's tone he thought Skylar missed. With one glance back at his team leader, Grady lifted his hand to give the man a signal to move in. Grady didn't want to be alone and unarmed with Wilson for any longer.

Before he could call back to his team, Wilson swung his arm around Grady's shoulders. He stiffened, but the man squeezed him hard enough he almost broke a rib. Or his collarbone. He hissed out a breath.

Wilson ignored it. "You're going to be surprised. That's for sure."

Grady didn't agree. Something about this didn't sit right with him. Despite the fact that Skylar seemed to have completely changed her mind about this man being up to nefarious activity—or at least she was pretending as much—he wasn't about to abandon caution that easily.

Wilson walked them down two flights of stairs. Grady couldn't step into the space without saying, "What was with the live rounds your men had? You could have killed one of us." He figured this guy was in charge but didn't know for sure.

"Bah." Wilson waved off his concern. "I

wouldn't have hit you. I was just trying to scare you. All part of the day's fun." His words had an edge to them that kept Grady from relaxing. Then he said, "Sorry if it upset you."

Right. Like that was the problem.

Skylar said, "Well, they did damage the White House." She pointed to the door frame they'd hit. A hole in the wood and splintered shards surrounded the silver end of a bullet embedded there. "I'm sure someone will take that out of your paycheck."

"I'm sure," he said with a humorless smile. "Now, where is my associate?"

They waited a full minute before the man entered.

Simmons.

She took a step back. Wilson nodded to his associate. Before Grady knew what had happened, the two men moved. He only got his hands up fast enough for them to brush the barbs of a stun gun flying toward him. Not fast enough to bat them away before they embedded in his shoulder and the skin of his neck. Grady had no time to brace for the voltage that surged through his body.

They'd practiced getting hit with Tasers and stun guns regularly in training. It didn't make it any less uncomfortable, though.

Grady hit the ground. He bit down hard and

tasted blood. He could feel Skylar on the floor beside him. "Take them to the van. Kill them, and get rid of the bodies."

FIVE

His entire body ached. He felt like he was coming off that monthlong flu he'd had a couple of years ago. Grady blinked and tried to move but quickly realized it wasn't a good idea. The ceiling of a van was above him, while the tires below rumbled against the road. No windows, just intermittent flashes of light from the front windshield. Streetlights. Cars. They were still in the city.

He looked at his watch. The time had frozen at 8:14 a.m., probably when he'd been hit by that Taser. Only the second time he'd been unconscious today, and it was likely still early. Not his best day.

They were tied up. Again. The only difference was that this time their hands were in front of them. *Good.* Anyone with training could get out of zip ties done like this.

The morning news played on the radio in the front, but that DJ didn't come on until after nine. Still, with DC traffic they might not be far from the White House. Skylar lay beside him, her dark lashes pressed against the top curve of her cheeks.

She almost looked innocent. Almost. Good thing he knew now the woman was a force to be reckoned with. Strong. Determined to succeed. She'd carried on and kept up with him, even after she'd been shot. Her will to follow through and get to the truth was something.

Then in that one second before the stun gun hit, he'd also seen a flash of what had almost looked like vulnerability. A glimpse of hurt. Fear. He'd known then that Skylar hadn't always been the resolute agent-in-training he'd spent the morning with. She had survived something that had forged this iron core inside her.

What was it?

Grady leaned up to get a look at the driver. The man who'd run from the usher's closet after Skylar had been shot, the one who had given the order to kill them. Still in his army uniform, Simmons drove the car with both hands tight on the wheel. Knuckles white, back hunched. Good, he was stressed. That meant he'd react. Maybe even make a mistake.

There was no way Grady was going to let this guy kill Skylar. Even if they were both tied up, and he had no weapon to defend them with. He was a Secret Service agent, and she would be soon enough. That meant they were on the same team, regardless of the fact that they'd only met earlier this morning. They were fellow agents.

She might be as strong as he was, but knowing that just made Grady all the more determined to protect her. He would hate to see the worst happen to Skylar, when she'd come this far.

She stirred. Grady put his hand over her mouth so she didn't give away the fact that they were both awake. Her eyes opened, and anger flashed there. She was ready to fight.

Grady then moved to press an index finger against his lips. When she nodded, he lowered his hand from her mouth and motioned to the driver.

"We can whisper." He waited a second, glanced at Simmons to make sure they hadn't been heard and said, "Are you okay?"

Her face twisted in a scowl. It almost made him smile. She was just as determined to get out of danger as he was. But this wasn't the time for humor. He could understand she wasn't happy about the day's events so far. This should have been a relatively simple exercise and it had quickly turned into something much bigger.

Wilson had dragged them from the White House to this van. What purpose did getting rid of them serve? Getting the clock without

Grady and Skylar causing problems? Wilson could be planning to plant proof they were the ones stealing this clock. Maybe they were nothing but scapegoats. Nuisances to get rid of.

Wilson would have to work hard to prove to the Secret Service Grady had been in on it. That wouldn't be such an easy pill for Stringer or any of the others to swallow.

"Are you okay?"

He shrugged. Should he be, when the driver was about to try to kill them? "Was Wilson part of your hostile team?"

"He was in the briefing." Skylar thought for a second, then said, "But he wasn't supposed to be the leader. He assumed the role all by himself." Her eyebrows drew together. "Do you think he was the man we heard talking with an English accent?"

He nodded. "There was something about his inflections made me think he might be trying to disguise an accent." Which meant the man wasn't a spy. If he'd been trained, Grady would never have been able to tell.

"And him?" Grady motioned to the driver. The man she had entered the White House with as part of a tour, who had shot at her.

The exercise had succeeded in flagging vulnerabilities that would take some time to unpack. Whether they could be used by real hostiles in the future was something Grady and his team would have to figure out. And that would have to be done *if* they survived the driver's coming attempt to kill the both of them. He'd been trained to deal with what was present first, then attack the periphery. That meant get out of danger now so they could fight the additional threat next.

Skylar's hands and feet were secured as his were. Even if they could get the back door open they still wouldn't be able to jump onto the street. He had no desire to cover his body with road rash, although that was preferable to being murdered.

He leaned closer to Skylar. "Wilson is drawing more attention to himself by sending us away from the White House and the cover of the exercise. If we show up dead in a field somewhere, he can't disguise that as an accident." He shook his head, trying to figure it out. "Whatever he's after has to be more important than the threat of having two murders pinned on him. He thinks he can get away with it."

Which meant Wilson knew something they didn't.

Skylar's eyes were distant, as though she were also trying to figure this out. "Once we get out of here we can go back to the White House and ask him."

Grady felt his lips curl up in a smile. She

wasn't trying to be funny. However, her bravado made her fiercely cute. Though he figured she'd rather he thought of her as capable. Good thing he did. "Deal."

She might not be a full-fledged Secret Service agent yet, but all the loyalty and determination was already part of who she was. A threat had been launched against the White House. He knew Skylar was going to fight against that threat as much as she could. She was going to bring these people to justice. He could see it in every fiber of her being and knew she would make an amazing agent. Not one day in the future but now.

From now until this was done, they would be a team. Yes, he was already part of a team. But his dissatisfaction with his job and his hobbies— and feeling like something was missing from his life—made him realize this might be just the thing he'd been looking for. Grady didn't need a new challenge. He'd only needed a new friend.

One who needed his help.

The driver made a right turn, and the wheels hit gravel. They crunched along the loose stones at a much slower speed than the man had been driving on the road. Where were they? Wherever it was, they were close to the end. The driver was going to stop the van soon. And then he would make his move. He would try to kill Skylar and Grady.

And if he succeeded, those guys would get away with everything.

Skylar watched the decision move across Grady's face. The resolve she saw there was almost scary, had she been the one on the receiving end of everything this Secret Service agent could do. She knew enough about him from this morning to know he wasn't going to let anything happen to her. He also wasn't going to let any of these people get away.

For a split second, she wondered what it would be like if there was something romantic between them. If the man was capable of that much purpose in taking care of the people around him, then it would be amazing to be on the receiving end of it, coupled with love. But she had promised herself that love would never cloud her judgment again. She'd made so many bad choices that she hardly even wanted to entertain the idea of exposing herself to the possibility of being hurt.

Despite the fact that she knew full well romance could be sweet and wonderful, there was no way Skylar would put herself in that position again. It didn't matter if Grady was the nicest man in the world. Skylar could not let anyone have that much power over her personal life and her emotions. Finding out her husband had been cheating on her had been nothing short of devastating.

The van slowed to a stop but the driver didn't put it in Park. Simmons got out and slammed his door. Skylar lifted her head and looked out the front windshield. She didn't see him. She looked to the back window, but no shadow darkened the frosted glass there.

"Where did he go?"

Grady shook his head, lifting up to sit. "I don't know."

Skylar sat up as well. Her head swam with the aftereffects of being zapped with so much electricity. Her muscles were tight from the quick spasms coupled with lying here on the floor of the van. She scooted across the floor toward the driver's side. As she moved she looked around for a toolbox. A knife. Even a sharp piece of metal would help her break the ties that secured her hands and feet.

Before she could reach for the driver's seat to climb in the front, the van started to move.

"What—"

"He's pushing us."

Skylar lifted up and looked in front of the vehicle. The wing mirror. "There's a drop-off, a boat ramp. It goes down to a river." Her stomach bottomed out.

Grady's gaze darkened. "Gravelly Point. He's going to drown us in the Potomac."

She hadn't wanted to say it and wasn't all that glad Grady had voiced it out loud. Skylar had never considered the fact that she might die like this.

She was going to be a Secret Service agent soon. She wouldn't be on the president's detail straight away, but intended to work her way up to it. And she could spend the interim years doing that, being the best agent she could be. It was supposed to be a long and impressive career, if she did say so herself. She was *not* supposed to drown weeks away from becoming an agent.

Skylar hauled herself up and climbed into the front. But it was too late. Water hit the hood of the vehicle. She was thrown into the driver's seat at an odd angle, her legs still twisted in the back. She reached under her knees and pulled up the emergency brake, but they were already in the water. The vehicle sank into the Potomac, and water started to pour in.

While Skylar wrangled her legs into the front seat, the water level outside hit the windows. This was a nightmare. It was every scary dream she'd ever had, wrapped up in one incident. "What are we going to do?" She looked back at Grady.

He was up by the back doors, working at the

latch. "I can't get it open." The wound on the side of his head bled down his cheek.

"We could wait until the van fills up with water and then get the windows open, right?" Weren't there pointy metal rods on the headrests they could use to break the glass? She twisted to grab one, but there were no headrests. Whether it would've worked or not, she didn't even have the tool to try.

"I don't know." He sounded more mad than scared to her. Because he didn't know how to get them out of this?

Skylar reached for the glove box. All that fell out was papers. Nothing she could use to cut her bonds or get them out of here.

Water splashed against her feet on the seat, and she gasped. It was freezing. She bent to reach down and felt under the seat, anyway. Just in case something useful had been stashed down there. As she reached under the passenger seat, the van jolted again. Her hip slammed against the dashboard, and she winced. That was going to leave a bruise.

Grady was still working on the back door. She agreed it was probably their best chance but was willing to try to find another option. The floor under the passenger seat wasn't any help either. She looked around the back of the van again and prayed she would find something.

There! "Hand me that wrench." When he didn't move, she said, "Grady!" loud enough to jog him out of his concentration on the door. "The wrench."

"What?"

Skylar pointed at it with both hands. "Give that to me. I'll use it to break the front window."

"That will just let the water in."

"And it will let us out, so give it to me."

He grabbed it and shuffled his way to her. "I'll do it."

She shook her head. "I'm closer."

He clearly didn't like it, but he gave her the wrench. Skylar held it with both hands and jabbed at the top corner of the windshield. It took a minute solid of her hard slams before the window cracked. Water started pouring in across the dash, right onto her lap. She punched out the rest of the window and hoped they wouldn't get cut up too badly swimming out. How far down were they?

The water was up over the seats now. She ignored that and hauled herself out of the window and through a torrent of incoming freezing water that took her breath away. She heard Grady yell something but just headed for the surface. She needed air.

When her head emerged, the cool air of morning smelled wonderful. A second later a gunshot pinged the water. She felt Grady move up beside her and shoved him away with her hands, then kicked at him with her feet. She heard him swallow a mouthful of air, then water, but there was no time to explain.

Skylar ducked underwater and pushed him, then she swam as best she could still tied up. He broke the surface again, and she followed. Two more gunshots echoed through the air. She felt something hot sting the back of her leg but kept kicking. It was hard to ignore the pain, but it was better than allowing herself to be killed here, where no one would know the truth.

"Go." They would have to swim to the other side of the river if they were going to get away from the gunman. The driver of the van.

"He's running." Grady gasped, water running down his face. "He's going to try to cut us off."

There was no escape. Whichever way they went, Simmons was going to find them.

And he was going to kill them.

SIX

Answering gunshots echoed through the morning air. She heard someone scream. Skylar's feet touched bottom as she reached a spot close enough to the bank she could quit swimming. Unfortunately, that meant dragging herself out of the water with her hands and feet still bound.

Grady coughed and landed on the dirt beside her. "Someone is here. They must've heard the gunshots."

Skylar glanced around, trying to figure out where their assailant had gone. Also trying to ignore the trickle of blood on her leg. Not a bullet wound. She must have scraped it on something under the water.

More gunshots sounded, and she fought for the strength to pull the zip ties apart hard enough to break them.

The whole area around them was flat, and there weren't many trees. Just cars and the footpath. Would someone riding their bike to work see them?

Grady said, "We're near the Pentagon, and the Mount Vernon trail runs close to here. That trail is as busy with bikers and runners at rush hour as the street is with cars."

Traffic whizzed past on the George Washington Memorial Parkway. She said, "A driver could see that we're in trouble. But only if they look over at the right moment."

Breaking free of these ties was going to hurt a lot. Thankfully Simmons had secured their hands in front of them and not behind their backs. With their wrists secured together, not overlapping one on the other, it was only a matter of snapping the ties. Tape was easier, but it was still possible.

The ones on her feet would be more difficult, though. Maybe impossible. Skylar prayed someone was calling the police from their car even now.

If they got free, would it only be so they could die unbound? Where had Simmons gone?

Grady lifted both hands, brought them down hard over his bent knee and snapped the ties. He winced, then glanced at her.

Skylar tried the same move but only succeeded in bruising herself. *Figures.* She hissed out a breath. "How are we going to capture him if we can't even get out of these ties?" Yes, she was mostly just referring to herself, but she needed to feel like they were a team right now. The only problem was she was letting the team down.

"We'll have to—"

An armed man ran from behind a tree, right toward them.

Simmons in his army uniform. Had he stayed to make sure they were dead? He lifted his gun. Grady yelled, "Don't!"

Skylar's breath escaped her throat, nothing but an exhale and a moan. She'd been sure she would die in the van, and now this? There was nothing they could do to stop it.

"Put the gun down!" Someone else was here?

Skylar whipped her head around in time to see a fourth person. The man who stepped through the trees into view held a Sig Sauer like it was the most natural thing in the world. He wore jeans and a blue button-down shirt, his age somewhere north of fifty.

Beyond the end of the barrel, Simmons's mouth crept up in a sneer. Didn't he care about this newcomer? She saw the gleam in his eyes. He was going to kill them anyway, despite the new man's arrival.

Skylar had to say something. "Don't—"

A single shot rang out. From the new guy's

weapon. Their captor dropped to the ground, and the man who had saved their lives kicked his gun away, while Simmons groaned and clutched his leg where he'd been shot.

Grady exhaled. "You just saved our lives. Who are you?"

"Niles Ford," the man said, holstering his weapon behind his back. "I think my ride-share spilled his coffee all over the interior of my new truck, but I never figured archivists were made of particularly stern stuff. They just look at paper all day."

Skylar stared up at their rescuer. "Is any of that supposed to make sense to me?"

Grady ignored her question and asked Niles, "You got a knife?"

Niles produced a pocketknife from a pouch on his belt. Grady used it to cut the ties on his ankles and then helped Skylar get free of hers.

Grady said, "If you have a phone, too, we should call this in. Get Secret Service police here." He pointed at Simmons. "He needs medical attention first, but I sure have a lot of questions."

Niles cocked his head to one side. "Secret Service?"

Grady nodded. "I'm Agent Farrow, and this is Acting Agent Austin." They both rose to their feet.

Skylar brushed herself off, but the reality was she had more bruises than friends right now. And she was soaking wet. They shook Niles's hand, and she thanked him for saving them. "We really appreciate it."

"Perhaps you can appreciate it enough not to mention my name in any of this?"

Grady said, "You discharged a weapon."

"When ballistics come back, my employer will take care of the situation. So long as your statement of events and what I explain to him matches up, everything will be fine."

Skylar shook her head. Who was this guy? Sure, this was Washington, DC, and he could work for any branch of government she knew about, or one that she didn't even know existed. But still, not waiting for the police?

Grady stepped closer to the man. "At least call it in for us. We have no phones, and only Simmons's gun to maintain this situation. If you hadn't shown up, we'd be dead right about now."

She wondered at him not telling the man about the hostage situation at the White House. Maybe it was to save face because the Secret Service had been outwitted during a mere exercise. But maybe Grady just didn't want the information leaked since it didn't need to be common knowledge. Niles definitely seemed like the kind of person who lived with enough constraints of his own that he might understand.

"I'll call in an anonymous tip. Should only take them a couple of minutes after that to find you." Niles glanced behind him. "I'm actually surprised no one else ran after me. You can't turn around in this town without finding a tourist with their cell phone taking a picture."

Grady started to speak, but Skylar cut him off with her hand on his bicep. "We appreciate your help, Niles. But really, if we don't know who you are, then where do we send the fruit basket to say thank-you for saving our lives?"

Grady looked at her like she was nuts, but Niles laughed. He pulled out his wallet and took a card out. He handed it to her.

On the card was the name *Niles Ford* and a phone number. Nothing else. "If you need anything, call me. I'll only be in town for a few days."

"Taking in the sights?" Skylar asked.

Niles laughed. "You kids take care." He disappeared almost as quickly as he had shown up.

Grady shook his head and went to retrieve the injured gunman's weapon. "That was probably the weirdest conversation I've had in my entire life. If I didn't owe the man my life, I would've probably tried to arrest him."

Skylar waved his card. "Maybe later when

we're done with all of our immediate problems." Yes, Niles had saved their lives, but Grady had been with her every step of the way so far. They'd saved each other over and over again this morning. And he was the one still with her now.

Simmons had passed out, blood coating his right pant leg. Niles had shot him in such a way that Simmons was hurt, but it wasn't life-threatening. Skylar checked his pulse just in case, and it was steady.

"He needs an ambulance." Not wanting to leave Grady's side, she searched through the gunman's pockets and found a wallet and cell phone. Even though Niles had said he would provide an anonymous tip, she called a number Grady gave her. A couple of minutes later, Secret Service Uniformed Division showed up, along with two Arlington County sheriff's deputies.

They debriefed with the officers, while EMTs checked them out. Skylar held the business card Niles had given her out of sight, not wanting to expose the man's involvement unless it was absolutely necessary. She would put it in her pocket, but she was soaking wet. As they loaded Simmons into the ambulance, he started to wake up.

Skylar went to climb in, but Grady brushed past her and moved to the gunman's side. "Tell me about Wilson. He wanted us gone. Is that his real name?"

The gunman just glared at him.

"Why did he want us dead?"

Simmons shifted his glare to Skylar. She shivered, and not from the cold. He still wanted them dead, but he would be in police custody now.

Wilson was calling the shots, and Simmons had carried out his orders. Was he a true believer, or simply being paid well? How many others had Wilson brought around to his way of thinking?

She said, "What were you going to get out of the deal? Whatever it is, I don't think you can spend it in prison."

Grady pushed out a breath and tried to calm his nerves. He wanted to wring this man's neck. The guy had pushed the van into the river and then waited around to make sure they were dead—just in case the river didn't claim them. He probably figured he'd have been long gone by the time their bodies were fished out of the Potomac.

And now Grady's life was in debt to a mysterious man who had called himself Niles Ford. This did not sit well with him, considering he was a senior agent. And that wasn't pride talking. It was his job—his responsibility—to ensure the safety of this junior agent.

He channeled the frustration into questioning this man. "Who is Wilson? Is he really the man with the English accent? Why does he want a clock from the White House?" There were a million things in that building worth stealing. And yet the guy was going after one particular item, ignoring countless other priceless artifacts.

Simmons said nothing. Just closed his eyes and kept his lips shut. He could exercise his right to stay quiet all he wanted. The Secret Service would get to the bottom of this. And when that was done, Grady would find out who Niles Ford was. He was fine with the idea that the man was driving by and happened upon an attempted murder in progress. What bothered him was that it was *this* man in particular. One clearly trained, and wishing to remain anonymous. The coincidental nature of his arrival didn't sit right with Grady. Something more had to be going on he wasn't seeing.

Did Grady or Skylar—or both of them—have a secret guardian they weren't aware of? This was Washington, DC. Backroom deals abounded. What it had to do with the English guy using the exercise as cover for a theft and a murder Grady didn't know. But he was going to find out.

"You're going to prison. You think he's going to retain his loyalty to you? You think he'd keep your name out of it?"

Army guy opened his eyes. "A job's a job."

"The clock?"

"You think I care about that? If the two of you aren't dead, I don't get paid. Wilson can go jump off a bridge, for all I care."

"That's his real name? *Wilson?*"

Surely when the man found out Simmons had failed, he was going to send someone else to finish the job. It was nearly all Grady could think about.

Simmons nodded, no longer caring how much he said.

Grady jumped out of the ambulance. He motioned Skylar to walk a few paces away with him, then said, "The English guy is Wilson."

She nodded, so he continued, not really sure how she was going to take his next suggestion. "I'll understand if you want to go home soon. Get cleaned up. The exercise is probably over by now, considering. An officer will hang out outside your hotel room—or wherever you're staying. Just until I know for sure it's all good."

"No way," she said, shaking her head. "I'm sticking with you until we get this Wilson guy in custody."

Surely she hadn't forgotten the day's danger so far. It wasn't even eleven in the morning yet.

Skylar lifted her chin, determination blanketing her features. "I figure the safest place for me to be is right beside a trained Secret Service agent. That's world-class protection right there."

"Sure, if Wilson hadn't also tried to kill me." He wasn't going to be flattered. He wasn't going to let her appreciation of him and the job he did go to his head. Still, he couldn't help but be a little puffed up by what she'd said. Especially after his most recent failure. "I appreciate your faith, but once you've given Command your statement, we'll be getting you into protective custody until Wilson and everyone working with him has been apprehended."

"So I can be at Command until then? Can I watch the exercise wrap up?" He ignored the look on her face.

It wasn't that he didn't want her with him. That wasn't it at all. The problem was Grady had a job, and Skylar wasn't even a rookie yet. She was still in training. Her ability to function as a Secret Service agent was hampered by rules. Ones that kept all of them—and the people they protected—safe.

"You know, the longer we stand here debating, the better the chance Wilson is going to get away with this." She lifted her chin. "We should be going back to the White House with those agents taking him into custody."

"Not *we*. Just me. Simmons is going to the hospital first. I've already called it in. They're looking for Wilson, and when I get there, I'll make my statement. You'll make your statement and the Secret Service will bring him in." She wasn't going to be racing around, gung ho, bringing down bad guys.

She would be safe.

He would be working.

There were plenty of agents and cops that could protect Skylar. It didn't have to be Grady. But the fact that she wanted it to be him definitely helped. He didn't know what exactly had happened between them so far this morning.

One of the Secret Service Uniformed Division officers rode with an Arlington deputy in the ambulance. The other one gave them a ride back to the White House before he headed to the hospital as well.

"You're just going to dump me off at Command and go risk *your* neck?"

Grady turned to her. He did want to know that she was safe. As in personally assure she was safe. He might be able to work more efficiently if she was with him and he didn't have to worry about her, but not enough that he'd give Wilson one target instead of two.

No way.

If Wilson was going to try again, Grady wasn't going to make it easy for him.

SEVEN

Grady strode into the command center bus parked across the street on Pennsylvania Avenue, Skylar right behind him. She gasped.

He nodded. "I know. It's huge."

And the whole place was abuzz with what was happening, agents talking low into their radio headsets. Directing efforts to take back the White House from the supposed hostiles.

"Director Tanner!" Grady called across the din. Both he and Skylar were soaking wet, and she was still dressed in her disguise clothes, as they walked to where his boss stood behind an agent at a computer. He pointed to the agent's screen and said something, then came over.

The director lifted his chin. "I've been wondering where you got to."

"No one saw us taken from the White House in a van?"

Tanner flinched. "I'm still trying to figure

out how they got you out. Must have been some smooth talking by that guy to get through the gate."

Grady agreed, considering the man had taken them out to try to kill them.

"Heads are going to roll for that one, I can assure you."

Grady wasn't sure if that was supposed to make him feel better about almost dying.

"I heard the call from Metro PD, but I could hardly believe it. The hostiles really tried to kill you?"

"Yes, sir." He explained about Skylar over-hearing the conversation concerning the theft of the clock and everything that happened after.

Tanner shifted his gaze. "Doing okay, Austin?"

Skylar lifted her chin. "Yes, sir."

Grady couldn't get the image of her in the van, with water pouring in, out of his mind. To say they'd been put through the wringer today was an understatement. And yet in all of it, Skylar had remained in control and alert. He was proud of her. "She did great today. Kept her cool, helped both of us stay alive."

Her gaze darted to his, and she smiled.

"Day's not over yet," Tanner said, then turned back to Skylar. "I'll need you to get together with one of our agents. We need to know who this Wilson guy is."

"What about the agents who were tied up in the Yellow Oval Room with us?" Grady asked. "Couldn't they ID him?"

"They called in," Tanner said, "but they're still in the White House, bringing in all the hostiles. They'll be at it for a while yet. When the dust clears and we have everyone in custody, we'll be able to differentiate who was simply here for the exercise and who the thieves are. With your help, of course."

Grady nodded. He was going to do everything he could to bring those men down and keep Skylar safe. He didn't want to relive the terror of thinking they were going to die. Not ever again.

There was something about Skylar. A…spark, maybe? And the strength he wanted to ask her about. Definitely, they should spend some more time together.

He wasn't interested in a relationship, but maybe she needed a friend. Or a mentor in the Secret Service. Someone she could call on when she needed help or had a question. He could do that.

"I'm happy to help," Skylar told the director.

Grady wished he could get her—and yeah, okay, him, too—some dry clothes. He was seriously uncomfortable. And dripping a mess onto the carpet. He moved from foot to foot.

"I know you're anxious to get back out there," Tanner said. "But first let's go through everything the two of you know. We need to pinpoint exactly how many of our hostiles are also thieves. And Skylar can help us ID them."

The director looked about as happy as Grady was about the idea of thieves posing as hostiles. If those guys seriously thought they could get away with this they would quickly realize they were wrong. The Secret Service was going to round up each one of the hostiles and make sure the would-be thieves were brought to justice.

Then there was all this business with the clock.

Grady could hardly believe someone wanted to steal from the White House. Weren't there easier places to break into, easier things to steal? But he'd been shot at. There was no other reason that made sense to try to kill them than Skylar and Grady knowing too much.

Enough to send them off in a van to their deaths.

"There's another problem, sir."

The director's eyebrow lifted.

Grady took a half step closer and spoke in a low voice. "I saw the main thief, the one they call Wilson, talking to a Secret Service agent."

"Be very careful with what you're about to say, Agent Farrow."

Grady nodded. He knew the implications of fingering another agent as a traitor. Not to mention being in league with those who would breach the defenses of the White House. But right was right, and wrong was wrong. And in the balance were his life and Skylar's. They all had to make their own choices.

And one of their agents may have made the wrong one.

"I didn't see his face. I have no idea who it is." He thought through his words, measuring them carefully. If he was to start everyone hunting for a mole, he could inadvertently make it so he implicated a teammate falsely. That would mean repercussions for both their careers. "Only what I saw. Wilson talking to one of us."

"A male agent. Or, at least, he was dressed like one of you," Skylar said, though there was a question in her voice. "Caucasian. About five-ten, dark brown hair cut short."

Grady frowned. "You saw him?"

"In the hall, and only from the back." She shrugged. "If it's even who you're talking about."

"It could be, but I didn't see hair color. So I can't corroborate."

The director folded his arms. "So all we have

is supposition? That isn't enough to do anything. Even if Skylar could identify the person."

Grady sighed. "We should at least watch out, just in case."

"I understand you would want to bring in anyone who was working with the thieves, but bringing in the thieves themselves is our top priority. If you want to play Internal Affairs in this scenario and you find evidence, I'll look at it."

Grady nodded. Had he been expecting more? Probably not, but it still stung that the director didn't see what he did. Or he couldn't, because Grady didn't have solid evidence to back up his claim.

He'd known it was flimsy.

That wash of ice water—the realization he really didn't have much of anything to corroborate his theory—shut off the slight he'd been dealt. He didn't blame the director for making this call. Reason dictated it was the right one, but part of Grady didn't like it—enough that he had no desire to someday ascend to director level. He didn't want to be the one who had to make those calls.

All he wanted was a simple life. He'd sworn off relationships for now, but maybe that was the pain talking. Losing his fiancée had been a blow he hadn't seen coming. It left Grady with the peaceful dream of one day having a nice place to live. Something comfortable that didn't look like a showplace. A good woman he loved to share it with. Paula had wanted more. She'd expected him to be a nine-to-five guy, which wasn't what being in the Secret Service entailed. Skylar understood that. She got the life they led here.

Or wherever they were going to post her when she finished training.

He wanted to say they should keep in touch after she left Washington and went back to training, but wouldn't that be weird? They'd known each other only a few hours, though it felt much longer. Did she have the same feeling about him?

He wanted to ask her that as well, but Grady held his tongue. Because Skylar was in danger, and so was he. After all this was done and dealt with, he could talk to her about keeping in touch.

First, he had to find the men who'd tried to kill them.

"You sure you're okay with this?"

His face was so soft Skylar almost wanted to ask him to stay. But what would that prove? It would be super awkward to have him sitting here in the command bus with her. Doing nothing while his people finished the exercise.

"I'm good." He needed to help them, didn't he? The irrationally scared part of her didn't want to be somewhere surrounded by people she didn't know. Mostly Skylar tried to ignore it, using a combination of what the Bible said and her own desire not to be ruled by fear in any situation.

He studied her for a minute, then said, "Stay here until I get back, okay?"

Skylar nodded. "Don't worry about me. Go do your thing. I'll be fine."

Who wanted to be the one who cramped someone else's style? He had a job to do. Skylar would be part of his world one day, but not today.

Grady had changed in the bathroom and then left kitted out in his full agent gear. At least he hadn't looked as though he liked the idea of leaving her all that much. She almost smiled. Maybe she should have clung to him and pretended she desperately needed him to stay so she could feel safe. Parts of that would feel nice. All the closeness. Probably some friendly hugging. She liked hugs.

Too bad she could take care of herself.

The dichotomy made her head spin. Kind of like being trained as a Secret Service agent, and then running away from gunmen in the White House because her life was in danger. Thinking in the van that they were going to die, then escaping. Facing down Simmons, and being saved by Niles. Why did she think that man had more of a story to him? Skylar shook her head and sipped her coffee.

"Skylar Austin?" It was the young man who'd brought her the drink. An intern?

"Yes."

"The director wants me to show you footage from the last few days, when the HVAC guys started arriving. To see if you can ID this Wilson guy or any of his friends."

Skylar followed him to the back of the bus, where he had a station set up with a laptop. She sat beside him and watched footage of the last few days, starting at the gate where cars came and went.

"Everyone who checks into the White House has already been thoroughly vetted. However," he added quickly, "we do get people who slip through the cracks. No one wants to admit they were at fault, but while we're experts, we are also human."

"I like that." Maybe she needed to think of herself in that way a little more. Skylar was forever pushing herself to do more. To be more. Testing the limits of her strength and capability, and then breaking through those barriers. One day she was going to fail. If she got the picture now, probably her failure wouldn't sting quite so much when it happened.

The intern grinned. "Now we get to play cat

and mouse, and figure out who this guy is." He scrolled through more footage to the arrival of a van. "When you see him, tell me. I can run the image through our facial recognition database. See if we can get a match."

Skylar watched the screen. Shook her head intermittently, when it wasn't any of the gunmen she'd seen. A few of the hostiles were HVAC people, but not all of them. Had the thieves recruited all, or only some? And how big was their team? She didn't believe it was only Wilson, Simmons and Johnson. Plus that mysterious agent—if he was even part of it.

Still keeping her attention on the screen, she said, "So, you like working with the Secret Service?"

"Sure, who wouldn't? Part of my poli-sci degree includes work experience, and I'm minoring in criminal justice."

"Wow, busy guy."

He grinned. "This was a fantastic opportunity. And yeah, I'm the coffee guy, and the 'watch these hours of footage until you want to scream' guy—"

She grinned back at him. It was kind of mind-numbing.

"But I'm at the epicenter of the country here." He motioned to the space at large. "These people have devoted their lives to protecting this nation.

They don't affect policy or laws, but without them, this whole thing we call America would just fall apart."

Skylar nodded. "I know. It's part of why I decided to become a Secret Service agent myself." She glanced around the command post. The hustle and bustle of personnel at work. There were no more than fifteen agents in the bus, but they were doing important work. They made sure the White House stayed safe.

It was heady stuff.

She said, "You like the people—the agents, I mean?"

"Sure." He shrugged. "Some of them are a little standoffish, and there are some I just plain don't like. But most of them are cool. Like Agent Farrow." He lifted his eyebrows like there was a secret underlying his words.

"He does seem like a nice guy."

"The best. Really helped me get settled here and feel like part of the team."

Skylar smiled, not sure what else to say. Grady had been nice to her today. And he'd helped keep her alive. But it wasn't more than that. The intern seemed to think something would develop between them, when Skylar couldn't even entertain the idea. What was the point?

The Secret Service could assign her anywhere, and she had little choice in it. And even if she were attracted to him—because what was the point in dwelling on that either?—who could say a friendship would even survive long distance? She'd probably never even see him after today or tomorrow.

Skylar sighed and set her elbow on the desk, her chin in her palm. The intern's cell phone gave off a series of beeps. He looked at the screen, then jumped up. "I'll be back in a second. Pause it if you see something."

Skylar nodded, not all that optimistic she was going to be much help. They might end up looking through days of footage. They didn't even know what time that morning Wilson had arrived.

A florist's delivery truck pulled up on the screen. Nope.

Nothing.

Someone tapped her on the shoulder. When she jerked around, she saw an agent in a ball cap and a bulky windbreaker behind her.

"Yes?"

"Grady needs you. He said come with me."

"I'm not supposed to leave the bus until he gets back."

"That's why he sent me. Because he needs you in the White House. Now."

Skylar paused the surveillance footage. "I'm really not supposed to leave."

The man's eyes hardened. Was this the Secret Service agent involved with the thieves? She opened her mouth to call for help.

He touched his weapon. It was holstered at his side, but unsnapped. "I could draw this and shoot you dead before you got a single word out. Then I would kill at least half the people on this bus before I ran out of bullets. Now get up and move."

Skylar's legs threatened to buckle, but she preceded him out the back doors of the bus.

The agent led her around the side of the building, probably toward a loading entrance of some kind. The White House was huge.

He kept her in front, his hand to the small of her back. It should have been a nice gesture that made her feel secure. It wasn't. Not when she could feel the pressure of the gun at her side.

Until they reached a long concrete tunnel. This was an entrance? "Where are—"

"Down we go."

EIGHT

Skylar looked down the long concrete tunnel. Only darkness waited down there…and apparently also a rear entrance to the White House.

"Come on."

She swallowed and started down the ramped walkway. *It's going to be fine.* This guy didn't need to know she had a teensy little problem with small, dark spaces. It wasn't like she'd have a panic attack. They'd never have approved her training as a Secret Service agent if she did. It was nothing but a garden-variety phobia.

One that was *not* on her file.

Skylar fisted her hands, racking her brain for what she could do. She was being held at gunpoint. But not led to her death—she hoped—just back into the White House.

For what?

Grady was there, doing his job. Maybe they were going to see Grady after all—but likely not for any good reason. Maybe they had him, and now her, and soon they were both going to die and the two of them would be implicated as thieves.

Each footfall of the agent's boots echoed down the tunnel. The sound made her shiver, even though she wasn't all that cold. She wanted Grady to be here with her now. So they could take care of this together. And not just because Grady had a gun and she didn't.

Skylar needed to figure a way out of this that didn't involve her being on the receiving end of another gunshot. One that would probably kill her this time, rather than grazing her leg. She'd taken off the protective vest and changed into an agent's gym clothes. She had no weapons, not even any unconventional ones. Still, there had to be some part of her training that could kick in and give her some indication of what to do.

She'd joined the army right out of high school, and Earl—her ex-husband—had been the sergeant in her squad. It'd been a bad idea from the start, but he'd managed to hide his extra-curricular hookups from nearly everyone—her included. Thus the memory of her military life had been colored by the failure of her marriage. It was hard to think about that time without also thinking about her bad choices.

Part of being a Secret Service agent was proving she was over it. That she wasn't the inadequate woman she used to be—at least, that was how she'd felt. And yet here she was with those feelings all rushing through her again. Insufficient. Naive, because she'd so thoroughly fallen for Earl's charms. Why couldn't she let the past go?

Now her entire career with the Secret Service was going to be colored by this. There was nothing stronger than the men and women who protected the president. The first time she'd seen an agent on a sightseeing trip, she'd realized that was who she wanted to be.

Would she even make it to graduation from training?

Getting there was everything she thought she wanted. But the niggling feeling remained. When she had everything she wanted, would it be all she'd imagined? For good or bad—and, boy, had she learned that one the hard way—she was going to live life on her terms.

Which meant she'd die on her terms as well.

He shoved her forward. "The door is just up here."

Skylar picked up her pace, since getting inside the White House meant she'd be where other people were. *Lord, please let one of the agents see us.* The last thing she wanted was to die alone. "Why are you taking me back in?"

"You ruined it all. Guess you'll just have to be the one who fixes things."

He said nothing more, she opened her mouth to ask another question, then thought better of the idea. Was he going to kill her, as Wilson had wanted? Frustration made her speak again before she could think. "I won't tell anyone I saw you. I don't even know who you are. I'll forget all about this, and Wilson is the one who will be fingered for attempted theft."

He didn't respond to that. Was he deciding if she was worth keeping alive, or would he really murder her in the White House?

Then she reached the end of the tunnel—and a ladder.

"Climb up, and flip the latch at the top. Do it quietly because if there's someone on the other side, they could hear."

Like that was going to happen. She wanted to make as much noise as possible if it meant someone hearing.

To keep from thinking about ways he would retaliate, she said, "Aren't the Secret Service watching this tunnel on surveillance?" They'd turned it back on since she and Grady were taken from the White House.

"Of course." He said it like she was some kind of imbecile. "They'll know it's been opened."

But would they know Skylar had been coerced at gunpoint back inside? He'd had to keep his identity secret through this whole situation. Maybe that was why he wore a ball cap now, to try to hide his face from the cameras.

The agent took her flashlight. Skylar climbed the ladder, her limbs shaky. She glanced back and saw the agent standing back, his gun aimed at her. At the top was a latched door no bigger than a foot and a half squared. If someone were on the other side, she wasn't going to be able to crawl through without him shooting her in the back before she could alert them to the fact that she'd kinda been kidnapped.

She pushed the door up, like the opening to an attic. Only this entrance went into the White House.

"Slowly. It'll hit the inside of a cupboard."

Skylar did as instructed, a knot in her stomach. The agent switched off his flashlight, then hers. On the other side of the door were two walls, a ceiling and the backside of a cupboard door. There were even holes in the walls where a shelf could be hung.

A slit of light shone around the edge of the door, which had been locked from the inside.

Skylar went up two more rungs on the ladder so she'd be able to reach the latch of the cupboard and then stopped. Listened. If bullets started flying, all the caution in the world wouldn't help.

Skylar unlatched the cupboard and crawled out…into the ground-floor Library.

"Good."

Skylar flinched. Wilson stood in the corner of the room with two guys. More hostiles she hadn't known about? The agent climbed out as well, and then there were two guns pointed at her. Two more were stowed but easily reachable. She would be dead if she tried to run or call for help.

The agent shoved her forward and asked Wilson, "Where are you at?"

"Still trying to locate the clock," Wilson said. "We'd be done if she hadn't jumped the timeline by eavesdropping. We're scrambling, but we'll get it done."

The agents were all rounding up hostiles, and the exercise was supposed to be over. What on earth was happening that they were able to move freely around the building still?

She'd thought Wilson was the one in charge. The Secret Service agent seemed to be calling the shots here. Did they have some kind of agreement, or was this all on the agent? Just a payday and some hired thieves to make it happen? They had to be insane. And worse, things were messy now that their plan had been ruined.

That would only send them scrambling to finish what they'd come here to do.

And it made them twice as dangerous.

"Go. Find it."

Wilson and the two HVAC guys with him—more hostiles she'd seen at the briefing as well—checked the hallway and then left.

Skylar faced the agent and raised her chin. "What are you going to do with me?"

He sneered, showing a flash of white teeth between his lips for a second. "This." He kept his aim on her, then lifted his radio. "Command, I have Skylar Austin in the Library. Looks like she's helping the thieves steal the clock everyone's talking about."

Grady heard the radio call when it came in. He was two floors above the Library, in the residence, searching for hostiles so far unaccounted for.

He glanced at Stringer, who looked about as confused as Grady.

Stringer said, "I thought you left her at Command."

Grady pulled out his cell phone so he could keep this conversation off the radio channel. "Let's head down there." He dialed as they headed for the stairs and descended. The intern picked up. "Skylar was with you. Why did I just hear a radio call that she's in the White House?"

"She's one of the thieves," the kid said. "And she's gone back to steal the clock. She must have run out of the bus while my back was turned." The words rushed out, the kid clearly exasperated.

Grady wanted to argue. He wanted to tell the intern he was wrong. No way was Skylar part of the thieves' group. But had he misread her? She'd seemed so innocent. They'd been chased, and then nearly drowned in the van. Had it all been nothing but misdirection, playing a part until she could show her true colors? Grady didn't want to doubt the kernel of trust in her he'd established so far today, but reality could prove him *completely* wrong.

Grady hung up and headed to the Library with Stringer. When they got there, Agent Barnes had Skylar's arm in his tight grip. Her lips were pressed into a thin line, and he thought he might've seen the sheen of tears in her eyes. Then she blinked, and there was nothing but anger.

Between Grady standing with Stringer and Agent Barnes holding Skylar were two agents. One was his team's lead agent, and the other was another of the agents who'd been tied up in the

East Room. These two didn't know an agent was suspected of working with the thieves.

Was Barnes the one who'd chosen to betray them all?

The man kept to himself, and Grady couldn't say he knew Barnes all that well. He was married, but Grady didn't even know if he had kids.

If Barnes was a traitor, this was a bold move. Discredit Skylar in the event she accused him of wrongdoing. She would have no credibility.

His team lead said, "I'll take her to Command, Barnes. You should get back to helping Alvarez round up hostiles."

Barnes didn't move. "She's a wily one. She'll say anything to convince you she's innocent, and believe me she's convincing. Nearly had me fooled. Don't listen to one word comes out of her mouth."

"Noted." The team lead secured Skylar's hands behind her back.

That was when she noticed him in the room.

Her mouth opened, but the tug on her arms caused a strangled cry to come out. Grady moved to go to her. Stringer shifted and whispered, "Don't."

He halted.

Skylar's eyes flashed with betrayal. Grady couldn't help her. Not when she could very well turn out to be part of this whole attempted theft.

It would damage his reputation. But it was still hard to believe a Secret Service agent capable of betrayal. And for a clock? It had to be more.

There were plenty of other things in the world that could be stolen much more easily if a person wanted a quick buck. He hadn't dwelled on it overmuch but figured this was true. This was probably the most secure house in the world.

Grady said, "I'll go with you." His team leader didn't need help, but Grady wasn't about to let the thieves hurt her any more than they already had. It was probably an irrational fear that she'd get hurt, especially when she could be one of them.

Stringer shot him a look. Grady ignored it and said, "Barnes should come, too. We'll need a statement on exactly what he saw Skylar doing."

"He dragged me in here," she said. "I wasn't *doing* anything."

He wanted to tell her he believed her. That he knew she was being framed. But he couldn't because he didn't know for sure. Wilson nearly had both of them killed, but who knew what the truth of the matter was?

The team leader frowned at her. "Your part in this remains to be seen, Ms. Austin. We don't like thieves, especially not ones who thought they could be Secret Service agents."

Barnes smirked. "She'll say anything to claim her innocence. Just like I told you."

Grady caught the curl of his lips and shot the man a frown. "You and I need to have a conversation."

Barnes lifted both eyebrows, cocky like always. "Too bad I don't have time. Not when there are hostiles to round up. Like I rounded up her." He pointed at Skylar, a jab of his finger in the air.

Grady wanted to slap cuffs on the man but couldn't. He had no evidence except Skylar's word that the man had forced her back into the White House. Just a sour feeling in his stomach. He put stock in intuition. Always had. Too bad it didn't provide evidence. Just a hunch, nothing more.

Had Barnes actually committed a crime—beyond being suspected of colluding with thieves? It wasn't much to go on. He wished he'd seen the man's face when he'd been speaking to Wilson in the entrance hall. All he'd seen was two people conversing. It might mean nothing or everything.

If what Skylar had said was true, and he had taken her from the bus, then he'd done it evading detection by the cameras. As one of their agents, Barnes knew where they all were. He'd brought her back into the White House to frame her. To take suspicion off himself and any accusations that might fly in his direction.

Nothing but a…

"Distraction."

"What?" Stringer turned to him.

"We need to find Wilson. Now." Grady turned to the team leader. "I'm going to find that Wilson guy. Can you wait on taking Skylar back to Command? I want to go with her."

"How about you do your job and I'll do mine, Agent Farrow."

He'd stepped over the line. "Yes, sir." Then to Stringer he said, "Let's go."

As much as he wanted the guy to hold off, the team lead would make sure Skylar got back to Command safely. Barnes would have to go along with it, or he'd be exposing the fact that he was a traitor.

They raced out and cleared all the rooms on this floor, then headed for the stairs. "Up or down?"

Stringer radioed Command for a status report on rounding up the hostiles and thieves. "Only places that haven't been cleared and secured are the second-floor bedrooms. They're working through those now."

"Let's go."

They headed for the stairs, beyond which was the curator's office. Why was the door open?

Grady didn't have time to check. Not when they had Wilson and his friends probably cornered upstairs. There were a limited number of ways they could escape from up there, though it was possible. What it required was extensive knowledge of White House secrets.

There were secrets.

And then there were Top Secret secrets.

How much did Wilson know?

Barnes could have told the man everything. Grady didn't want him to be a traitor, but it was possible. He could have been the man Grady saw talking to Wilson.

And he also had to admit it was just as possible Skylar might be one of the thieves as well. That she'd deceived him.

The report of gunfire could be heard, but he couldn't pinpoint the origin. Somewhere in the White House, one of the Secret Service agents was fighting back. Those involved in the exercise who weren't hostiles or agents were employees who had volunteered. Grady prayed nothing bad had happened to any of them. For their sake—or the sake of the White House and the agency. Reputations were earned over time, but they could be lost in a single moment. He didn't want anyone hurt.

What was far more likely was that Barnes had maneuvered the situation so the Secret Service's attention was divided between Skylar and Wilson.

Grady hit the second floor at a run.

Gunshots echoed through the hallway.

Answering fire.

He reached the bedroom door and saw two of his team facing Wilson and another man. Another HVAC guy Grady hadn't seen yet. How many of them were there? Both agents went down.

"Drop your guns!"

Clock or no clock, these men had shot Secret Service agents. He didn't care about a theft right now—just these men who had his back every day.

And Grady had theirs.

"I said—"

One fired. Stringer squeezed off a round.

Grady was already falling.

NINE

They made their way down the hall, Skylar at the center of the huddle of three agents. The one who had told Grady he wasn't going to wait for him; she guessed he was the guy in charge. The other agent was along for the ride, but seemed astute enough to keep an eye on Barnes—the traitor.

She wanted to plead her case. To tell them she was innocent. She'd scream it from the roof of the White House if it made them believe her. Being falsely accused was the scariest thing she'd ever endured. Even worse than the possibility of dying in a volley of bullets. She could end up in jail, and Barnes—not to mention Wilson and anyone else involved—would get away. Free and clear, with all the blame placed on Skylar.

The team-leader agent halted. He thumbed his radio. "Copy that." Then turned to them. "Shots fired upstairs. Agents down."

"Grady." His name was a whisper. What about his friend Stringer? Were they hurt?

"Let's go," the other agent said to Barnes. "We need everyone's help."

Barnes's deadpan face didn't betray one bit of his true motives. "I could take Austin to Command."

Her stomach knotted. "There's no time to lose, right? You have my word I won't do anything but what you tell me."

She wanted to lift both hands. To placate the team leader, like empty palms would make her seem more innocent, but her hands were tied tight behind her back.

Thankfully the team lead didn't make her go with Barnes. He said, "Let's go."

The agent held her elbow as they raced up the stairs, the man in charge leading the way. Skylar took a second to thank God they didn't have the time to argue with her when their teammates could be hurt.

At the top, she glanced back to where Barnes should have been.

She gasped. "He's gone."

His eyebrow lifted and he shot her a look. "You wanna be the one to go look for him?"

"No," she told the agent. "I want to know if Grady is okay."

"Me, too. So let's go."

"Barnes is a traitor. He can't disappear." She decided to go for it. "He hauled me back in the White House at gunpoint, and Grady and I think he might be working with the thieves."

Would he believe her?

To her surprise, the agent got on his radio and called for Agent Barnes to be detained if he was seen. And added that no one was to let him leave the grounds of the White House.

"Thank you."

Then he told Command that Barnes could just be the mole for the exercise, and nothing more. Skylar gritted her teeth, but there was no time to argue. He probably had to cover all his bases.

They reached the hall upstairs, and she saw Grady's head and shoulders sticking out of a doorway at the far end.

"Grady!"

She didn't care at this point if they realized she cared about him. Why would she? He could be seriously hurt, and she wanted to see his condition for herself.

The two agents stepped over him and entered the room, where Wilson stood.

"Drop the gun!"

"You have nowhere to go!"

Stringer eased up to a sitting position and grabbed his gun, his gaze not settling on anything. Like he couldn't focus.

She crouched beside Grady but couldn't touch him with her hands bound. "You okay?" She called over to Grady's friend.

"Hit my head on the way down." He shook off the confusion and turned to her while Wilson placed his gun on the ground and surrendered to the two agents.

Two more lay on the floor, along with an HVAC repair guy. Dead? Was he one of the guys who'd been with Wilson in the Library when Barnes had brought her in there? She couldn't see his face, but he'd been shot as well.

Her breath was coming fast. Too fast. "All this for a stupid clock?" There had to be more to it or none of this made sense. Then again, when did violence ever make sense?

Grady could be dead, and she couldn't even check. Why did that suddenly feel far more devastating than going to prison for a crime she didn't commit? One that, at this point, hadn't even happened yet. Wilson had tried, and here he was. Captured. But at what cost?

His glare shot daggers at her. "Meddling girl."

She hadn't been a girl for a long time. "You didn't have to kill these men."

The agents were looking at her differently now, grudgingly respectful. Great. Or it would be, if she could actually help them.

Grady groaned and shifted. That was when

she saw the blood, high on his left shoulder. "Can someone cut these plastic ties so I can *help* him?"

Stringer got the okay from the agent in charge, and she was cut free. Then he moved to the other agents who were down. More Secret Service personnel stepped over Grady and into the room.

"Watch it." She frowned at them and tried to help move him out of the doorway, but the man weighed a ton. "Grady." She patted his cheek. "Grady, wake up."

She needed to find the source of the blood. Needed to put pressure on it, after she figured out exactly how bad it was.

"Skylar?" He actually looked pleased to see her leaning over him.

She breathed out the tension she'd been holding even while she was yelling at Wilson, and everyone else. "Are you okay?"

He nodded. "Winged."

"Which is macho-guy speak for *Yes, I got shot, but I'm going to pretend it doesn't hurt that badly.* Right?"

Stringer cracked a laugh. He was back over by one of the downed agents. Would he be laughing over a dead man's body? That didn't seem—

The man sat up, touching a bleeding knot on his forehead.

Beside her, Grady sat up as well. "Seems like

that's the second time you've saved me today. Are we even now?"

"Don't be cute." She shook her head, not realizing what she'd said, and continued, "I don't think my heart can handle you making light of this right now."

A couple of the agents looked at her. Why were they staring?

She caught Grady's gaze and saw his look had softened. No, that wasn't good. Why was he so handsome? Grady leaned over and whispered, "I wouldn't want to cause your heart any problems."

He was joking, right? Her heart was beating so fast it felt like it was going to give out from the strain. "I'm *not* going to have a heart attack, I want to graduate from Secret Service training first. And that's not going to happen if you keep getting knocked unconscious." She pointed to the top of his arm, the fleshy part of his shoulder. "And shot. And scaring the life out of me."

Stringer grinned at her from across the room.

Skylar decided to stop talking. That was probably the best course of action. They were all staring at her—and Grady—like they'd both suddenly grown wings.

Grady put his good arm around her shoulders and pulled her to his side in a quick hug. "I'll see what I can do about that."

"Thank you." She knew she sounded like she

had an attitude, but it was that or cry. And her father had never tolerated tears. Although right now it seemed like getting emotional over this man served to change the other agents' estimation of her. It wouldn't clear her name, but it was a shot toward them actually trusting her instead of simply giving her the benefit of the doubt and letting her help Grady. At least, she could hope it was.

Stringer, his face now devoid of humor, stood over one of the agents on the floor. He shook his head.

"Oh, no."

Grady squeezed her shoulder. "First we work. When the job is done, then we remember."

That was how they deal with stuff like this? Get on with things, and push the grief away for later? She'd lost friends in combat before. And her mom, when she had been barely old enough to remember her. Grief hit when she least expected it. There was no pushing it aside. But these agents were pure professionals. They would power through and expect their emotions to fall in line like everything else.

Skylar got up. Grady did the same. The feeling in his eyes made her wonder if he wasn't as adept at what he'd said as he wanted to be. And honestly, that lifted him higher in her estimation.

When he was already pretty high up there.

* * *

Grady glanced at Skylar and saw she was ready. Alert. Her attention had switched from him to the room at large. Namely, Wilson and the threat to White House security he represented. He knew from her file that she'd excelled in training. Seeing it on paper was one thing, but he'd always preferred practical application. He strode over to Wilson even while he thought about her interesting reaction to his having been grazed on the shoulder by that bullet.

Namely, those tears he'd seen in her eyes when he'd regained consciousness.

He'd been worried for a second that the bullet had hit something important. He'd actually wondered if today was his last day alive. And the one thing he would die regretting? Not getting to tell Skylar he really did believe she was innocent.

That had been the only thing in his mind when he'd hit the ground. As he'd gasped through the pain. When he'd realized the wound wasn't mortal, he'd wanted to see her again.

Something about Skylar Austin had grabbed him. And didn't seem to want to let go.

Then she'd gotten all emotional over the fact that he'd been hurt. Again. He'd seen what was underneath the frustration. The helplessness—a mirror of his own feelings. She cared.

She cared about *him*.

In that moment, she hadn't blamed him for doing nothing while she was detained, suspected of being one of the thieves. It'd been all about Grady and whether he was okay.

Later he would think on it. Figure out what it meant for this burgeoning friendship they seemed to be developing. For now, he needed some answers from Wilson as to what on earth was going on.

He faced off with the man. "Tell me about Agent Barnes."

Wilson stared him down. Subdued, for now. Whether he would be cooperative was another matter entirely.

"Were you working together?"

Silence.

Skylar said, "One of your men is dead, two are in custody and Barnes ran off. You've been captured. There isn't any reason for you to keep all this covered up any longer."

Grady didn't begrudge her needing to have her say, but he was the one who was going to take point on this. She'd earned the right to be part of it, though she had no legal standing as an agent. He gave her a nod and then asked Wilson, "Who are you covering for?"

Something about what Skylar had said bothered Wilson. As much was clear from the twitch in his eye when she'd mentioned Barnes making a run for it.

Grady said, "There's no reason to protect Barnes. He ditched you to face this alone."

The reality was they had no idea if Wilson was the mastermind of all this or if Barnes was. They didn't know if it was a onetime thing or one in a series of thefts from the White House. Maybe they had a whole business going. Here and in other high-profile buildings.

Grady said, "A good man is dead. Now we're going to take apart your whole life to get to the bottom of your role in this. There's no way for you to escape justice at this point, so you might as well tell us what we want to know."

"I want my lawyer first."

"Nobody said you were under arrest." He would be, but Wilson hadn't been read his rights yet. There were legal procedures in place, but if he could get Wilson to talk before an official arrest they would be one step closer to figuring all this out.

"You pointed a gun at me and pulled the trigger. You killed an agent in here. And you sent me and Skylar out of the White House to kill us. Seems like a pretty elaborate plan for…" He looked around, saw a clock on the shelf behind Wilson.

This room was basically a sitting room with

feminine decoration, though minimal. Much of the White House had the appearance of a museum—beautiful but impersonal. This room was no different.

"This?" Grady pulled the mantel clock from the shelf and tested the weight of it in his hands. "There are other clocks. Maybe this isn't the right one. Without going through the curator's files for a list of all the clocks in the White House, it's my best guess. Since you guys were in here and all and went to so much trouble."

Wilson had spent time trying to find the clock. He'd tried to kill Grady and Skylar in order to cover up what he was doing. Then when he did find it, he'd killed a man. Grady couldn't believe one clock was worth so much trouble.

"Tell me," Grady said, "is there something special about this one, special enough for you to go to all this fuss? Or is it just about the money?"

The back of the timepiece had a tiny door to hide the internal workings of the clock. Still, it didn't look like anything special. Grady wasn't an art historian, though. Or a curator. It could be worth millions for all he knew. He figured so long as he didn't drop it, he'd be okay.

On the other side of the room, Stringer helped the injured agent out. Grady and Skylar had plenty of backup here with his team leader and the other agents remaining. He didn't want her in danger but had to face the fact that they were both at risk until he got word that Wilson had been found and detained.

Not to mention any other thieves still trying to escape custody.

"It doesn't look like much of anything to me." He shifted it from hand to hand, then pretended to drop it. Wilson didn't even flinch. Worth a try. At least now Grady knew Wilson had no personal connection to the clock. He wasn't trying to steal it because of an intrinsic value. Nor for nostalgic reasons. Probably just for the money, then.

Wilson made a *huh* noise in his throat.

He looked at him. "Something to say?"

The man's brows furrowed, as though he was processing this whole situation. "Turn that over again."

Grady showed him the back.

"That's..." His voice trailed off. "You said Barnes left?"

Grady strode from his spot beside Skylar over to Wilson and said, "If he had, what would it mean?"

It wasn't likely Barnes would get far. Not with the agents all looking for him. More were on their way, those not already on duty this morning. Soon the whole place would be swarming with more Secret Service. Barnes would have nowhere to go.

"Would it mean he's left you to take all the blame?"

"Left me with nothing but a fake I was supposed to steal, and a trap that's well and truly snapped shut now." The English tone to his voice sounded sardonic. He'd given up caring. He was just mad. "Guess I know where I stand."

A fake? Grady's head spun. "Barnes didn't take the real clock?"

Wilson's face twisted. "He told me to steal this one."

Skylar said, "And now there's nothing left to do but tell the Secret Service everything you know. Who you are. Who got you into the White House. All that."

Wilson had been thrown to the wolves by Barnes. Kind of like Skylar, and Barnes's attempt to implicate her as working with Wilson. Barnes and Wilson had already tried to have Grady and Skylar killed this morning. Would Barnes now do the same to Wilson?

It was a good reason the man might stick around, instead of fleeing. Unless he had a partner to do the deed for him.

Barnes had turned on everyone and then left. Which made Grady wonder what the man was into. Theft, yes. But there had to be a deeper reason he was betraying the badge. Maybe it was more than this one clock—maybe it had been a whole string of thefts.

If multiple thefts had taken place over the past months, or even years, Barnes had worked here and then he'd covered his tracks so no one noticed. Whatever the truth was, it was serious enough he'd found it necessary to confuse the situation completely before making his escape.

The theft of a clock didn't seem to warrant this level of scrambling to misdirect everyone.

Wilson's expression turned belligerent. "Just don't file an insurance claim on the thing. You'll probably get about thirty dollars."

It really was a fake? "You didn't know?"

"I was assured everything was legit. Guess I got played."

"This was a onetime gig?"

Wilson shook his head. Not in the negative. Grady figured he was just done talking. "I want a lawyer. And I wanna to-talk deal."

The team leader spoke up then. "No deals. Not when one of my agents is lying dead on the floor of this room and you're the one responsible."

"Barnes is the one responsible."

That might be true, but Grady figured he wasn't going to get away with anything either. Both men would be brought to justice.

The Secret Service agents led him from the

room, and Grady turned to one of his team. "Did we get everyone?"

The guy nodded. "All the hostiles are now accounted for. We just have to figure out which ones are real thieves."

This was shaping up to be a long day.

Grady thumbed his radio. "This is Agent Farrow. Has Agent Barnes been located yet?"

The call came back. "This is Agent Mills. I've got a dead guardhouse agent here. I think Barnes might be in the wind."

TEN

Investigating agents had shown up to deal with the bodies. Likely the FBI would also need to be informed of everything happening in the White House. They'd hit the point now that an agent had been killed where regulation would demand another agency take the lead on investigating.

At the bottom of the stairs, Grady remembered the door to the curator's office having been open. He glanced at Skylar. "One second. I just want to check in there."

She hung back but looked about as reluctant to let him out of her sight as he was to let her out of his. Good. This way he could make sure she was safe. Likely at the same time she endeavored to make sure he wasn't hurt any more either.

His arm stung, but other than needing a bandage over the gash on the meat of his shoulder, he was okay.

Grady pushed the door to the curator's office all the way open. The interior was packed with artifacts. Things that hadn't yet been catalogued, and others scheduled to be sent to the Smithsonian or the National Archives for storage. So many items were gifted to the president they didn't have enough rooms to hold them all here.

He spotted the White House curator at her desk, sipping tea from a china cup. What was she even doing here in the middle of a situation?

Kristine Bartowski was originally from Ohio. She wore thick-rimmed glasses and had wool sweaters in every color. Her usual work uniform was completed with a knee-length skirt and brown Mary Janes. Grady had only mentally filed all this when he'd brought one of his sisters through the White House on a tour and she'd tried to give Kristine fashion advice. It hadn't gone down well.

Would she even talk to him today?

The sight of her was so incongruous to everything that had happened so far today, he almost laughed. What came out was a cough.

Kristine looked up, then tugged the earbud from her right ear. "Agent Farrow."

"There have been gunmen loose in the White House all morning, ma'am. It's not safe for you to be here." His tone came out grouchier than he liked, but his shoulder stung.

"You having an exercise does not supersede the fact that I have work to do, Agent."

"Yes, it does. Especially in light of everything that's happened."

There was a traitor in their midst, and now Kristine was here. Grady couldn't help the thought that she might have something to do with it. Of course he would think so right now. But how did he get her to come to Command for questioning? There was no way she'd just go with him.

Considering she was here, he might be able to garner information on this clock. Would the curator know how a fake had made its way in? She wasn't going to like the insinuation underlying his words when he brought it up.

But this was about more than just her pride. Skylar's life could still be at stake, which meant Grady had to be his most charming self if he wanted answers. The alternative didn't bear thinking about.

He glanced back at the door where she stood. Skylar's big blue-gray eyes had broadcast her fear loud and clear today, and that hadn't changed now they'd caught Wilson. Yes, she could take care of herself. Yes, he'd seen her calm and collected through the most dangerous of situations. Now she was probably exhausted, the fatigue bringing her emotions close to the surface. It made him determined to find Barnes and make her safe.

"Can I help you? Or are you going to let me get back to my work?" Kristine's eyebrows had risen above the rim of her glasses.

Grady cleared his throat. He sat across from her at her desk, even though she hadn't invited him. "I'll be quick. I don't want to disturb you, but I do have a question."

Kristine took a sip of her tea. "Perhaps you could email me whatever it is you want to know, and then I could get back to my work."

"I'm in a time crunch. I need to talk to you about a mantel clock that was in the one of the sitting rooms in the residence. A group of thieves have been trying to steal it all morning."

Horror washed over her face.

"It was a fake." That should make her feel better, right?

She sputtered.

"At least that's what one of the hostiles claimed."

"Your exercise allowed one of my artifacts to be *stolen*?" She was as aghast as one of the guards at the National Archives would be if a tourist touched the Declaration of Independence with greasy nacho fingers. After they broke into the display case, of course.

"No, it's still there. But the thief claims it was a fake." He didn't really know where to go from here.

Kristine pulled a cell phone from her purse

and swiped at the screen. "I should have been *informed*. I should be the first one to know."

"I really am very sorry. It's just what the hostile said, something about not bothering to sell it at a yard sale…" He figured sticking as close to the truth as he could was a good plan. "And since there's a good possibility he wasn't lying…"

She glared. The sensation was like a rush of cold air. "This amounts to an accusation of incompetence."

"I assure you, that's not my intention." He swallowed, his mouth dry. "I don't have much to do for the rest of the day except fill out reports. I was wondering about the clock. About how something like that might have been switched out ahead of time." Never mind the fact that it had been done without the curator's knowing about it, leaving a fake behind that Wilson was supposed to steal. "And what kind of person might want to take it."

She eyed him suspiciously. "The most heinous kind of person, Agent Farrow."

"I assure you, this isn't about putting your job at risk," Grady reassured her. "I'm a curious person, and I love mysteries. What better than one that might have happened right under our noses?" He let that question hang in the air for a moment, and then said, "Was the clock maybe sent out for cleaning, or repair, at one time? It could have been switched then, and a replica sent back to the White House. You have records of that stuff, right?"

He knew there were, but not where they would be. Right now he just needed her to think through the problem. Help him maybe get some ideas as to why it was chosen, out of all the items in the White House.

"The mantel clock from the sitting room in the Residence?"

He nodded.

"That was from before my time, I'm afraid. I inherited the piece along with the Wentworth collection the previous curator acquired." She shuddered. "Ghastly paintings, the lot of them."

Never mind that the previous curator had dropped dead of a heart attack in the Blue Room. Grady had actually liked the old man. "Where would the records from the previous curator be?"

If it had been switched out for the fake some time ago, that meant an ongoing operation. Planning. Maybe even multiple artifacts from the White House had been exchanged for replicas and then sold on the black market.

"The Archives. You'll have to request copies of his records if you want to find out when the clock might have been switched with a—" she leaned forward and whispered *"—fake,"* then shivered and straightened. "Though I find that extremely hard to believe. I thoroughly vet every item in the White House. I have examined that mantel clock myself…"

"But you weren't trying to determine if it was genuine, right?" He tried to tread carefully now. "You inherited the clock and, after the Wentworth collection, you were probably glad you had a nice item already on a shelf. Maybe you didn't look too closely at it."

Kristine sniffed. Took a sip of her tea. "Get out, Agent Farrow."

So much for her helping him. He heard a light giggle from the doorway and skedaddled before the curator could ask Grady who was there.

He led a smiling Skylar down the hall, and they made their way outside.

"What was that about?"

He glanced around, scanning their immediate vicinity. "What?"

"That lady, she's the curator?"

He nodded. "I figured I'd take the chance, try to get more information. Didn't work, though." He frowned.

"You think this has to do with the clock being a fake? Wilson seemed pretty convinced it indicated this all might be a ruse to trap him. You really think that's true?"

"Could be."

"So Barnes just set him up, and Wilson fell for it?" She shook her head.

"Guess we'll have to ask him why when we find him."

Skylar shivered. "I won't mind if I never see that man again. It was like he could twist anything, say anything, and it would sound believable. If he's been hiding the fact that he was a traitor all this time, then he had to have learned how to lie about *everything*."

They walked down the path and crossed the street to the command bus. This time it was even more packed with personnel. Each chair was occupied by an agent, busy at work. Half of them were on their cell phones.

Someone noticed her, and within seconds the whole room had gone wired, everyone now on edge. Did they really think she might have betrayed them? She glanced aside, but Grady moved closer to her. Was she not willing to let them see whatever hurt was probably on her face? The clock on the wall indicated it was almost one in the afternoon. It had been a long day so far, but hopefully they wouldn't have to endure much more.

The intern rushed over. He pulled her in for a hug Skylar apparently hadn't been expecting.

"Uh…" She blushed and glanced at Grady.

"Glad you're okay." The intern paused. "Also, sorry for thinking you were one of the thieves."

The rest of the agents didn't look so convinced. At least the intern seemed to feel bad that he'd left her open to get abducted. Not that he could have done anything to stop Barnes. The guy wasn't armed, and he wasn't an agent.

"Any word on Barnes?" Grady asked.

"We're still searching for him, and we need your help. The director said to tell you he wants you at a computer, so you can finish up ID'ing the thieves. That all right with you, Agent Farrow?" The intern glanced between them, including both in his question.

Grady nodded. "I have to get patched up." The look on Skylar's face said she didn't want him to walk away. He squeezed her shoulder. "You're in a room full of armed agents. You're safe."

She squared her shoulders and turned to the intern. "Let's go."

Grady found Stringer and asked his friend to help him get his wound cleaned up.

"You don't want EMTs to do it?" Stringer waved him to a corner free of people.

Grady shook his head, already unbuttoning his shirt. That would take too much time, and he wasn't hurt badly.

Skylar glanced over, and Grady gave her a small smile. She returned it. He didn't know what her look meant, but he wanted to see more of it. There had been enough crazy today. He was ready for quiet. For soft conversation, maybe laughter.

Between friends.

The shoulder of his undershirt had a hole in it. Grady pulled it off. Agent Stringer touched a cotton bud soaked with antiseptic to the wound on Grady's shoulder. He hissed at the sting but caught himself before he jumped out of his seat.

"Baby."

"Watch it," Grady shot back. An inch to the left and he'd have been shot on his vest. But, no.

Stringer's lips curled up. He was smaller, but bench-pressed more—a lot more—so Grady had to challenge him in other ways. "Hurry up so I can go help find Barnes."

"You mean so *I* can find him." Stringer secured a bandage on Grady's side. "It doesn't look good. It's probably infected. Badly. You'll die, but not until later, of course. So no suspicion can be laid on me."

"I'll leave a deathbed note so everyone knows your poor medical care killed me." Grady shoved him away and hopped off the stool to go find a new shirt. His phone buzzed with a notification. "Let's go."

"Sure you don't want to stay?" Stringer whispered, motioning toward Skylar, who was talking to the intern.

"Why?" He had a job to do. She'd had one as well, and Skylar had been amazing today even when things had gone crazy.

Stringer just looked at him. "Dude, if you need me to explain it to you…" His words trailed off, and he shook his head.

"Fine. I'll go get this guy myself."

He didn't wait for Stringer, he put his vest over the T-shirt he'd found and geared up. Skylar would be fine here. He didn't need the distraction she posed right now. Not when he had decided attraction wasn't real, and relationships didn't last. He'd been convinced in the past that romance was real. He'd believed love was forever. His ex-fiancée had cured him of that affliction.

Wherever Paula was, with the friend who was supposed to have been his best man, he hoped they were happy.

Okay, so that wasn't true. But he *was* trying to make the best of the whole thing. Trying not to dwell too long on how he'd obviously failed in some way. Done something. Or not done enough. Why else would she have dumped him for his friend?

"You're thinking about her again."

Grady ignored Stringer and headed for the door.

"Paula."

"Stringer…"

"Is this like word association?" He heard the smile in his friend's voice. "Because I could keep going."

"It's not a game. It's my personal life."

"And it was a year ago, dude. Time to get on with things."

Grady sighed. "I thought that's what I was doing."

"Dating?"

"I'm not signing up for one of those online things."

"That's not what I'm suggesting," Stringer said. "Although—"

"No."

Stringer sighed. "Brooding isn't going to get you to the next season."

"The calendar does that." Grady spun back, right before the door. He was ready to get out of this box. Buses were fine, but not filled with people. He was getting claustrophobic crammed in here like sardines in a can.

"I mean the next season of your life. One that's hopefully a whole lot happier than this one. Because, I gotta say, looking at your hangdog face all day is getting old."

But a new relationship wasn't the answer to

his restlessness, right? He hadn't wanted a rebound. "No one told you to be here."

Stringer lifted his free hand, rifle hugged against his chest. "I'm just saying."

Grady pushed open the door with his free hand and they stepped outside. "I know what you're saying."

He did. That was the problem. No one was fooled by his "moving on" talk, or the fact that he'd changed nothing about his life since Paula had called off the wedding.

Wallowing clearly wasn't working for him—or anyone around him. Grady walked between cars and they headed to the entrance that led into the small parking structure under the West Wing. It was a quick exit for the president, or any of his staffers, when they needed it to be. Or a private entrance for visitors.

Barnes had killed a guardhouse agent and fled. Would they find any evidence to point to where he'd gone?

Commotion back at the bus brought his attention around. Wilson was being escorted from Command by the director and a group of agents. Probably so he could be taken to a more secure location where he could be questioned.

Grady and Stringer walked back over. Extra cover in getting the man to the transport vehicle probably wasn't a bad idea.

Skylar stepped out behind them.

Gunfire erupted across the parking lot. The reaction was instantaneous. Except by Skylar, who didn't duck quite fast enough. Grady ran over, slammed into her and got her out of the line of fire.

They hit the ground. He rolled to displace the force, then covered her as bullets hit the pavement all around them.

ELEVEN

"We're taking fire!" Director Tanner yelled into his radio. Grady scrambled to a crouch, his rifle tight against his chest, and got Skylar up against a car, out of the line of fire. She had no weapon. He'd have to cover—

A bullet hit the car window above and tempered glass sprayed on them. She screamed, and he covered her again, tenting his body over hers and praying neither of them got cut by broken glass too badly.

Two vehicles away, a gas tank exploded. What on earth? The ball of fire whooshed into the air. Was this more than one sniper?

"Find cover," the director yelled to an exposed agent.

"Come on." They had to move or else they'd be sitting ducks. It wouldn't take long for the shooter to find a better angle. Right now he seemed to be aiming randomly, but an agent was down and another man lay dead on the pavement.

Wilson.

Had Barnes taken out the leader of the thieves, or his former partner? Wilson was the one who could thoroughly implicate him in any wrongdoing. This wasn't good. Not when his testimony would be needed for a conviction.

"I want men on that shooter. Now!" his boss yelled. The man wasn't known for his calm demeanor under stress, but everyone else's ears were probably ringing like Grady's.

The director was right, though. They needed to get the shooter in custody before more people were hurt. Agents were dispersing, headed for the point of origin. Agent Stringer was already gone, probably hunting the gunman as well. It was where Grady would be if it wasn't for Skylar being unarmed in a gunfight. Grady didn't want to check the roof of the building he thought they were coming from. He'd risk getting shot in the face for his trouble.

The director rose from his crouch. "Men on the west—"

A red mark spread out from the center of the director's chest, and he dropped to the pavement.

"Two shooters!" Grady's radio burst to life, multiple voices calling in a second shooter. "We have two shooters. Everyone off the street! Get these people out of here!"

The command bus was too obvious a place

for them to hunker down. They'd be better off just getting out of Dodge. Like in this old car.

"Get in," he told Skylar, figuring he'd have to hotwire it. "Let's get out of here."

Another shot came, this one farther away. Then a second from the original shooter's direction.

Grady squeezed off two shots in response, and got a look at the roof then. Barnes raced along the wall at the top of the low building on the north side of Pennsylvania Avenue. Grady's next two bullets chased him. He shifted his gun to track with the man's movements.

A shot pinged off the rear quarter panel of the car.

The engine fired up. "I did it! Come on, Grady. Let's go." Skylar was in the driver's seat, hunkered down so she could reach the wires under the steering wheel.

Agents on the roof in pursuit would get Barnes. The rest would get the second shooter. Grady's priority was keeping himself and Skylar alive long enough to help provide the Secret Service with what they needed to prove Barnes was a traitor.

The man had disappeared from the roof now. Grady jumped in the driver's side as Skylar scooted over to the passenger seat. He shoved the car in Drive and shot away from the curb, sideswiped a parked car and straightened out. He burst through the barrier at the end and turned right.

He drove with one hand on the wheel and passed his gun to Skylar, then handed her another clip. "Reload for me."

He braked to avoid hitting the car crawling in front of him. Traffic, seriously? He didn't need this right now.

Skylar ejected the clip onto her lap and the back door opened.

Barnes dived into the seat before Grady could react and pointed a weapon at the back of Skylar's head. "Hand me the gun." He turned to Grady. "Drive."

"This isn't going to win you any favors. Just get out, Barnes." Traffic moved forward. Grady moved with it, and then said, "We aren't going to help you escape the Secret Service, so just go."

"You will when I shoot both of you and dump the car."

"That's hardly going to convince anyone this was all a mistake." Seriously, what was the man thinking? "Do you have the real clock?"

He needed something to distract him from the fact that there was a gun to Skylar's head. Again.

"Pretty sure that ship sailed when I shot at the team," Barnes shot back. "Cat's out of the bag now. There's no stuffing it back in. Might as well make the best of it. Clock or no clock."

"So you don't have it."

Barnes huffed. "The clock isn't even the point."

Grady wanted to ask who else he'd been working with. Like Kristine? There had to be more people involved they didn't know about, and he didn't like surprises. Especially ones that came at the end of a loaded gun. Barnes had to have had a plan to get away.

Skylar said, "I can't believe you'd throw away your career like this. Destroy lives you've sworn to protect, and for what?"

They couldn't be very good thieves—or have a sophisticated operation going—if they hadn't realized it wasn't a valuable item. Could Barnes really be so dumb? Maybe Wilson had been duped, as he'd seemed to think happened? Maybe this was all nothing but a double cross between Barnes and Wilson that had gone wrong. Get Wilson arrested. Barnes would be free, no suspicions. He could take what money he'd already earned and split.

Maybe that was why the clock wasn't the point.

It was a theory, but one Grady had no proof of. And now wasn't the time to work it out. Saving their lives came before evidence collection or figuring out Barnes's motives.

Grady gripped the steering wheel, racking his brain for ways to get out of this. Whatever it was, it was going to have to be drastic. "You wanna get yourself in deeper? Be my guest."

Skylar shot him a look.

He didn't know what to tell her either. He was supposed to have protected her, and yet here she was. In the line of fire. Again. Barnes had bested him so many times today it was getting seriously frustrating. Grady didn't have time for anger that would cloud his judgment.

"Seriously," he said to Barnes. "Just get out at the next light, and we won't tell anyone we saw you." Barnes would know Grady was lying, but he just wanted the man to go already. "We aren't your ticket out of here."

He prayed the man took that direction. *Please, Lord. Don't let Skylar get hurt. Help me protect her.* It felt right to ask God for help, even though it had been a while since he'd done it. God wasn't one to hold grudges about ignoring Him. He was all about grace and mercy—which Grady and Skylar would need plenty of in order to get out of this alive.

Barnes snorted. "The minute I get out, you'll call Command and tell them exactly where I am."

"Then leave us. Take the car." He had to protect Skylar. Saving her life was more important right now than making sure Barnes didn't get away.

"And lose the opportunity to kill you so you can't make my life worse?"

"You said yourself it's too late to go back. Shooting us won't keep us from implicating you. Shooting Wilson and then Director Tanner already did that."

"Hey, that wasn't me who hit Tanner. It was the other guy."

"On your orders, no doubt."

"You have no idea what you're talking about. So why don't you shut up and just drive!"

The man was mentally unhinged, swinging the gun around. Skylar was reaching new heights of scared-for-her-life today, and all of it had to do with the man in the back of the car. The one pointing a gun at her. *Again.*

She could hear the constant buzz of Grady's phone in his vest pocket. The Secret Service were probably calling, wondering where they were. Had they caught the other shooter? Hopefully that meant people were looking for them.

If there was some way she could get free, and out of the car, Barnes wouldn't have this power over either of them. She hardly wanted to leave Grady with him, but it would help bring this situation to a close. It would be one against one. No distractions for Grady. While Barnes was desperate enough he wouldn't be thinking straight. That gave Grady the advantage, even with the risk of getting shot.

Barnes held the gun on Grady while he continued to drive. The man was out of her reach, and he'd see it coming if she tried to swing her arm back and hit him with the unloaded gun. She'd handed him the clip, and figured he'd simply been too distracted by conversation with Grady to ask for the rest. But she couldn't knock him out without giving him three seconds warning while she maneuvered into position to make an effective swing toward his head with the butt of the gun.

Grady glanced at her, just once. Skylar didn't wanted him to see how frightened she was. She didn't want to let down their side, or be the weak link. How else could she bring this to an end?

Barnes and Skylar both leaned toward the front of the car as they slowed. The driver of a car behind them lay on his horn. Barnes barked out, "Why have we slowed down?"

"Traffic," Grady said. "It might be just after lunchtime, but this is DC."

"I know. I grew up here," Barnes said. "I'm not some tourist who knows nothing about this city."

Skylar jumped on the opportunity to get him

to talk. "What about Wilson. The guy was British, right?"

He said nothing.

"And the clock? Why that, when there are plenty of other artifacts in the White House you could have taken that are far more valuable?" Skylar shrugged. "I mean, it's practically a museum."

"It is a museum," Grady said.

She shot him a look. The side of his face at least. He was driving, so he couldn't look at her every second. Didn't he realize she was fishing for information? Kind of the way he had done, asking Barnes questions.

"See what I mean?" she told Barnes. "Plenty of other things. Why that clock?"

"Because."

Skylar sighed. *We're not getting anywhere.* "It must hold some value to you. I refuse to believe it was simply an easy item to take. I mean, it's not huge and bulky like some of the paintings. Or a vase."

"Or a chair. Do you have a point—" Barnes's eyes had darkened "—or are you simply attempting to talk me all the way to an insanity plea?"

She shrugged, like this was all no big deal to her. "There has to be a reason why you wanted Wilson to take that particular thing. I'm just curious."

"That killed the cat. Didn't you know?"

Skylar glanced at her door. He needed to believe she was kowtowed, and not about to jump free of the car. That she wouldn't make a fuss, and Grady would do what he needed to in order to save her. Barnes had to keep believing he would get what he wanted. Why they had to go on a joyride through Washington, she didn't know. Nor did she want to think about what he'd said about killing them and taking the car.

No one would ever know who did it. Or why. She didn't want to be a corpse at the morgue. Her father and uncle would never rest until they found the truth, which would put them in Barnes's crosshairs as well. She didn't want to believe that her whole life and everything she'd gone through in the military—and, yeah, her unhappy marriage—had all led to…this.

Nothing but the victim of a dirty Secret Service agent and a man who'd been handpicked to take part in a Secret Service exercise. Both had been vetted. Both had been investigated. Whoever he was in real life, Wilson's profile had to have come back clean. The alternative was he'd bought his way in. Used Barnes to get on the exercise roster.

Wilson had possessed a regal nose, not to mention that high-brow accent. She couldn't really tell one regional UK accent from another. More than the more well-known ones, at least.

There were so many variations it wouldn't help her figure out who he was. But now he was dead, and Barnes was determined to kill more people in order to get away. And to what end, a life on the run?

Grady would hunt him down.

Grady and the rest of the Secret Service.

The White House had been nothing but a source of terror all day. She thought she wanted to be on the president's detail, but maybe she didn't want to go back there later on in her career, after all.

Maybe Skylar would see her career as a Secret Service agent soar in financial crimes, and she'd never set foot in the White House again. She hadn't decided where she wanted to end up, not wishing to put limits on what she could do. Or on who she could be.

Faced with Barnes here and now, she couldn't say her modest upbringing had prepared her to deal with this guy. But at least he didn't use his masculinity or—like her ex-husband—his perceived oh-so-much-higher intelligence against her. Earl had always talked down to her, then got frustrated that he had to explain things.

It was part of the reason she'd studied so hard for all the Secret Service tests. There was no way anyone would ever be able to take that tone with her again.

Unfortunately, that attitude had landed her here in this car, afraid for her life again.

Skylar shifted her hands toward the door. Unlike the van they'd been in this morning—a smaller-model utility truck—this was a regular car. If she could pull fast enough on the handle, could she jump out? Road rash was preferable to death—assuming he didn't shoot her before she hit the pavement. What choice was there?

Skylar shifted another inch. Barnes's attention was on the front window, and Grady's driving. They were moving slow but steady, rolling at maybe fifteen or twenty miles per hour. That was good—it would hurt less when she jumped out. And hopefully give the driver in the vehicle behind theirs time to hit the brakes so he didn't run her over.

It was always the small things that counted.

Skylar glanced at Barnes. The gun. At Grady. She wasn't going to be a pawn. Was she really going to do this? She reached over with one hand, braced to pull the handle and dive out.

A gunshot blast boomed in the car. The noise exploded her eardrum into a high, loud whine. The windshield shattered. *Barnes, trying to stop her.* The noise in her ears was deafening, ringing like high-pitched electronics, while Grady seemed to be yelling in a muffled tone behind it all. She screamed but couldn't hear it over the firework sound still in her ears. Nor could she hear what he was saying.

The car jerked to the right. Skylar's head hit the frame as they careened to the side. She tried to hang on, but with the disorientation she couldn't grasp on to anything. Barnes had fallen to his side on the seat and was now fighting to get back to a sitting position. A gash on his temple trickled down his face. Grady gripped the wheel tightly, and then she saw it.

They were headed right for it.

Twenty miles per hour.

Thirty.

A second later, they slammed into the concrete barrier.

TWELVE

Grady punched down the airbag. His face felt like it'd been hit with a two-by-four, and the air smelled like the gun range. He cracked the door open, stumbled out and nearly went down on one knee. Caught himself on the frame of the door and managed to stay standing.

"Dude, are you okay?" The young man who ran up couldn't have been more than nineteen and had a camera slung around his neck. "That was crazy."

Grady only nodded. "Call the police."

Sirens were already headed their way. The noise cut through the din of traffic and people approaching in conversation. Plus the ringing in Grady's ears. He'd been close enough he'd felt pain from that shot in his own ears, but Skylar had to be hurting. He ignored the discomfort and rounded the back of the car. It wasn't worth looking at the front end, now smashed like an accordion against the wall of this building.

The rear door was open.

He looked inside, even though an armed Barnes tucked behind the driver's seat would shoot him without a second thought if he stuck his head in, no warning. But he had to see.

Sure enough, Barnes was nowhere to be found. Skylar lay across the center console, sprawled at an odd angle. Like his sister's old rag doll. There was no visible blood, not even after he shifted her back upright.

He wanted to stay with her, but couldn't. He winced at the thought of her reaction to what he was about to do and asked the people around him, "Did anyone see a man run away from the car?"

A couple glanced at each other like Grady was nuts. The young man lifted one hand. "Secret Service jacket, brown hair?"

Grady nodded. "Which way did he go?"

The young man pointed.

"Stay with her until the cops get here." Grady took off after Barnes. He didn't want to leave Skylar, but he had to catch this menace who had threatened their lives so many times today.

When he finally saw him, Barnes was already half a block ahead and running fast. People saw his gun and got out of his way.

Grady used his cell phone to call whoever was now manning the command post. "I'm in pursuit of Barnes." He gave the location and then hung up after backup was promised.

Someone got in Barnes's way, and he shoved them roughly against a building. The man slumped to the ground.

Grady yelled, "Get down! Get out of the way!"

Barnes now knew he was in pursuit, but it couldn't be helped.

The man who'd been hurt lay propped against the wall of a building, clutching the left side of his head. Grady couldn't see how bad it was, but the older man was pale. His eyes wide. There were enough people around that he'd get help.

So Grady left him to stick with his chase.

Just like he'd had to leave Skylar behind in the car. Was she okay? His head was foggy from the impact, and his ears were still ringing. But he wasn't about to let her continue on with the threat of being killed hanging over her head. He had to do this. And he figured he had the where-withal to stick with the pursuit. *Thank You, Lord. Help me catch him.* He would bring Barnes in.

He had to.

The alternative was to have a homicidal traitor running around Washington. One who evidently didn't know he was headed right for the FBI building.

They were on the other side of the street, but

still. He was crazy if he thought he could actually get away with this.

Barnes ran across the street, headed toward a familiar stone building. It almost looked like a palace, or something constructed by the Greeks. Statues flanked the rear door, over which hung a sign indicating it was not the visitor's entrance of the National Archives.

Grady followed him. Passed in front of the statue to the right—a seated man, one arm clutching a book that lay across his lap and the other holding a scroll. The inscription on the statue said *STUDY THE PAST.*

There was no time to do so now, though. Not when he was in pursuit of a murderer and traitor. Besides, he'd been over and over what happened with Paula so many times he needed to quit thinking on it.

A security guard had the back door open, a staff member having just gone through it.

Barnes shot the guy and went inside. Before the door swung closed, Grady heard two more shots.

Gun raised, he entered the archives in pursuit of a man who was supposed to have been on the same side as him. Inside, one security guard was down, as well as the staffer who'd gone through the door ahead of Barnes.

The injured guard whimpered, and her gaze

darted around the hall. She saw Grady approach, and her eyes met his. *Save me.* Her eyes practically screamed.

Grady said, "Where did he go?"

The guard pointed.

Grady found Barnes in a hall, with way too many sightseers hanging around. Even one in the line of fire was too many. "Drop the gun, Barnes."

The man's whole demeanor screamed bravado. He wasn't worried about getting caught? They were at a standoff. The man should at least be concerned this might not go his way. What did he know that Grady did not?

Barnes grabbed a woman and held his gun to her head.

"No!" Grady took two more steps. Gritted his teeth. "Let the woman go, and we'll talk." He paused. "Share information. Figure out a way to help each other." Never mind the fact that this guy was in serious trouble. There was no way Grady would actually let him get away.

"I find that hard to believe, considering all I've done this morning. But go ahead," Barnes taunted, "bluff all you want, Agent Farrow."

Grady bit down on his molars. He couldn't risk a shot hitting the woman or anyone else in the hallway. The crowd had backed up and gathered against the walls. They shifted slowly, all headed for the exit doors.

Barnes dragged the woman back two steps. He glanced around, saw precisely where he was—a fact Grady's brain clocked as interesting from a tactical standpoint—and pulled the fire alarm on the wall right beside him.

He shoved the woman at Grady just as the alarm blared to life. The reaction was instantaneous. Shouting. A rush of people.

Grady caught her and used the momentum to rotate them both. He sent her on toward the people crowded against the wall. "Get out of here."

Grady wasted no time running in the direction he'd seen Barnes go—toward the stairwell.

When he punched the safety bar and emerged to the marble staircase, he stopped immediately. Gun up, finger down the barrel, he listened. Barnes could be waiting here for him, but he wasn't.

An elderly lady rushed up the stairs, wide-eyed. She took one look at Grady's uniform and pointed behind her. "They went that way."

He'd gone down the stairs, then. Not up.

Grady raced down after him. At the bottom of this staircase was a small cafeteria and an auditorium. As he raced after Barnes, Grady prayed no one would get hurt here. Both areas on this sublevel might be full of people. The last thing he needed was Barnes opening fire in a crowd and murdering innocent civilians out of desperation.

People filed past him, headed for the stairs. For a second, Grady thought he saw Niles—the man who'd saved them from Simmons. Probably just someone who looked like him, though. The alarm was earsplittingly loud, but he ignored the discomfort and tried to locate Barnes in the crowd.

There.

Barnes wove between people. Families. A couple, two toddlers in tow. Thankfully, he left them alone and crossed what was a small lobby of sorts, through a set of doors that had been propped open and then cut right. Grady sped up in time to see him head up a hallway that rose in elevation between multiple people who didn't notice the man's gun.

They noticed Grady's.

Several screamed, until they noted his searching for someone—not them. Then they screamed and glanced around—looking for the real threat. Grady ran on, undeterred by their reaction.

Two security guards followed suit, calling for the crowd to part as they made their way up the incline behind them.

Grady emerged into the auditorium, empty now except for two rows of kids, all wearing neon yellow T-shirts. The last thing he wanted was Barnes using a class of school children as human shields.

But Barnes ignored them. He raced between rows toward the far end of the huge room and a lit sign.

EXIT.

Grady yelled over his shoulder to the security guards. "Call in. Get someone at that exit to cut him off."

He didn't wait around for them to call it in. Barnes jumped over a row of seats, ran two feet and then jumped again. He was headed for the door to the side of the stage. Not the back entrance on the far side of the auditorium.

Grady raced around the rear, an arced walkway behind the last row of seating. He knew he was fast—fast enough he'd beaten several other Secret Service agents in the last Marine Corps marathon. Was he fast enough to get all the way across the back and down the stairs at the far side to the stage door before Barnes?

He pushed all thoughts of the morning, Director Tanner's prognosis and Skylar—not to mention her pretty face—from his mind. Those things would distract him. Grady pumped his arms and legs and tore across the carpet behind the auditorium's back row.

The teacher squealed. Seconds later, she ordered all the kids to follow her, though several seemed more interested in the scenario playing out. Grady would have made them stay where they were but didn't fault her for getting them out of the way. There was an armed man running toward them.

Barnes reached the front row, leaped and landed right in front of the stage. The kids were more or less out of the way now, watching. Grady rounded the corner at the far end and hit the stairs. A couple had phones out, no doubt videoing Grady to post on social media later. He didn't have time to object—or tell them that probably wasn't wise.

The stage was raised maybe half a foot off the floor. Barnes skirted the wooden rise and headed for the door. He grasped the handle just as Grady reached the second-to-last step of the tiered auditorium.

Barnes ran through the door.

Grady hit the door before it could latch shut.

The green room was empty. Grady ran for the door at the other end. The hallway was quiet. No Barnes.

The security guards followed him in, red-faced and huffing. Grady didn't blame them. His breath was short as well. The noise from the auditorium was a muffled roar as seats bumped up, kids struggled to collect their belongings and their teacher continued to shout orders.

"Where does this hall let out?"

The security guard frowned. "It's a maze of rooms and hallways. Some go upstairs, but there are two ways he could get outside from here."

"And backup?" Grady asked. "We need to cut him off before he gets away."

The security guard got on the radio again, but Grady didn't have time to find out what their response was going to be. Barnes had to know how to get out of here. Otherwise he'd never have taken the risk of getting out this way when he could have left the building in a crowd of people evacuating.

Grady had to figure out which way he'd gone.

Then he was going to bring Barnes in.

He crouched beside Skylar and brushed hair back from her face. That was nice. Her head swam, but she didn't want to wake up. It was a nice dream.

"Ms. Austin?"

She blinked and found herself staring at the ceiling of an ambulance. The man beside her wasn't Grady.

Stringer looked down, concern on his face.

"Where's Grady?" She didn't care that she sounded desperate. "Is he hurt? I want to see him." She pushed up from the stretcher, but Stringer and an EMT pressed on her shoulders.

"Easy," the EMT said.

Her arms buckled and she laid down. "Where is he?"

Stringer frowned. "He went after Barnes."

Just left her? She didn't know if she was more worried that he'd get hurt or hurt that he'd made her worried.

Okay, somewhere in her mixed-up, probably concussed brain that actually made sense.

"He had to go."

"You don't have to justify his actions to me. I understand what the job means. I'm training to be a Secret Service agent. He had to go after Barnes." Really, she got that. Grady needed to do his job and make sure no one else got hurt.

Maybe he was even making sure she didn't get hurt as well.

The EMT touched something to her forehead. Her eyes flicked to him, and she scrunched up her nose. "Ouch."

The man looked like he wanted to chuckle. "I know. I'm sorry I had to do that, but you're a mess."

Everything came rushing back. "That's what happens when you crash into a concrete wall."

The risk had been substantial. Even if it was probably Grady's only workable plan.

Skylar had been wearing her seat belt, but the crash had tossed her around. She prayed Barnes had been slowed down enough that Grady, the cops and the Secret Service could catch up to him.

"There's a nasty bump back there. You'll have a headache."

She closed her eyes and said, "And an earache. And an 'everything else' ache." She smiled at the EMT but didn't open her eyes. "Still, it beats being dead."

Stringer laughed. "It really does."

Despite the moment of humor, she couldn't let go of the worry. Skylar opened her eyes and looked at Stringer.

His attention was on his phone. "Skylar—" He saw she was looking at him.

Was Grady hurt?

"It isn't bad," he said. "Grady did it. He caught Barnes."

THIRTEEN

Grady pushed the door open and walked down the hallway to the room where the doctors were examining Skylar. The rest of his team had shown up, and they'd pinned Barnes in a corner. He'd given up. Thankfully, he hadn't chosen to end his life—or forced them to do it. Grady hadn't wanted to kill him when the alternative was watching justice play out.

Still, worry over how Skylar was doing remained foremost in his mind. What had she thought when she woke up and he was gone?

Stringer pushed off the wall and walked toward Grady.

"How is she?"

"A mild concussion. Scrapes and bruises." Stringer checked his phone. "Nothing major... and I have to go back to the office." He stuck his hand out again. "Congratulations on bringing Barnes in."

Grady nodded. Shook his friend's hand. "I

can't relax yet." He motioned to her room. "I need her off the street, in a safe house. Just until we know for sure there's no threat."

Stringer nodded. "Then you should take her somewhere safe. Now. Barnes is too much of a wild card. We have no idea who he was working with beyond Wilson and those guys. Not worth the risk. The second shooter killed himself before we could capture him, so we have next to no information on this operation."

"You think Barnes will talk?"

Stringer shrugged. "You think more people are involved?"

"I wouldn't discount the possibility. Barnes must have friends or a place he could've gone to hide out." And yet he'd headed for the National Archives. Trying to disappear in a crowd? It hadn't worked.

Grady said, "I'd have figured he was the kind of man who had a whole plan in place. That he'd try to flee to an extradition-free paradise to spend whatever money he'd amassed."

"But he didn't," Stringer said. "And now we can ask him about all of it."

"Keep me posted."

Grady wanted to work with his Secret Service team on this. Help bring Barnes's entire operation down. But Skylar was hurt. He'd have to figure out how to keep her safe from any other threats and pray he could trust the agents and cops assigned to protect her.

"What are you thinking?"

Grady said, "I should stay with Skylar, and make sure she's safe."

Stringer nodded. "I'll run things on my end and call you."

He gave his friend a nod and knocked on Skylar's door.

"Come in."

He cracked the door and got a look at her. Hospital gown. That blond hair down, all around her face. She looked…young. "How's your head?"

"I had them give me regular painkillers. I'll be okay."

He shot her a look. "Is that even true?"

"He said it was a bump, and it'll hurt, but he didn't even think I had more than a little concussion." She lifted her hands. "Gave me some things to watch out for. Like slurring or getting dizzy. Said I shouldn't push too hard."

He pressed his lips together. "A little concussion is still a concussion."

"Honestly, the bruise from getting shot is worse than the bump on my head." She tipped her head to one side. "You brought in Barnes?"

He nodded.

"And you're okay?" She looked him over. Was she worried he'd been injured?

"Everything's fine." He settled on the end of the bed. "And I'm good to stay long enough to get you home once the doctors are done."

"You want me to go home? You think I'm going to just sit around there by myself, when Barnes will probably tell the Secret Service I'm as guilty as he is?" She almost sounded like she was going to cry. Grady figured she wasn't upset as much as just tired. She'd been through the wringer so far today. She needed rest, not another stressful situation.

Grady reached for her hand and folded his fingers between hers. "Barnes might try to get you in trouble, but he isn't going to succeed. Do you have anything to feel guilty for?"

She shook her head.

"Then why are you worried?"

Skylar sniffed, then wiped her eye. "Sorry."

"For what?" He shifted closer and touched her cheek. "Lie back and rest. I'm going to get some coffee, and I'll be back, okay?"

Skylar obeyed, but not without a flash of rebellion in her eyes. "Fine."

Grady hid his laugh behind a cough and shifted blankets that didn't need fixing under the guise of tucking her in. "I'll be back."

A few hours later, Skylar was released. The evening sky was darkening when he pulled up to the curb to collect her. She looked battered and worn-out but not in enough danger of serious complications for the doctor to admit her overnight.

Grady drove her home. He held her hand the whole way, just like he'd held it the whole time she waited to be examined for release assessment.

The man didn't have a lot of words sometimes, but those he did have spoke loudly enough for her to get his meaning. Grady didn't like the fact that she was in danger. He didn't like the fact that, even going with him, she would *continue* to be in danger. He couldn't change that. But he'd backed down and taken care of her. Shown her comfort when she needed it.

That alone made her busted-up heart begin to knit back together.

"We'll have people outside, just in case there's still a threat. We'll be making sure you're safe."

Skylar nodded at Grady's statement but couldn't muster much more feeling. Music played low on the car stereo. He'd been surprised when she gave him a residential address instead of the name of a hotel. Not many people knew her uncle was a senator. Nor was it a secret, necessarily.

What were they going to talk about? Sure, she'd pushed for him to stick with her. But that didn't mean it wasn't going to be awkward. She knew she was keeping him from work. Maybe he wanted her to tell him it was okay for him to go.

"The house has an extensive security system. I'm sure I'll be fine until everyone working with Barnes is caught." If she needed to, her uncle could probably pull some strings that would make Grady's head spin. But she'd rather it was him. Her uncle—and her father—were both fiercely protective of her.

Skylar was going to tread carefully, but that didn't mean she was going to walk into a relationship. She wouldn't discount a good, solid friendship, though. It might be nice to have a friend she could count on. And if there was anyone who fit that bill in her life right now…it was Grady.

She'd already given him her number, and Grady had called her so she had his on her phone waiting for her when she got home. Why was she so excited about that? It wasn't like she was going to start texting him like some eighth-grade girl with a crush.

The GPS announced, *You have arrived at your destination.*

Skylar pointed at the brownstone two doors down, her uncle's house. "Right there."

He pulled over and parked under a tree that

had been planted last year. It was still being supported, tied so it stayed upright. Skylar had been like that for a long time. Joining the Secret Service had been her way of breaking free of the restraints. Going her own way. Proving to the world she was strong on her own.

She shifted in her seat to face Grady. "You probably have to get back to the White House."

He frowned, his gaze on the house. "I'm not going to leave, Skylar. So you don't have to try to convince me to go. For the time being, I'm here and trusting the rest of my team will get the answers we need from Barnes. That's what being part of a team means."

Skylar pulled off her shoe and got out the door key from where she'd hidden it that morning before the exercise, then put her shoe back on and climbed out of the car. Grady walked her up the steps. She let them inside, then entered the code on the alarm panel. When he left, she would rearm it to alert her if any doors or windows were opened. For now, Grady was here. She might not have her service weapon on her, but there were guns in the house she could access. And Grady had his on his hip.

Safety was relative, she knew that. At least she could appreciate the fact that she was okay right now. She'd learned firsthand that was what counted most: the present. Let the past go. Don't worry about a future that was out of her control. Right now, she was okay.

She and Grady stood in the hallway together. The grandfather clock ticked each second.

"Do you," she began, "want a drink?" She motioned over her shoulder in the direction of the kitchen. "I could make tea. Or coffee."

"Coffee sounds good."

Why that pleased her so much, Skylar didn't dwell on. She strode down the hall and pushed through the door to the kitchen. The housekeeper had already come this morning, so the place was pristine and smelled like lemons.

"Senator Richard Farringdon? That's the connection?"

"Guilty as charged." She chuckled, and glanced over to see him eyeing a framed photo of the two of them. She had her army uniform on, and her uncle's arm was across her shoulders. "I'm his niece."

"I saw a footnote in the file they sent me about a familial connection. I didn't get that far before the exercise started."

"He's at home in Montana, so…" She didn't really know how to end that, so she said, "It's my father's birthday in a couple of days. Uncle Richard said he'd go since I couldn't make it."

Grady said, "Are you close?"

"My father and uncle are all the family I

have." She'd pushed away from them for the year she'd been married. Since then they'd well and truly made up for it, barging in and making her connect with them. She smiled, thinking about her last camping trip with her father. He hated fishing, but he'd pretended well enough to enjoy himself. "We've worked so hard to be close it seems strange to think of my dad getting older."

Grady frowned. "I can't say I've ever thought to work on my relationship with my parents. It just is."

She nodded. "Most people feel that way. We've been through a lot, and we had to work some things out. Especially when I told them both about Earl, and…" She paused. "Do you even want to hear about this?"

"Yes," he said quietly. "I do." Grady pulled two mugs from a mug tree.

He was being so gentle. She didn't realize it then, but he'd given her time to work things through in her head. He wasn't probing, just seeking to understand. Of all the things he could have done or said… "Thank you."

"For what?"

"Letting me talk." She shrugged.

"You're part of the Secret Service team now. There is no way we're going to let him get to you." Grady stepped closer. "Don't worry, okay?

I know that sounds trite, and it might not be helpful, but you really can trust we've got your back."

She nodded. "My ex-husband cheated on me. It hit me hard, made me doubt myself."

"How long have you been divorced?"

"Two years."

"I understand having your confidence shaken, but you have to know that's not the woman I spent time with this morning."

She felt her eyes widen.

"You faced down the danger, Skylar."

"*You* faced it down." She smiled. "I'm pretty sure I was just running the other way."

He smiled back, captured by the amusement on her face.

"And then you threw yourself on top of me outside, when we were under fire, like a total Secret Service agent hero."

Grady shrugged one shoulder in mock humility. "It's what we do."

Skylar laughed. The sound was like sleigh bells in winter and felt like hope. She poured two cups of coffee, and they sat, chatting about nothing and everything. Soon enough he'd get word that agents were stationed outside.

Right now there was nowhere else in the world he would rather be than here with her.

Had he ever felt that way with Paula? Grady didn't think so.

At a pause in the conversation, he said, "I was engaged a while back." He knew about her past relationship. It made sense to tell her about his. At least, that was what he told himself.

"You were?"

He nodded. "Paula ran off with the friend who would have been my best man. Three months before the wedding."

Skylar gaped. "Why did she do that?" Like she couldn't believe anyone would consider not marrying him.

Grady tucked the feeling away and shrugged. "She wanted a nine-to-five guy who took the boys to football practice on Saturday mornings. That's not what this job is."

"Even with the relative stability of being stationed in the White House—"

"For now, at least."

"You still can't guarantee hours or weekends off." She shook her head. "She really thought you were going to...what? Get a new job?"

"Maybe."

"Change, anyway. She wanted you to be someone else."

"Not the man she'd said *yes* to."

Skylar nodded. Were those tears in her eyes? "That's nuts."

"I'm glad you think so." He lifted his eyebrows. "It means I'm not crazy because I think the same thing."

"Wow." She shook her head. "Just…wow. I can't believe a woman would do that to you."

Grady nearly laughed out loud. He'd come a long way since Paula had left. But the sting of betrayal was still there. It had marked him. Not just the loss of their relationship, and the marriage they should have had, but also the loss of his best friend. He'd kept everyone in his life at arm's length since then. Licking his wounds.

He didn't want to start dating again. What if the same thing happened? He couldn't guarantee there wouldn't be another situation where he'd get hurt all over again, so what was the point? It wasn't worth the risk.

Grady walked over to the sink and set his mug upside down. To his right, there was a shuffle. A flash of movement reflected in the kitchen window. He turned, drawing his weapon and thumbing the safety as he turned. Skylar gasped.

"What is it?"

He stared out the window into the waning light of sunset and motioned for her to move away. "I don't know."

"Is someone out there?"

Grady pulled out his cell phone and led Skylar to the living room instead. He called in a possible threat. She sank into the couch, but quickly got back up to pace. "Maybe it's nothing. Maybe we're just jumpy because of everything that happened this morning."

He caught her when she reached where he stood and drew her into his arms. "Skylar. I'm here, and I won't let anything happen to you. Threat or not, you're safe."

She nodded.

Grady couldn't resist. He leaned down and planted a kiss on her forehead. He shouldn't promise she would make it through this when Barnes could show up at any moment, guns blazing. But he would do everything in his power to keep her right here.

In his arms.

FOURTEEN

Skylar started to get up off the couch, thought better of it and sat back down. Blew out a breath. It was just after seven in the morning. The disturbance outside last night had turned out to be nothing more than the neighbor's cat. But still, Grady had been here with her. He'd stayed.

"Everything okay?"

"Sure."

She'd slept, though he'd woken her up every thirty minutes. They'd had sandwiches for dinner last night, eggs and coffee already this morning. Barnes was in custody. Why wouldn't everything be fine, with Grady here to keep her company?

Skylar tapped her fingers on her leg and looked around her uncle's living room. Should she suggest they watch a movie this morning? Would that be too date-ish? He'd been so sweet, keeping her company. He made really good food and even washed the dishes. What kind of man did that? Certainly not her uncle or father. They had housekeepers who took care of those things.

Did he wish he was back at Secret Service Command, interviewing Barnes? Maybe he wanted to be part of what was happening there. And yes, her brain had been going around and around on the same things all night, churning up the same worries. But once she started to even consider the idea of having real feelings for him, then came the anxiety.

Would he betray her the way her ex-husband had?

She couldn't believe Grady capable of dishing out that kind of hurt to her. But then, she'd never believed Earl would cheat on her either.

Grady had told her about his ex-fiancée. She had cheated on him. Left him for someone else. If anyone knew the sting of betrayal she'd felt, it was him. Maybe she should talk to him about it. But the idea of admitting she felt something for him was scarier than all the guns she'd faced down yesterday.

He was a full-fledged Secret Service agent. When she graduated, he was going to be her superior.

This time was nice, but it wasn't their lives. Just one day spent together, and then they were going to go their separate ways.

Maybe he knew. Maybe that was why he'd

gotten steadily quieter since she'd woken up an hour ago to the smell of fresh coffee. Wishing he was somewhere else, perhaps?

Even now he scrolled through whatever feed on his phone had his attention. Emails. He didn't seem like a man who was all about social media. Federal agencies didn't want their people on sites like that, anyway.

Anything to save himself from having to talk to her, apparently.

His phone rang in his hand.

Grady jumped up. "Agent Farrow." He listened for a minute, then his attention shifted to include her. "Hang on, I'm gonna put you on speakerphone." He tapped a button and lay the phone on the coffee table.

"Like I said, this is Agent Ramirez, from Secret Service Intelligence." The voice was female, and she sounded around Skylar's age.

"What do you have?" Grady asked.

"I dug up some information about the clock's history, if you're interested." She paused for half a second. "Barnes is in custody, and everyone's working the thieves' angle. I just got to thinking about the clock itself, and I couldn't let it go."

"Information would be great," Grady said.

A rustle of papers came over the line. "I looked into the background of that particular clock. It was gifted by a foreign dignitary from the United Kingdom a number of years ago."

"So there's a British connection?" Skylar sat up straighter. "Which could link this dignitary to Wilson."

Grady nodded, but looked like he was thinking it over. "Makes me wonder if there isn't some personal connection between Wilson and this dignitary."

"He isn't old enough to have been there, like on the man's staff, when the clock was gifted to the president," Ramirez said.

"But he could be related to him some other way. Maybe even family," Skylar said.

"The dignitary and the president evidently fell out of favor with each other. The dignitary tried to retrieve the clock from the White House—I found an article in the *Washington Post*. There wasn't anything more than an awkward scene. By then the clock had become a piece of White House decor."

She paused. "The dignitary was…well, he'd been into the grape juice, if you know what I mean. And the president wasn't going to acquiesce to his drunken drama. I'm not sure what the president did—you'd likely have to ask someone who worked for him back then—but the whole situation was brushed over. Nothing else was mentioned about it beyond the scene the dignitary from the UK caused."

"Thank you, Agent Ramirez."

Grady said, "Yes, thank you. That was very helpful."

"Not sure it gives you much about the thieves and this whole situation, but there's a man at the Smithsonian who has been there almost as long as—" she kicked a few keys "—agent-trainee Skylar Austin has been alive. Might be worth talking to him about a fake artifact in the White House."

"Thank you," Grady said.

"Not a problem. I'll email you his info." Ramirez hung up.

Grady lifted his phone and tapped it against his leg. "I already talked to the curator." His eyes were distant, as though his attention was miles away from Skylar. "Maybe this Smithsonian guy knows more about why they might've picked that clock and if it bears significance."

"You want to go see him?" She pulled at a thread on the blanket on her lap. "I'll be fine."

Grady sighed. "You probably didn't mean that to look quite so pitiful." His lips curled into a smile. "But you are the epitome of sad right now. Like you just lost your best friend."

Skylar looked away. "It's fine."

The couch moved and he settled beside her. "You're lying."

She gasped.

"It's very cute." He was studying her. "You don't know what to do with me here, but you don't want me to leave either?"

She shrugged.

"Why don't you come with me?" He stood and looked at his watch. "I'll call over there, and if he's in then let's go talk to this guy."

Skylar stood, not wanting to admit that an outing was probably the best medicine for feeling down. Her head hurt, but it was more of a dull ache. The sleep she'd had seemed to have cleared the fog in her head. But why spend time with him when it would only be more torture over the things she didn't want to say?

"Come on." He chuckled. "Grab your shoes. We can get some lunch while we're out."

She didn't tell him she was still full from the breakfast he'd made her. If a big, strapping man like him needed to eat again, who was she to stand in the way?

Grady glanced at her for the fiftieth time during the drive. "Doing okay?"

She sighed. "Do I not look like it?"

Great, he'd made her mad. Grady took the turn for the Smithsonian Facilities. Basically where they put everything not on display at the museums in DC. "Uh… You look great. That's not what I meant."

She chuckled. "Thanks, I think."

Grady pulled over to the side of the street, determined to get his foot out of his mouth. Otherwise, he was going to ruin this fledgling friendship they had happening.

Could he deny he was interested enough to wonder if they could have more? She was the most interesting woman he'd met in a long time. Yesterday afternoon and evening had been quiet, but not in a weird way. It had been nice, hanging out with her. Not doing much of anything. When had he ever done that?

He put the car in Park, shifted on his seat and faced her. The wound on his shoulder smarted, but he ignored it. "I didn't mean you look bad. And I didn't mean I changed my mind about you coming. I wouldn't have brought you all the way out to Maryland if I didn't want you to come with me."

He waited for some kind of acknowledgment, but she held her thoughts close, not giving anything away. So he said, "I'm enjoying spending time with you and getting to know you. Even with the dunk in the river and being shot at yesterday. I'd rather do it over dinner at a nice restaurant, but spending time with you has been good, too. This life is who we are. But the danger should be over now that Barnes is in custody."

She sat up a little straighter, so he continued, "We're not the kind of people whose lives are quiet. We jump in, both feet. We're the premier federal agency. And the FBI might not agree, because they think they're better than us, but we'll just let them live in their fantasyland."

Her lips twitched.

"I'm sorry you were in danger yesterday. I didn't want you to get hurt but, now that it's done, we can do something else."

"I'm good with that."

"Which part of it?" He waited on her answer, unsure whether he'd be satisfied with it. If she said she was okay with the work, did it mean she didn't want to see what else he might have planned? They'd already shared dinner and breakfast, but that could hardly erase the stress of the day before.

Maybe he was reading this whole situation wrong. What if she wasn't attracted to him at all? He didn't want to be insecure, but his ex-fiancée had left him questioning every feeling. And every motive. Skylar had proved herself trustworthy and a reliable part of the team. What more could he ask for?

Grady knew, though. For a split second, he wanted to ask her for *everything*. But that was ridiculous. They'd only met yesterday. It wasn't like he was in love with her.

He just wanted a date. Dinner somewhere nice, like he'd mentioned.

"I'm good with the other stuff." The look on her face said something entirely different than what he'd thought. Maybe he wasn't far off base. She smiled. "And not being in danger."

Okay, so she isn't going to elaborate. He sighed. Would a woman ever make sense to him?

Grady pulled back onto the road, and within minutes they reached the security guard for the Smithsonian site entrance. The man was skeptical but, given Grady's credentials and his call ahead, the official made quick contact with Secret Service Intelligence to confirm Skylar was who she said she was and they were ushered through the gate.

Skylar gaped at the building. "Pretty big, considering this place is basically the Smithsonian's attic, right?"

"Maybe it's secretly run by a bunch of hoarders." He parked the car, then shot her a grin. "At least, I might believe that if I hadn't seen pictures of drawer after drawer all neatly arranged."

"Good." She cracked her door open. "All that organization is probably going to help us."

At the front desk, they asked for Daniel Painter. The man who strode from a hallway did so with a gait accompanied by the click of his cane on the tile floor. The sound echoed through the lobby. He peered around, then found them. His grin revealed a mouthful of teeth so even and straight they had to be dentures. The man reminded Grady of his grandfather in a way that made his chest tighten.

He rubbed the front of his vest, then stuck his hand out. "Mr. Painter?"

"Daniel, please."

"Grady Farrow." He motioned to Skylar. "This is Skylar Austin."

Daniel lifted her hand and pressed his lips to her knuckles. "Mademoiselle."

Skylar flushed. Grady wondered if maybe he should try that—see if he got a similar reaction. She cleared her throat. "Nice to meet you."

The older man didn't let go of her hand.

"Mr. Painter?"

Daniel smiled, not taking his eyes off Skylar. "Where have you been hiding all my life?" He glanced at Grady, a mischievous look on his face. "Surely not with the Secret Service."

"Actually, she is Secret Service." Grady was getting annoyed now. Not that he was jealous this man was showing Skylar such intense attention. That wasn't it. But still... "When she finishes training, she'll officially be an agent."

"Assuming I survive that long." She grinned. "I had a rough day yesterday."

Daniel's eyes widened. "How mysterious! We'll have tea. You can tell me all about it."

Skylar chuckled. "Actually, we came to ask you about an entirely different mystery." She tugged on her hand, but Daniel now held it in both of his. "A mantel clock from the White House."

Daniel's gaze flicked to Grady, then back to Skylar. "That old thing? It was mentioned to me, but I hardly remembered it. Not the most exciting thing I've been involved with in this business." He leaned closer to Skylar. "Ask me about the work I did unearthing ancient artifacts in Egypt. Anything but a completely uninteresting clock from jolly old England."

Skylar finally extricated her hand from Daniel's. She could have pulled it away at any moment, but that would have seemed rude. This she did with grace. Especially when she wound her arm in Daniel Painter's and said, "That clock was the reason why my life was in danger. It's why we're here."

"Say no more, my dear." They strode down the hall, the click of Daniel's cane echoing again.

Grady figured he'd been relegated to following, so he brought up the rear. Skylar glanced over her shoulder at him, an *eek* look on her face. Then she smiled, so he smiled back.

"Tell me all about this danger, and I shall come to your rescue with the force of my extensive knowledge."

Grady nearly rolled his eyes. The older man's flirting was outrageous, but if Skylar hadn't shut it down—and she didn't seem to want Grady to either—then he was content to follow her lead. If she wanted to use the opportunity to get the answers they needed, it was okay with him.

Did he want to be the one with her arm wrapped in his? Sure. Did he want her to smile at him, then laugh like that at something he said? Of course. But Grady was also good with stepping back and letting her decide what she was okay with and what she wasn't.

Daniel headed for a corner office, testament to how long he'd been working for the Smithsonian. On the wall was a plaque commemorating forty years of service. It had to be more now. Was the man planning for retirement, or determined to live as much of his life until that wasn't an option anymore?

He led Skylar to a couple of wingback chairs. Grady leaned against a file cabinet and folded his arms. It wasn't easy over his bulky vest, but he made it work. He wasn't going to let Daniel know he wasn't perfectly comfortable with what was happening here.

"When the Secret Service called," Daniel said as he settled into his seat, "naturally I took a look at my files."

Grady nearly rolled his eyes. "The Secret Service" had called. Like Skylar was the one here to see him and Grady was the help instead of point on this entire business.

Skylar said, "Did you find information about the clock we were asking about?"

Something Grady couldn't name washed over Daniel's face. "Of course." Was he going to lie to them? Daniel pulled a paper file from the desktop. "The clock was of German design but manufactured in England before the turn of the twentieth century. I cleaned it, performed some minor repairs to the mechanism and then sent it back to the White House." He looked up and pressed his lips together in a smile. "All quite routine, I assure you. Except for one thing."

"Which was?" Grady was glad Skylar asked the question. He would have done if she hadn't, but she seemed to have the conversation in hand. Had she noticed what he had about Daniel's change in demeanor?

"A note regarding a shipping problem." Daniel paused. "Happens all the time, but it got back there in good time, so all was well."

Skylar shifted in her seat. "If I were to tell you that the clock in the White House was, in fact, a fake, what would you say?"

Daniel blanched. "Good gravy. Are you sure?"

She nodded.

"It certainly didn't happen on my watch, I assure you."

Grady wasn't so sure. It was Skylar who said, "We certainly don't think you had anything to do with it."

"Well," Daniel huffed, "of course, I didn't."

Grady's phone vibrated in his pocket. He slid it out, saw the number was from Intelligence and moved toward the door. "I'm going to take this."

She nodded. No nerves, no silent communication. He figured that meant she was good and stepped into the hallway.

"Agent Farrow."

"I know you said to email, but I spoke with Agent Stringer, and he told me to call you right away."

Was Stringer outside? "What is it?"

"There was an accident early this morning during transport to the federal prison where they were going to hold Barnes. A truck blew up, and he escaped."

FIFTEEN

Daniel leaned back in his chair. There was something about the old man Skylar couldn't quite put her finger on. It bothered her, nonetheless. He grasped his cane and stood. "Would you like a tour of the facility?"

"I should catch up with Agent Farrow." Not that Grady had left. He was just in the hallway on his phone. "We have another appointment after this."

Just lunch, actually. And probably fast food. Some drive-through. But Daniel didn't need to know that.

She felt strange not being with Grady. Clingy wasn't her thing, but that didn't mean she wouldn't feel a whole lot safer with him in the room. What was it about this man that weirded her out? She hadn't felt it in the hall. She'd simply thought he was a charming old man practicing his rusty flirting skills. Then Grady had excused himself and…something had changed.

"This way." He led her to a door at the other end of the room, but it didn't lead back out to the hallway.

"Um…"

"There's something I need to show you, Ms. Austin. It won't take long, and I think you'll be *very* interested to see what it is."

Skylar glanced back at the door. Daniel tugged on her arm with more strength than she'd thought he would have, and moved into the hallway. It was darker than the hall they'd walked down to get to Daniel's office. Deserted.

Something clattered to the floor. She looked at him and found he'd discarded his cane. In his hand he held a palm-sized derringer, pointed at her.

"I've been waiting years for someone to come asking about a fake artifact." His voice was soft. Not angry, more resigned.

"I'm not here to expose you." She swallowed. "You can put the gun down, because I have no interest in telling anyone what you may or may not have done." She was only asking about one clock, not whatever had spooked him.

She took a step back, instinct screaming at her to run.

"Not one step."

"Please, don't kill me. You'll only make things worse for yourself." He couldn't think murdering her would be a good idea. If he let her go, he might actually get away with this. He could run.

She lifted both hands and tried to look helpless. She wasn't close enough to grab the weapon. Not to mention, the thing was old. Who knew what damage it would do? It could backfire, or Daniel might have kept it maintained all these years. Skylar was more scared of a historical, relic weapon she knew nothing about than a weapon she'd handled—or knew how to fight against.

Where was Grady? Surely he was done with his call by now. She didn't need a knight in shining armor, but his entrance might be distraction enough for her to get the derringer from Daniel.

Grady. She wanted to yell his name, but that meant he'd get shot as well when he showed up.

Daniel said, "What do you know about the clock?"

"Only that the one in the White House was a fake. Nothing else." She used the distraction of her pleading to get an inch closer to him. She had to close the gap without him noticing, if she was going to have a hope of stealing that gun. "We don't know anything about you."

"It figures you'd stumble across it and not even know what the business was. I hid it so well no one ever found out. And if you hadn't come here, asking about that stupid clock, no one ever would have."

"What are you going to do now?" He couldn't shoot her. It'd make him the target of a police investigation that would have them examining every part of his life. Was he going to kidnap her? Grady would come looking. He wasn't going to just accept her sudden disappearance.

Daniel grasped her elbow and hauled her down the hallway. Their footsteps echoed against the bare walls. Whatever limp he'd had before was gone now. Was this man's entire life a lie?

"Let me go," she pleaded. "Please. You don't have to do this. I won't tell anyone." Even though the minute she got back to the Secret Service she would tell them everything he'd said. "I promise. I'm not here to get you in trouble. You've obviously kept the secret this long. We can go our separate ways, and you can live your life."

Until the feds caught up with him, that was. Her whole argument was flimsy, but what else did she have that might get her out of the line of fire?

"I will live my life," he said. "Don't worry about that, Ms. Austin." He hauled her around another corner. Were they going down?

She glanced back. The floor was declining slightly. What was at the bottom of this hall?

He continued, "I'm going to get out of this

place." He stopped at a door with a number pad on it. "And you're my insurance. Now enter these numbers."

Daniel took half a step back and held the weapon aimed at her as he relayed sixteen digits. When the door clicked, he said, "Open it."

Skylar pulled on the handle. It was heavy, like a fire door. As she opened it, a rush of distinctly cooler air blew into the hall from what looked like a cave. A tunnel stretched before them, lined with wires and halogen lights along the walls. A railing. The tunnel descended down even farther.

"I'm not going in there." She'd never been spelunking, but this likely wouldn't be fun the way that could be. Something about this tunnel made her *not* want to go down there. *God, help me.*

Daniel shoved her forward, the gun pressed against her side. Her feet landed on slick steps, on worn stone. The tunnel looked like it was used frequently, or had simply been used regularly for years. Maybe even hundreds of years. By who? Why did the Smithsonian need to go underground?

At the last second before the door shut, Skylar glanced back over her shoulder. The breath of a prayer crossed her lips.

Grady.

He rounded the corner and their eyes locked. Too far away for her to convey a message. If he

came down here, Daniel would shoot him. Or
her. Or both. She couldn't let Daniel do that to
either of them.

*Please don't let Grady get the combination.
Daniel will shoot him.* She had to get out of this
without getting hurt. She wasn't a Secret Service agent yet. What did her career matter? She
wasn't one of them. Yet. Sure, the potential was
there, but right now—in the balance—it was
Grady who came out on top. Not because he was
worth more than her. She knew her value. The
problem was that she understood how much the
world would lose if the worst happened to Grady.

And there was no way Skylar was going to
let that happen.

Grady saw the determination in her eyes right
before the door shut. He knew that look—Skylar
was determined to protect him. Too bad for her
there was no way he would let her die just so he
could live. What was Daniel thinking? He'd left
them having a nice conversation, where Daniel
had been shocked to hear about the fake. Something had changed.

Grady pulled his phone back out and tapped
Stringer's number on Favorites. He explained the
situation in as few words as possible, then said,
"Get me the code for this door."

Something must have happened because it

seemed Daniel was intent on escaping into a tunnel system under the facility. Holding Skylar at gunpoint. He'd only stepped out into the hallway for a few seconds.

His head was still reeling at the news Barnes had escaped.

Had the man been working with Daniel Painter?

He was supposed to be protecting Skylar... and he was doing an awful job at it. Now her life was in danger—again. She was determined to save him—again. He'd think it was endearing if he wasn't scared to the marrow of his bones that she could get hurt. Again.

Grady blew out a breath and leaned his forehead on the door. It was cold enough that the sensation shocked his skin. Metal overlaid with paint. He couldn't just kick the door in. He had to wait.

Daniel was long gone with Skylar. He kicked the door, purely out of frustration.

Grady ground his teeth. He shifted his feet. Was Skylar okay? Was Daniel hurting her? She needed not to fight back, or he would pull the trigger. Did she know to just play along?

He squeezed his eyes shut. Not being able to help her left a sour taste in his mouth. *God, don't let her get hurt.* No, that wasn't fair for him to pray. It wasn't asking too much of God, but it was setting Grady up for bitterness if God had a different way of aiding her out of this situation. If Skylar was alive, but she got nicked by something sharp, then Grady could claim God hadn't answered his prayer. All because he hadn't prayed for God's will to be done.

That was setting himself up for failure.

Help me. Use me. I need to save her—You know that. Help me to do my job here.

Faith was a whole lot more complicated than he'd ever thought as a child, but that was okay. He held tight to a simple trust in God, but God Himself was not simple. His ways didn't always make sense—and that was okay as well. God was God, and Grady didn't need to understand everything He did.

Grady's phone rang. He swiped to answer and before he even said anything, Stringer said, "Six, seven, four, three…" The numbers continued. Sixteen digits Grady entered, hammering each number on the panel with every ounce of frustration he felt.

The door clicked. "Got it. Thanks."

"Don't thank me. Some agent named Ramirez already had it."

Grady hung up, yanked the door handle and darted through, weapon first. *Thank You, Lord.* They might have saved Skylar's life.

He trailed down a hallway lined by cave walls. The air pricked at his skin, making him shiver.

The tunnel leveled off at the bottom. He stopped before the end and leaned his shoulder against the wall.

Checked his phone.

No signal. He was on his own down here.

Grady stowed the phone and pressed on into an open area, the ceiling a little higher than the one in his kitchen. Eleven feet, maybe. What was this place? It was freezing down here.

Several dark openings encircled the space. Grady stopped in front of each of the five tunnels and listened. He caught some slight sound at the third. A whisper. The shuffle of a shoe on stone. A yelp in a higher tone. *Skylar.* He prayed it was her—that God had given him these sensory cues for a reason—and pressed on down the tunnel.

It ended sooner than the first had, and he emerged into a wider tunnel, like a tributary draining to a rushing river. A golf cart was parked in this tunnel, which wider than two lanes of highway. Lined along its walls were more halogen lights, again strung together with wires, lighting the whole place with a bright white glow.

How long did these tunnels go for? Would they emerge from their ends in different states? Grady didn't particularly want to find out. There were so many tunnels under the ground in this part of the country—and he wasn't just talking about the metro system.

"Get on." Daniel's voice was hard, his tone inviting no argument. "Now."

Skylar stood straight. "Tell me where the real clock is."

"You think I remember?" Daniel scowled, quite a change from the congenial man who'd walked them into his office. "I did so many forgeries back then I lost count, started recording them in a logbook."

"Where is the book?"

He laughed. "Turning into a real investigator, aren't you?"

"Tell me where it is and you can go wherever you want," Skylar said, hoping he'd at least consider it. "You don't need me."

"You think they'll just *let* me out of here?" He grabbed her arm and pressed the barrel of the gun to her chin. "It's hard enough to get in a government building these days, but what do you think they do to us to make sure no historical items walk their way out of here?"

Skylar didn't say anything.

Grady didn't know the answer to that either. He could guess more scanners and a security checkpoint, but it wasn't like they actually worked there like Daniel did. Were they supposed to know?

"I told you I'll need insurance, and you're it."

Grady stepped out into the tunnel. "Not so fast."

Daniel, the gun still pointed at Skylar's chin, whirled around. She yelped as he dragged her in front of him. Grady had no better shot than he'd had from the smaller tunnel. Daniel was determined to use Skylar for cover.

Grady took a couple of steps closer. "I agree with Skylar. You leave, *we* stay." They were a team, and Daniel needed to know. "So let her go, and *go*."

Daniel lifted his chin. "One more step toward me, and I'll kill her."

Grady stopped.

"Lay your weapon down."

"No."

"I'll shoot her."

"I'll shoot *you*," Grady said. "Which means you shooting her would be pointless, since you'd both be dead." There was no way he would lay his gun down. That was not part of his training, and Skylar knew it.

His gaze snagged on hers. Wide eyes, full of fear—and a whole heap of anger. Good. Mad was good. It meant she wasn't going to cower or back down.

He was proud to see the backbone he knew she had now.

Her eyes darted around. Not erratic. He realized she was motioning high and to the right—at the light on the wall of the tunnel. The light? He glanced back at her and saw her nod.

Grady took aim and shot the light out, praying she had a solid plan. One that didn't end in her diving in front of a bullet.

The whole tunnel went dark. He heard a thump.

And a gunshot.

SIXTEEN

The second the tunnel went dark, Skylar moved. Launched herself at Daniel and slammed into him, full force. The older man yelped and started to fall back. They landed on the ground, her on top of him, and the gun went off. Skylar grabbed for his wrist, missed a couple of times, and finally found his arm in the dark.

After a second, there was a hum. The lights turned on, green now like the neon glow of night-vision goggles. A backup system. Presumably the interruption in the lights would have alerted security, and they were on their way now. At least, she hoped that was the case.

Skylar grasped his hands in a grip he wasn't going to get out of. "Get his gun!"

Hopefully Grady would do it, not argue with the fact that she'd just given him an order. They were partners in this, even though he had seniority.

Daniel moved so fast she didn't have time to

react. His head slammed into hers and the momentum shoved her to her back.

She lost her grip on the gun as stars flashed across her vision.

"Drop it!" Grady's voice brooked no argument. She heard him move over to them, then he said, "Keep your hands where I can see them."

Skylar felt across her forehead and found the spot where Daniel had slammed his forehead into hers. She winced. "Ouch."

"You okay, Austin?"

Why was he using her last name? Skylar lowered her hand and looked over. Grady's face was all business. She wasn't sure she could speak a whole sentence. All her brain wanted to do was think about Grady for days. Like a song stuck on repeat.

She shook her head, then had to swallow the bile that jumped up from her stomach. Skylar groaned.

"Austin."

"I…" She sucked in a breath of cool tunnel air. "Okay." If she said more, she was liable to lose the last thing she'd eaten. She'd be put off Grady's cooking for life.

"Can you get up?"

Skylar rolled onto her hands and knees and then stood. A dull ache rolled through her head.

"Think you can secure our friend here?"

Grady pulled a zip tie from the back of his belt. She secured Daniel and then tugged on his elbow until he got the message and stood. She was going to breathe through her nose until the nausea passed. They'd just have to figure out what she was saying without her actually speaking.

"Walk." Grady held his aim on the man and she followed the two of them up the tunnel, back toward the ground floor of the facility. Without turning back to her, Grady said, "You still okay, Skylar?"

She swallowed, then said, "Yep." The word was short, but she figured he got the message, considering he wasn't about to take his attention from Daniel, even if the man was secured.

This should have been a simple conversation. Trying to discover if there had been some significance in stealing that particular clock. Instead, they'd uncovered yet another mystery, this one involving an employee of the Smithsonian. Daniel making fake artifacts for years. Selling the real ones on the black market.

And he'd likely done that with the clock Wilson had been looking for.

Skylar didn't think Wilson and Daniel were connected, though she could hardly think straight. They'd stumbled on Daniel's illegal activity, nonetheless. Hopefully the man would cooperate with them. They needed access to that logbook he'd mentioned if they really wanted to find out if it was all connected. Was Barnes part of this?

Skylar stumbled. Her face smashed into the back of Grady's vest, and she realized he'd stopped. "Sorry."

He didn't turn, but she could feel the stiffness coming off him in waves.

"Accident." Skylar closed her mouth before she said anything else embarrassing.

There was a click from the hall and the door opened. Grady motioned Daniel through first. Into the middle of a waiting crowd of Secret Service agents. Or just four. Maybe she was seeing double.

"Got here as quick as we could," Stringer said.

Grady nodded, still mad at her apparently. "Skylar needs medical attention."

Stringer frowned, glancing from Grady to her. She said, "I'm okay. Daniel head-butted me, is all."

Stringer winced. "I see that. Let's get you an ice pack." He waved her over. She glanced back at Grady while he escorted Daniel down the hall. Away from her. Skylar sighed.

"Come on," Stringer said. "You can tell me what happened."

Like she was just another witness. Just another trainee agent, not someone Grady had said he was friends with. She'd thought they were a team, but maybe she was wrong. Maybe he didn't like when she tried to fix things, considering her nothing more than a wannabe. A liability.

"I'm not even going to ask." Stringer chuckled. "None of that looks good."

She glanced up at him. "What?"

"All the emotion on your face. You're gonna want to work on not giving away everything you're feeling." He grinned, his teeth bright against his dark skin. "It's a little overwhelming, to be honest."

"Apparently getting hit in the head means I have no filter." She paused. "On my face." How on earth could that make sense to anyone?

"I get it." He patted her shoulder, then yelled, "Where's my ice?"

An agent hurried over, a bundle of ice wrapped in a damp dishcloth. "This was all they had in the break room."

Skylar resisted the urge to wrinkle her nose and balled it up, then pressed it against her forehead. "Ah. Better."

Stringer smiled again.

"You're a very smiley person."

He chuckled then. "I'm what?"

"Happy. Though, it seems like it's mostly at my expense."

He glanced at Grady. "Not all you. And not because you got hurt."

"Then, why the humor?" She leaned against the wall. "If you don't mind me asking."

Stringer shrugged. "No problem. It's just great to finally meet the woman who can give Grady's iron-fisted self-control enough challenge to shake it."

Skylar stared at him while her brain exploded with questions. She didn't even know which to ask first.

Stringer only laughed. "Maybe you've met your match as well." He paused. "Sorry. You're hurt, and your head probably doesn't need this. But I have to say, I'm happy for you guys. Things have been crazy since the exercise, and the job isn't even over yet. I can't believe all you've both been through. But I just think maybe it's also been good. For both of you."

"Is that supposed to be a riddle? Because it really sounded like one."

Stringer's laugh echoed down the hall as he strode back toward Grady. She didn't know what on earth was so funny, but whatever. Let the man have his private joke. She wasn't going to care when her head hurt this much. Grady didn't seem all that impressed by the laughter either, given the look on his face.

A look he sent her way as well.

Did he not like the fact that she'd figured out how to get the jump on Daniel? He couldn't really be jealous she'd thought of it first, could he? That was way more of a petty idea than she'd figured he would have. Which just proved to her how much about him she still didn't know. They'd only met yesterday, even though a month's worth of excitement had happened since then. Most of it had been full of danger and stress. Not a steady basis for a relationship. Friends or otherwise.

Skylar looked away to stare at her feet. Grady could think what he wanted. She'd done her job, and she was proud of it.

It didn't matter how many times Stringer motioned toward Skylar, Grady wasn't going to go over there. What were they, twelve? This wasn't the lunchroom in junior high. Grady was a grown man who didn't need encouragement to go talk to a girl. Not when Skylar was a woman he wasn't going to play games with. She deserved better.

It didn't matter how he felt about her—or how that feeling had grown exponentially all day. He'd hardly been able to speak, knowing she was behind him. Feeling the heat of her there, in the tunnel. Knowing she could have been killed. So easily.

Or moment minutes before then, when everything had gone dark and the gunshot rang out. He'd nearly had a heart attack, not knowing if she was dead or alive.

The whole thing made him cognizant of the fact that he might just be more into her than he'd thought. What was it about Skylar that made him feel like he'd come alive? Her determination alone scared him more than he'd thought possible. And amazed him.

He'd worked with female agents before, so he knew it wasn't just the fact that she was a woman. It was the fact that it was *this* woman. Skylar.

Grady pushed off the wall beside where Daniel sat in a folding chair someone had found. He rounded on the man, determined to get some answers. "Making fakes. All these years."

Daniel didn't look at him.

"But I don't think you did it alone, did you? Who were your partners?"

Something flickered in the older man's jaw.

Grady pulled up a picture on his phone, one from when they'd reinstated White House surveillance at the end of the exercise. He turned the screen so Daniel could see an image of Barnes. Then Wilson. "Know either of these men?"

Daniel looked at it. His eyes flickered to the side. "No."

It wasn't enough for Grady to state conclusively if the man was lying or not. But he didn't react strongly enough to be working with either of the two men. So either he didn't know them, or he did but it was amicable. Which meant he was probably covering for them—keeping their secret.

"This is about national security."

"That's what you guys *always* say." Daniel smirked. *"National security."*

"It is. Because an agent you might know, Peter Barnes, killed the other, Wilson, yesterday. And he escaped custody this morning. I think you know him. And you know what? If he was your partner, you think he's going to let you live when you could ID him?"

"I want protection."

"So he *is* part of this fakes ring."

It didn't explain why Wilson had been sold out with a faked item to steal, probably figuring he'd get caught in the process. But it did open up a little more of this so that it might start to make sense.

"Did you help him escape custody?"

"No information unless I get protection."

"We'll keep you safe so you can stand trial. Don't worry about that." Grady folded his arms. "What I want is what you know about Barnes."

"I want a deal."

"Talk to the DA about deals. I just want Barnes."

"You aren't going to arrest me?"

Grady shook his head. But that didn't mean someone else wouldn't. The man had held Skylar captive and almost killed her.

Daniel said, "I have proof of everyone involved. All the players. Names. Information. Bank account numbers."

"Where?"

"In a logbook."

"Where?" He barked the word. Had he stayed silent, the man could have cost them their shot at evidence. Details of all Barnes had done, just because Daniel didn't want to go to jail for what *he'd* done.

"Okay, fine. It's at my house, with a brown leather cover."

"And if we tear your house apart looking for the logbook?"

Daniel gasped. "You can't do that!"

"It's national security. Remember? We can do a lot of things."

The man blustered. Grady figured the logbook was at his house—probably hidden away. He glanced at Stringer. "Get me Mr. Painter's address."

Stringer nodded. "Already on it."

He looked back at Daniel. "We will find it, and you'll go to jail for attempted murder and forgery."

Daniel blustered.

"If you tell me where the logbook is, I'll square things away. Make sure you only answer to what we can prove." He paused. "But send me on a wild-goose chase, and it won't be good for you. Not after you held Skylar at gunpoint."

Grady pulled back, realizing how loud his voice had gotten. Yes, she'd been in mortal danger. Did he have to shout about it? No. Because now everyone in this hallway knew he cared.

Grady said more quietly, "Think about it." Then turned to look down the hall, where a crowd of Smithsonian employees had gathered. He scanned each of the faces, wondering if one of them knew Daniel Painter had been making forgeries for years—taking artifacts worth millions of dollars and selling them on the side. Someone had to have noticed something.

At the back was a familiar face, a man he'd seen several times. And not just when Niles had saved them from being shot by Johnson.

"Hey!" The word exploded from Grady's mouth as he trotted down the hall.

Niles blanched. He backed up, turned and strode away down the hall. Thirty people minimum stood between them. Grady turned to the nearest agent, one on crowd control. "Find that guy. Don't let him leave the facility before I talk to him."

The agent jumped into action, and Grady turned back. Daniel Painter was on his feet now, his face close to Skylar's.

Stringer was there as well, which was the only reason Grady didn't shout and race back down the hall. "Back up." He dragged Daniel away from Skylar.

"Back. Up." The words were short, but she needed to know he was serious. What was she thinking, letting Daniel get in her face?

Their eyes met for a second, and he saw a measure of hurt there. Grady ignored it, despite the pang in him. Her safety was more important than her feelings—and he needed to keep reminding himself of that or he was going to end up hesitating. Sparing her feelings but opening a window where she could get physically hurt.

Or…more physically hurt than she'd gotten so far today.

Stringer settled Daniel back in the chair and turned to Grady. "I got a call from Intelligence. They looked deep into Barnes and found he's swimming in money he didn't earn as an agent."

Grady felt his eyebrows rise. "You think he's been making fakes and selling them?"

"Trafficking in artifacts from the White House. Could be big black-market business."

Grady blew out a breath. "What about the curator? She had no idea, but how is that even possible?"

"You think she's involved?" Skylar asked.

Grady shrugged. "The alternative is that she's kind of incompetent."

Stringer's phone rang. He talked for a second, then said, "Thanks," and hung up. "Barnes was spotted down in Crystal City. I gotta go."

Grady nodded.

"Also the warrant came in. You're clear to search Daniel's house."

Skylar glanced between them.

"Let's go."

She hadn't moved.

"Are you coming?"

She tipped her head to the side, the question on her face. "I don't know. Am I?"

Grady wasn't in the mood for riddles. Didn't she know he wanted her right beside him so he could make sure she came through this in once piece?

"Let's go, Austin." He started down the hall without looking back to see if she followed. "We have work to do."

Seconds later, he heard her footsteps. Grady smiled.

SEVENTEEN

Skylar followed Grady up the front walk of Daniel Painter's house. Stringer had left with the rest of the agents, all out on the hunt for Agent Barnes in Crystal City. The lead was supposed to be solid, and Grady hadn't even wanted to entertain the idea they might not catch him. As far as he was concerned the whole thing was a done deal.

Skylar was going to hold her feelings in reserve until they actually captured him. At least the pursuit was all the way to the south, across the river. Miles from here. Skylar shivered, glad the cops had sent officers to the house already.

Grady glanced at her. "You okay?"

Like she was going to admit she couldn't handle this? "Fine." She sniffed and lifted her chin. Maybe that was an amateur move, but she wasn't officially a Secret Service agent. Yet. "Ready?"

Flipping it back on him reinforced to Grady the fact that he was in control. She didn't have much say here, in his world, but she wanted to see this through to the end. What she *didn't* want to do was sit at home and hear about it all later.

She'd be scared out of her mind at home. Besides, if anything happened here, she would be standing next to Grady when it did. Who better to protect her than someone trained to give his life for the president?

A local police officer stood at the open front door with his partner.

Grady said, "Did you go inside?"

The older officer said, "All clear. We had fun kicking the door in." He grinned.

Skylar's head was still pounding, despite the painkillers. She touched her fingers to her forehead.

Whatever was on her face stopped him, and his eyes softened. "Skylar."

"I don't…" She didn't even know what to say. Cutting off her words was better than suddenly admitting she didn't want him to die. He would think she was a clingy weirdo.

Grady sighed and pulled her into his arms. Her face smushed against all the paraphernalia on his vest. Not super comfortable, but she wound her arms around him and just held her breath. Felt what it was like to be in the embrace of a man who cared. One who had, time and again in the last two days, fought like she was important to him.

"Thanks."

He leaned back. "You're welcome." Those brown eyes were warm again. "Sorry I was short earlier. I just don't like when bullets start flying."

"Isn't that your whole life?"

He grinned. Leaned closer. "I meant at *you*. And I'm sorry you got even more banged up."

Skylar could feel the warmth of his breath on her face. Was he going to—

Grady's lips brushed against hers. Just a whisper, but it spoke louder in her life than any other gesture—no matter how big.

She waited for him to go for more, determined not to overthink this. Just a nice interlude in an otherwise stress-filled day. Why would she object? He was a good man.

But Grady stiffened.

Did he regret—

He let go of her and spun in one movement, strode across the lobby toward what looked like a living area.

"What is it?"

He glanced at her and placed one finger over his lips. Skylar closed her mouth. The softness was gone now, replaced with a professional determination. So much for their nice interlude. Probably better this way. She'd have read more into it than he meant, and then her heart would be crushed to powder—nothing left of those broken pieces—when he explained how he really felt about her.

She followed him to the edge of the living room, where the hall tiles met wood flooring. Then she heard what he had. A rustling.

She surveyed the couches, the TV unit packed with DVDs of black-and-white movies. A lamp, its twin on the other side of the room. In the corner, disguised as an end table, was a dog crate.

"Puppies," she told Grady. "Daniel Painter has dogs." The crate was open, but the dogs weren't running around the house. Where were they? "That's probably what you heard."

Grady stepped back and looked into the hall, up the stairs. "Maybe. The officers should have given us a heads up. Stay behind me."

Skylar wasn't going to argue with that. Stringer had given her a gun, just in case, but she prayed she wouldn't have to fire it. The dogs had been secured in the kitchen with a tall baby gate. Skylar watched while one barked at the intruders, and the other raced outside through a dog door. She kept pace with him as he checked each room.

"We should look for the logbook."

Grady nodded. "I saw an office back there."

He motioned down the hall to an open door. Inside were walls of bookshelves.

"These all look expensive." She winced. "I'd be scared to read them just in case I folded the corner of a page down because I misplaced my bookmark." She'd referred to it as a *quitter strip* more than once before. "I much prefer a good secondhand bookstore. Worn books that have been devoured over and over again. That's real life."

"Worn pages?"

"We all have them, don't we?" She motioned to the walls of books. "Being…*preserved* like that? It's not natural."

The corners of Grady's mouth curled up. "Maybe you could help me look for a safe among the shelves."

"I really hope it's in a safe." She didn't want to know how long it would take to check each one of these pricey books for the logbook that would be the evidence they needed to get Barnes. "Although hiding it in plain sight would be a genius idea."

"I'll check the books," Grady said. "You look beyond the obvious for something hidden."

"Deal." She grinned at him. Had they really kissed only minutes ago? Who knew whether the logbook was even hidden here? When he'd finally opened up about it, Daniel Painter hadn't given them much to go on past the fact that it had a brown leather cover.

Skylar was glad she had the book to focus on. Being with Grady was distraction enough.

Among other things, Grady tried to factor in Daniel's height. He'd want the book within reach, but not anywhere obvious like eye-level. In the end, he sighed. "Maybe it's not even in here."

"I'm beginning to think it isn't in here. Maybe he hid it under his mattress…or in his underwear drawer or something." Her nose wrinkled at that. It was very cute.

But Grady couldn't dwell on that. On her. Otherwise they'd be right back with her in his arms, their lips meeting ever so gently. Not even a real kiss before the dogs had disturbed them. Sweetest almost kiss of his life.

Too bad he had a job to do, and that wasn't part of it.

"Here."

He rounded the desk to where she'd crouched behind it, in front of a low cupboard. With a safe inside.

"It's open." She swung the door to the safe wide. "Nothing but papers." She lifted out a couple of small boxes. "Jewelry."

"Valuables, but nothing he couldn't handle losing if they were stolen."

Skylar spun, staying crouched before the safe. "What are you thinking?"

"That I watch way too many old detective movies. It's making me crazy, like there's a backup safe somewhere in here."

"Two safes?"

"One easy to find, some valuables inside. But nothing too precious. Like a decoy. The second contains the real prize."

She straightened. "That's not a bad idea." Skylar circled the room, pulling pictures from their hooks.

Grady moved to the books, checking randomly across shelves to find a hidden compartment. "Come on," he muttered to himself. "Come on."

"I'm not finding anything on the walls."

He wanted to give up. Maybe this wasn't even the right room. But why hide a book anywhere else than as a needle among a stack of other needles? Only Daniel would know which book it—

He tugged on one of the books. "What…" Grady's voice trailed off. He checked the books beside it on a low shelf, one up from the bottom in the far corner of the study. "Look at this. The whole row is stuck in."

He reached for the outermost books on the

shelf and tried to pry his fingers into the space between the books and the wooden sides of the shelf. The left edge had no gap, but on the right side he could get his fingertips in there.

He pulled. Did it again with both hands. "Stuck."

"Try pushing it." Skylar crouched beside him and laid a hand on his shoulder.

Grady touched his fingertips to the spines of the books and pressed. There was a quiet click, and it popped open.

"Great." Skylar sighed. "We need the combination for this one now." She hadn't moved her hand away, and the light weight of it felt nice.

Grady turned. She smiled at him, and he returned it.

"No." She shook her head. "Focus on the safe."

"What?" He laughed and realized it sounded a little embarrassed. As though she'd caught him with his hand in the cookie jar.

"You're getting distracted. I can see it." She moved her hand, but he caught it gently in his and placed it back on his shoulder.

"Maybe you're helping me think."

It was her turn to laugh. "I don't believe that for a second."

"Okay, so maybe not." He called Intelligence from his phone and asked for the same agent he'd spoken with before. Ramirez. "Pull up the file for Daniel Painter." It was likely less than an hour old, but they were good at their jobs. "Give me anything you think might be the combination to his safe."

They ran through a couple of combinations, then a couple more. "No dice." Grady sighed.

"Try this." The agent on the other end of the phone rattled off another combination.

Grady entered it. "I thought we did his dogs' birthdays."

"This is a combination. If I work through this pattern, there are three thousand plus more possibilities."

Grady didn't like the sound of that. It would take forever to try them all. "Let's pray this is it."

Sure enough, the safe clicked open.

Another click sounded in the room. This one came from the other side.

Grady shot up, pulling Skylar behind him. "Kristine?"

"We really should stop meeting like this." The White House curator's tone was as stiff as her spine as she strode halfway into the room. Gone were the skirts and heels. She wore jeans, boots and a bulky jacket. "Now hand me the contents of that safe. You'll have to thank whoever was on the line for cracking the combination. Very handy, your help."

Grady didn't have time to say anything before

Kristine said, "Give me the contents. Now, and I won't kill the two of you."

That made no sense, since killing them would actually make her life simpler. Wouldn't it? Grady figured she'd only said that so they'd be lulled into some false belief that they might get out of this alive. Then Kristine would kill them, anyway.

She shifted the gun to Grady, then said, "Skylar, the safe. Toss me the logbook."

"You won't get away with this." Grady couldn't check, but the phone line could still be open with Intelligence. He hadn't hung up, and he prayed the other agent hadn't either. Grady had no idea if help might be en route, but they certainly could use some. The officers outside. Other agents. Anyone. *Please, Lord.*

Anything to keep them alive and the logbook out of Kristine's hands.

Help us, Lord.

Skylar stood up, a book in her hand. She held it out, and the log shook.

Kristine snatched up the book. "Barnes came to me with the idea for the job. Wilson is too much of a loose cannon. It was necessary to get rid of him so we could continue our work elsewhere. Then, when I realized making you the scapegoat could help confuse the Secret Service so they wouldn't know who was and wasn't part of this, I agreed to it."

"Didn't work, though, did it?" Grady said as he moved back in front of Skylar. The curator was the one behind all of this? He could hardly believe it, but it made sense given she had the knowledge and inside position to pull it off. Barnes was probably just the muscle.

Grady's head spun.

If he didn't think Kristine would shoot one or both of them, he'd have pulled his gun. But a gunfight wasn't how he wanted this day to end. Far too many bullets had been fired already. Grady had a gunshot wound to the shoulder, and Skylar's forehead would be bruised for a week.

The Secret Service would find her, but if she killed them no one would be able to undo it.

"Take it and go."

Skylar clutched the sides of his vest.

"Just go," Grady ordered.

Kristine started to smirk.

Down the hall he heard the sound of the front door opening. "Agent Farrow, you still in here?" It was one of the police officers.

Grady wanted to shout. To warn them someone was in here.

The second Kristine's attention was diverted by this newest threat, Grady pulled his weapon.

She ducked into the hall.

Grady fired.

The officer shouted to his partner to call for backup. They met in the hallway. The officer saw it was Grady and lowered his weapon. "Where did she go?"

"Who?"

Grady quickly explained, then went to the back door and looked out. Didn't see anything. Couldn't hear anything. The dogs barked, running circles around his feet. If Kristine had come this way, she'd have disturbed the animals.

Grady ducked back in. The officer stood behind him. "Why don't you go search upstairs? She might have gone up there and then climbed out a window."

"Right." The officer jumped into action.

Grady walked back through the ground floor, looking for a possible basement access. How would Kristine know about that, though? She could have followed them here, but she also could have gotten to Daniel Painter before them. That meant she'd have warned Painter they were on their way.

A trap set for them.

"It's clear up here. No windows open. They're all painted shut."

"Grady!"

He followed the sound and found the room

Skylar had called from. A tiny living room—formal. The kind with no TV.

She stood beside a small cupboard in the corner. "Just like in the White House."

"She went out a tunnel."

EIGHTEEN

Grady went first down the tunnel. Skylar couldn't help the sigh. "Again?"

He chuckled as he moved. "Seems like it."

"Maybe after this I could put in a request. No tunnels for at least six months." She sighed. "I've really had enough of them, you know?"

His laugh continued to echo down the stone corridor. His flashlight bobbed ahead of them, illuminating the tunnel. Not the end though; it was too long for that. Beyond fifteen or twenty feet there was nothing but darkness.

"At least this one could have had lights like the last."

"And yet your idea was to shoot one out and make everything dark." He actually shivered.

She shuddered herself. "After this, I won't be in a hurry to go spelunking." Grady stumbled, and she grasped on to him. "Sorry. I shouldn't run so close behind you."

"It's no problem. Just uneven ground." The

ground was rocky down here, and his light was on the terrain ahead of them.

After that he went even faster. Skylar didn't blame him. She likely wanted to catch up to Kristine as much as he did.

"How far ahead is she?" Her voice came out breathy from running so fast for a good half mile now.

Grady said, "Can't be too much farther."

"Where does this tunnel even go?"

"Could go anywhere."

"But we're not ascending to the surface. Not yet, anyway."

He slowed. "Shhh." It wasn't rude. She was babbling.

Skylar whispered, "What?" as low as she could. He had to have heard something, though she couldn't make out more than their footsteps. And the low rumble of a phone vibrating. "I think your phone is ringing."

He didn't pull it out.

"How do you even have signal down here?"

He shrugged. "I heard something else."

After another minute, they came across a metal door. Grady held his weapon up, ready. Skylar pulled on the handle and muscled the door out of the way, while staying out of the line of fire.

Grady stepped through.

Skylar couldn't deny the fact that she wanted to be what he was. Skylar wasn't willing to let that dream go. Especially now that she knew the kind of men and women who did this job. She'd met so many of them over the last two days, and she admired them all.

Grady hit the top of that list.

Skylar only hoped once this trip to DC was done, they would stay in touch. She would likely be stationed across the country somewhere, or maybe even overseas. No one got into the White House on their first assignment. Which meant they wouldn't work together again. Maybe not for years, and possibly never in her career.

And why did that make her sad?

"Come on."

Skylar hustled to catch up. This day was wearing on her. She was getting emotional, probably because she was tired. All the adrenaline rushes of the past two days had drained her. Grady, too, but he wasn't acting like he was exhausted. Not like she was—muscles heavy, no strength. No reserves. The kind of fatigue caffeine wouldn't help—if she could even find a coffee shop. She didn't even know where they were.

Until she heard it—the distant rumble of a train.

"The *Metro*?"

Grady said, "I think we're close to a station."

"Kristine is going to head for a train. We'll never catch her."

"We'd better hustle, then."

Grady trotted away, down another tunnel. How did he know which way to go? Skylar followed mostly so she didn't get left behind, out of range of the flashlight. Not that he would leave her, but the man was resolute. And Skylar was still just as determined to continue to pull her weight.

She didn't care so much about whatever report would be written on her actions in DC. She'd stand by every decision she had made, and figured extenuating circumstances would be taken into account.

Plus, if they found Kristine—and the others brought in Barnes again—then they'd have finished this. Daniel would corroborate their story, if he continued to talk in exchange for a deal. And Johnson could testify as to what they'd all been up to. Simmons as well.

Now all they needed was the woman.

Up ahead the noise was louder. Grady stopped by another door.

"Have you seen any sign of her yet?"

He shook his head. "No, but this door is ajar. I think she went through here."

Unless she'd left it open just to throw them off. Skylar held her hand out for the flashlight and shone it around the space. Just stone walls, then concrete. Bare floor. Nothing to hide behind, and no other places Kristine could have gone.

"Let's go." She wanted to tell him to be careful, but figured he already knew that.

Grady stepped in first, again. Skylar followed. A short hall led to another door, and then a storage area. Boxes. Stacked crates. Even cleaning equipment. Then another, and they were out in the hall between the elevators at the entrance and the platform of whatever Metro station this was.

The bustle of passengers was a low din. A couple of people looked askance at Grady in his uniform. Not that an armed Secret Service agent was an uncommon sight in DC, just that it was uncommon outside of the vicinity of the White House.

One of the people, a tourist by the look of him, took a cell phone picture. Skylar pointed her index finger in their direction and said, "No!" in her most stern and authoritative voice. They would probably still post it, though. Maybe Intelligence could use it to track their location and send backup.

"This way." Grady turned in the direction of the train platform.

Skylar trotted behind him, gun held in front of her. How did he know where to go?

Maybe he didn't agree with her practically

yelling at an innocent bystander, but they didn't need the publicity. People were too quick to write off honest law officers trying to do their jobs to the best of their ability. They didn't need their pictures all over social media.

A train rumbled into the station, but she couldn't see it. They raced down the elevators and she scanned the platform as they emerged. She looked both ways down the platform, but obstructions between them and the people dotted about made visibility difficult. Plenty of places for Kristine to duck behind something—or someone—and blend in.

Grady was a ways down the platform, darting between people. Skylar checked the other side, where folks waited for trains going in the other direction. Had Kristine gotten on the train?

Down the platform she saw a familiar man, blond hair. Half a foot taller than everyone else. Niles? What was he—

She heard Grady yell then, "Kristine's on the train!"

Grady raced along, eyes peeled on every woman inside the train. He'd seen her get on board. How far down the train had she been? Where was she now? Grady didn't want to be stuck in one car if she'd moved to another—or got off right before it left.

Skylar was somewhere behind him, searching as well. Pretty soon he'd have to answer his phone and check in, but Secret Service Intelligence had probably tracked his phone. Even with a likely break in his GPS in the middle of the tunnel. He couldn't have had a signal that whole way.

The cops back at the house hadn't followed them. He figured they'd assumed other agents would be backing up Grady and Skylar. So right now, they were on their own.

The doors began to close.

Kristine darted out of a car at the end of the train, glanced in Grady's direction once. Saw him following and started to run.

"Skylar!" He yelled for her even as he sprinted after Kristine, bumped two people apart, muttered "Sorry" and kept going. Had she heard him? At the other end of the platform was an escalator—probably to a street exit. Or would the woman they were pursuing head for another platform and pretend to get on another train?

Kristine took the steps two at a time, not even appearing to be winded, despite the fact that they'd all run this far. Heading outside was a good way to get free of Grady. Too bad Grady wasn't going to stop until Kristine was in cuffs and explaining this whole thing.

His phone started that steady vibration against

his chest again. Grady clicked on his wireless headphones as he ran and stuck one earbud in in time to hear his battery level was high.

Kristine raced away from the top of the escalator, toward the gates where ticket holders swiped their way out of the station.

Three of them, none with tickets.

The cops who worked here were going to have to figure out fast what was happening. Grady didn't have time to stop and explain. Thankfully his badge was on full display with the rest of his insignia.

Grady clicked the button on his headphones. "Farrow."

"It's Stringer."

"I'm pursuing Kristine now." He sucked in a breath. "Headed out of…" He found the station name on the wall and told Stringer.

"We're on our way. The cops at Painter's house filled us in on what happened." Stringer paused. "We're probably ten minutes out."

Kristine could be long gone by then. "Drive faster."

"Copy that."

The woman herself hopped the ticket barrier. One of the officers on guard hollered at her to stop. Grady raced over and did the same. The officer started to yell, realized who Grady was and waved him on. With a shake of his head, the older cop got on his radio. Grady was good with that. He'd take all the help he could get right now.

Before he continued his pursuit, Grady glanced back. Skylar hit the top of the escalator.

He yelled over his shoulder, "She's with me!" Then kept on running.

"Sounds like you're in the thick of it."

Grady had forgotten Stringer was still on the phone with him. He'd need Stringer to have up-to-date intel when he showed up, so Grady didn't end the call. Though he did say, "There a reason why you called?" Even while he ran through the huge tunnel to yet another escalator.

"Sure, talked to Intelligence about Daniel Painter," Stringer said.

His legs burned, but his lungs were happy to accommodate this uptick in his cardio routine. It wouldn't last, though. Pushing this hard and this fast for any length of time would leave him quickly drained. He hoped Skylar was doing okay, considering he'd basically left her behind. Forced her to keep pace with him when her head was probably pounding.

It wasn't exactly what partners did, but it was how things had worked out in this situation. At least she had the vest and gun. She wouldn't look official to someone who knew what to look for, but then again she wasn't a full agent. That time would come, and Grady wanted to be there to see it. To congratulate her.

The escalator to ground level was twice the height of the one from the platform to the ticket barrier. Grady pushed and huffed his way up each step. "And?"

"Had them look for connections between Painter and Agent Barnes."

"And Kristine Bartowski?" Grady kept running.

"Bingo."

Grady hit the concrete step off the escalator and glanced left—where Kristine had gone.

She waited by the curb down the street. Tapping her foot, she glanced back toward Grady. Blanched.

Where was the logbook? She wasn't carrying it, but she could've stashed it under her jacket. Or dropped it. What there hadn't been time for was for her to destroy it, which meant wherever it was the thing was still intact.

Grady started toward him. "Hands up, Kristine. Time to stand down." He crossed to her in a fast-walk stride.

"We're six minutes out," Stringer said in his ear.

"Hands, Kristine. Now."

She didn't lift her hands. She glanced away, down the street.

A car raced toward them, weaving through traffic. It stopped so fast Kristine stepped back, like she was wondering if it was going to hit her.

Barnes sat in the front seat.

And Grady had no backup.

"Don't get in." Grady strode over. "Barnes, get out of the car. You're both under arrest!"

Grady couldn't fire at an unarmed woman—not that she had no weapon, just that she hadn't pulled it out and threatened Grady's life with it in the last minute or so. Kristine was getting into the car. Did Barnes have a gun? Then again, neither could he fire at a moving vehicle fleeing the scene. He could hit a bystander.

Kristine had the door open. She glanced back with a smirk as the front passenger window whirred down. Barnes pulled out asemi-automatic. Grady dived and rolled to the side on instinct.

"Gun!" That was Skylar.

"Everyone—" His words were drowned out by the volley of gunfire, louder than fireworks on the Fourth of July.

"Go!" Kristine yelled.

The car engine revved, and the tires screeched. It tore away from the curb before she even had the door closed. Grady put two bullets in the back quarter panel while it was still close enough there was no chance he might hit a bystander.

When it moved too far away, he read off the license plate aloud so Stringer could hear it.

"Copy that," came his muffled reply.

Grady climbed to his feet, looking around as he did so. "Skylar?"

Before he even found her, he heard her scream. Niles had ahold of her arm, dragging her away.

NINETEEN

Skylar sputtered. "Let go of me!"

Niles huffed but let go. "You should be thanking me."

She shoved him away as Grady ran over. He had gravel on the side of his face. Was he okay?

"You're bleeding," Grady said. All his attention was on Niles, his gun pointed at the man.

Where had Niles come from, anyway? And why did it seem like the guy was following them?

"Skylar," Grady said, his voice a command.

She glanced from Niles to Grady, her head still spinning. Maybe she should sit down. "What?"

"You're *bleeding*."

"I am?" She pulled the zipper of the sweater down and peeled it aside. Warm wetness trailed from the inside of her bicep down to her hand, where it dripped to the ground. She swayed as she stared at the drops.

"Time to catch her." Niles's voice sounded far away.

Grady didn't lower his weapon, though he sidestepped toward her. Close enough her nose bumped into his bicep.

"Whoa." She sucked in a lungful of the very nice scent of him.

Grady wound his arm around her back. "I gotcha."

"Yes. You do."

Niles chuckled. Or was that Grady?

Multiple cars pulled up, and people ran over. "She okay?"

Skylar turned to wave toward Agent Stringer's voice.

"Her arm is bleeding down my back."

She pushed off him and looked. Oops. The trickle was still coming. Was that bad? A lot of her blood was going everywhere. Skylar clapped her hand over it. Weren't they supposed to put pressure on it?

"Here." Stringer handed her a folded square of material, which she applied to her arm.

"Who carries a handkerchief anymore?"

"It belonged to my grandfather."

"Oh." She pulled it off her arm.

"No." Grady shifted and laid his hand over hers. "Keep it on." Then he glanced at Stringer. "Arrest this guy."

They grasped Niles, who said, "I saved her life!"

Grady didn't answer. Questions filtered through her mind again.

"I see this is the gratitude I'm going to get for saving your life."

Skylar tipped her head to one side. "You did…" She glanced at Grady. "He pulled me away. I'd have been shot in a much worse place. I'd be *dead*."

Grady's gaze on her softened.

She smiled, liking the look of that emotion on his face. "You're going to let him go?" She lifted her hand, wanting to trace her fingers across those full lips. Pain shot through her bicep. His arm banded tighter around her.

"Easy." His eyes still locked with hers, Grady said, "Stringer, any word on when the ambulance will be here?"

"Couple minutes." She could hear the smile in Stringer's voice.

Skylar turned. Why wasn't Grady answering her question about Niles? He shifted, and she felt his fingers over hers again. He shifted the handkerchief and she hissed out a breath. Why did Stringer think this was so funny?

"It's not bad. A nasty graze that's going to be uncomfortable, but it could have been a whole lot worse."

Stringer nodded, his gaze dark. "A lot worse."

"Worse than Grady's shoulder?" She lifted her chin, determined not to allow them to sideline her just because of a graze. A bad graze, but still a graze.

Stringer chuckled. "Yes."

Niles glanced between Stringer and Grady. "One of you guys want to let me go?"

Grady nodded, and the agents let him go.

"You saved my life. That makes twice." Skylar studied him. "Who are you?"

Niles nodded, as though he approved of her question. "Private security."

"Pri—"

"Your uncle hired me to watch out for you."

Skylar pulled her arm from Grady's. It hurt, but she had to stand up for herself right now. She couldn't be clinging on to him, even if he was warm. And strong. And steady. And...

She shook her head and focused on Niles. "Private security?"

She couldn't believe this, but regardless he nodded. "Your uncle keeps tabs on you. He wanted to make sure nothing happened."

"I was at Secret Service training."

"We figured you were safe there. It was light duty," Niles said. "Then you were sent here for the exercise—congratulations on that, by the way—and we realized you'd be much more out in the open." He gave her a small smile. "Turns out he was right to be concerned."

Skylar didn't know whether to scream or hug him. Or call her uncle and do the same—but just the screaming part since hugging him was impossible over the phone.

"I suppose I owe you a thank-you." Even though her gratitude was totally grudging.

Niles shook his head. "All part of the service."

Stringer and a couple of the other agents scoffed, but Grady stuck his hand out. "Thank you, Niles."

Niles shook with him, then turned to her. "Expect to have a shadow until you return to training."

Skylar blew out a breath. She didn't have time to argue more, since the ambulance pulled up at the curb. While they cleaned the wound and put some cold antiseptic goop on it, Grady chatted with Stringer by the door of the ambulance.

Her father and uncle really thought she couldn't handle life? That she needed this level of protection? The last couple of days hadn't been anything like normal. Half of it, she hadn't even seen Niles. He had saved their lives, but the fact that her uncle and father both didn't think she would be okay on her own stung. Of course, it stung. Them being overprotective was one thing, but it was like they didn't trust her.

Stringer said, "I had a couple of agents question Daniel some more, since we know he's connected to the curator. He spilled everything. A few months ago he had an attack of conscience, got saved and realized he had to mend his ways. But he'd already made the last of his fakes, so he sent the music box back to the White House anonymously. Like it was yet another gift given to the president."

Grady shot him a look.

Stringer shrugged. "Kristine never exposed him, even though it became clear he was out of their little arrangement. Daniel said if she had exposed him, he'd have accepted the consequences as God's will. She never did."

"And then this happens," Grady said. "Wilson is set up to take the fall for stealing the clock, right? Barnes gets away with Kristine. Daniel is in custody."

Stringer nodded. "Makes you wonder if this wasn't one big plan to get back at Wilson and leave Daniel swinging in the wind while the two of them make their getaway."

Skylar couldn't believe what she was hearing. "Daniel didn't act like a humble man trying to make amends."

"Said he was sorry about backsliding and dragging you into it," Stringer answered. "He asked for a minister to come see him so he can get back on the right track."

"Anything else?" Grady asked.

Stringer nodded. "Family sentimentality aside, Daniel said that clock was worth millions. It's a unique English/German design, which is only significant because it was constructed late in 1938, only about a year before World War II started. It was very controversial, given the times. No one wanted to touch something that represented cooperation between those two countries—there was too much resentment."

Grady glanced between the two of them, his gaze landing on the EMT taping a bandage over the wound on her arm. It still stung, but if they tried to sideline her she was going to kick up a serious fuss.

To keep the conversation going, she said, "So they made a ton of money. The curator, the Smithsonian employee and the Secret Service agent? Plus Wilson, though they wanted him out of the arrangement enough to have him try to steal a fake so he'd get arrested." It was a guess, but there was a chance she was right. "Or am I missing something?"

"It's all looking like that's what happened. Daniel got out, so Kristine and Barnes came up with a plan to force Wilson out as well so they could get away just the two of them." Grady nodded, his look speaking plainly that he was proud of her deduction.

Stringer said, "Intelligence turned up money transactions between the three of them. And they all have offshore accounts with the same amounts of money in."

"So they are a team. Or they were." Skylar thanked the EMT, then climbed out of the ambulance.

There was no way she was going to the hospital again with things coming to a head. All this was actually getting interesting. Though, maybe that was because this part was about solving the mystery and not about running from danger.

Barnes and the curator were together and in the wind.

"Which begs the question," she said aloud, even as she thought it over, "where are they going to go?" She wanted to fold her arms, but settled for holding her injured one up. "An airport, a train. A boat somewhere. Or just off the grid, and they stay in the US…"

Grady said, "We have to consider all the options with something like this."

Maybe it was just the tiredness in his tone, but she didn't like it. "You don't have to placate me. I was only trying to help brainstorm." She started to walk away.

* * *

Stringer pointed at Skylar's back and mouthed, *Go after her.* Grady wanted to pummel his friend, but that would take time. He didn't need help. And he didn't need pushing toward Skylar. His heart was doing that job fine all by itself.

Grady reached for her arm, realized it was the one with the injury and jogged instead to get in front of her. "Where are you going?"

She lifted her gaze and halted. Shrugged.

Grady moved close to her, not within kissing range, but not much farther away either. "Skylar."

"Yes?"

"Those were good ideas." He could see on her face it was going to take some convincing to get her to believe him. Grady touched the sides of her neck gently, his thumb tracing her jaw line. "We all pull our weight, and I want that from you as well. It's what you've done so far." He let go for a second to motion behind him at the rest of the team. "And you have to know I wouldn't have gotten through everything if it wasn't for you being with me."

"I made things worse."

"I don't recall that."

Skylar rolled her eyes. "Maybe that's because you see what you want to see."

"You think I'm a dreamer."

She was silent for a moment, then said, "Yes. Actually, I do."

Grady scoffed.

"Your fiancée left you, and you went into, like…relationship hibernation. All so you wouldn't get hurt."

He wanted to retreat, but he didn't. Grady forced himself to see this through, even if it wasn't what he wanted to hear. "Is that bad?"

She smiled. "Not from where I'm standing. That is, if you're willing to emerge for something that could be good."

"I already know it could be."

"I do, too."

Were they really talking about what he thought they were talking about? "Skylar?"

She smiled. "Thank you for looking out for me, Grady."

He studied her, trying to figure out when all this had happened. Between chasing suspects and taking cover from fire. And yet, he wondered how he could have missed it until now.

"Are you going to kiss me, or what?"

Ten feet away, Stringer laughed. Grady thought he heard one of the agents say, "Kiss her!" but he couldn't be sure.

Grady wasn't one to turn down the offer of a lifetime, so he leaned in. But he kept it short. Just a quick, soft press of his lips against hers

254 Defense Breach

before he leaned back. "Considering your idea, I think we should go to the curator's house. I don't want you by yourself until Barnes and Kristine are brought in."

He sighed to himself. *That was super romantic. Come with me so you don't die.* Grady wanted to kick himself but couldn't figure out how to do that without it looking bizarre. He settled for saying, "I want you with me, Skylar. Where I can keep you safe."

Her eyes narrowed, a gleam there. Was she wondering how long that would hold true? Maybe forever, if she would have him. Skylar didn't need anyone giving her half-baked promises. Not after the marriage she'd had. Grady figured that—with God's help—he could be the right man to make her a promise that would last forever.

"Okay."

Grady figured that was the best he would get, given so much had been left unsaid. Now wasn't the time for forever discussions, though. Not when the danger was still real. Barnes and Kristine were still out there.

He held out his hand. She put hers in it, and they walked back over to where Stringer was pretending he hadn't listened to everything they'd said.

Stringer rocked back on his heels. "All good?"

Grady shook his head, while Skylar said, "We're fine, thank you."

Her tone made Stringer laugh, and he said, "Ready to head back to the curator's house?"

"Yep." Skylar nodded.

Grady said, "We have a BOLO out on the car. Either that'll turn up a lead we can follow, or we'll find something at the house that can tell us where they're going."

"Either way, we'll be there?" Skylar asked.

Stringer nodded. "Now you're getting it." He turned and headed for his SUV.

Grady and Skylar headed for one of the other vehicles. He opened the driver's door and said over the hood, "When we're done we should take a night tour bus. I can show you the sights, if you want."

She nodded, though it was tentative. "If not tonight, then tomorrow."

It was a getting late in the afternoon. Had he really only met her yesterday morning? "Tomorrow. For sure."

She smiled. "Okay."

They climbed in and set off.

He wanted dinner as well, if she agreed. And another one of those kisses. He'd like to explore that as well. Whatever she wanted. Because while he was looking for forever, Skylar would be headed back to training. When she was done, she would be assigned somewhere. Their lives would be difficult to mesh, even if they managed to sustain a long-distance relationship.

But those issues were for later.

Stringer drove them to the curator's house. There was no way Barnes or Kristine would come back here. They'd know Secret Service would be watching the place. Grady didn't expect to find too much. Besides the fact that Kristine had hidden a huge secret long enough no one even suspected her as a party to this, the place was nearly immaculate. One of those electronic vacuum robots even worked its way along the baseboards in the dining room.

The BOLO would catch them trying to flee the country, or local law enforcement somewhere would spot the car. Barnes and Kristine would be found. It was only a matter of time. But would they come without a fuss?

"Look at this." Skylar picked up a paper on the curator's home desk. "It's a receipt for a chartered aircraft."

Grady walked over and scanned the page. "From three months ago."

"They could be falling back on old plans. Using a known entity as a way of escape, maybe."

"I'll call it in to Intelligence. See what they can dig up."

Ten minutes later he had the answer he needed.

Grady motioned Stringer and Skylar back over to him. "They're at a small airport just outside of Richmond. They're trying to flee."

TWENTY

Grady took the turn for the airport, their SUV right behind Stringer's. In total, there would be six Secret Service vehicles, filled with agents on hand to stop Barnes and Kristine from fleeing the country. They'd used false names—the same names listed on the paper Skylar had found—and filed a flight plan.

They were going to Aruba.

Grady hit the brakes, and they parked in a huddle of three vehicles behind a hangar, in a support-staff parking lot. The rest of the vehicles peeled off, so those agents could approach from different angles to stop the targets from escaping another way.

It was a small, private airfield. Not huge like Ronald Reagan, which was close to the heart of DC. Thankfully that meant there was little human or air traffic this late in the evening. None of them wanted anyone innocent to get hurt.

The plan had been laid out en route, with Secret Service Intelligence coordinating the attack on a conference call. Skylar had never heard anything like it and had been in awe as they laid out the general location, possible exits, choke points, or ways the targets could fight back. She'd also heard surveillance information they'd gathered, which confirmed one woman and one man. Barnes had a pilot's license so they didn't need a third person to fly them.

The game plan was simple enough, and the time it had taken them to formulate it impressive. They were treating Skylar like she was one of them, with Agent Ramirez even putting her right in the heart of it. Of course, that included the most protection, since there would be agents all around her.

Skylar took a second and prayed for everyone's safety and that they would capture these two who had caused so much havoc. In just two days, she'd gone from being so determined to prove herself as capable that she couldn't see anything else, to willing to let go a little in the moments before a coming operation to offer up a prayer.

She needed to put God first, even in work situations. She needed His help, and would accept it gladly, considering He'd given her Grady. The man had stood at her back through all of this.

She didn't have enough words to say how

thankful she was for him and the fact that he was in her life right now. Skylar didn't know where it was all going to go, but what she did know was that it had been a blessing she hadn't realized she needed. God had known, though.

"Ready?"

She nodded, and they got out. Grady opened the back of the SUV and pulled out a vest. She strapped it on while he did the same, then he handed her a ball cap. "Put your hair up under there. You have the training to be here, and I want you to see Barnes taken down. But I don't want him recognizing you in the crowd of agents and getting any ideas. That okay?"

She nodded. While she wasn't specifically Barnes's target here—the man was trying to escape, not still kill her—that didn't mean she was out of danger. They were Secret Service. Danger was what they lived, day in and day out.

Skylar couldn't wait.

They met up with the group crowded against the side of a hangar. Only hand signs were exchanged. At the appointed time, everyone's phones vibrated in their pockets, and then the signal to move was given. Skylar laid her hand on Grady's right shoulder and followed him along the side of the hangar, her rifle snug in front of her.

The hangar was lit up, shining light onto the

runway in front of the building. The plane was inside, a small craft that could probably fit a dozen people. She didn't know much about planes, but this one looked expensive. The interior lights were on, but there was no noise from the engine.

Kristine and Barnes weren't ready to go yet. Where were they?

Grady looked at a handheld device. Red dots on the screen surrounded the area. Two dots at the center, one a little dimmer than the other.

Positions were established, and one of the agents got on a bullhorn.

"This is the United States Secret Service. You are surrounded." His voice carried through the otherwise quiet hangar. Everyone braced for what was about to happen. "Put any and all weapons down, and come out with your hands up, immediately."

The alternative would be messy. The steps up to the door of the plane formed a funnel. Barnes and Kristine could pick off anyone who climbed them, shooting before the person even reached the top. Creating mass casualties without ever leaving the plane.

No one wanted things to go that way.

From inside the plane there was a scream, and then a gunshot.

Skylar gasped. Nothing else came. Just that

one shot. Who was dead? The agents were all braced. To breach the funnel and give their lives? She wasn't okay with that. None of them should have to sacrifice so much. Too high of a price to pay. *God, help us.*

Barnes emerged through the door and stood at the top of the stairs, gun in his hand. Had he left Kristine behind to die so she couldn't tell anyone the extent of what Barnes had done? There was evidence enough. Skylar needed to get in the plane and see if she could save Kristine. The woman had held a gun on her earlier today, but that didn't mean she shouldn't live in order to pay for her crimes.

Leaving the other agents to their cries for Barnes to put his gun down and surrender, Skylar lowered her weapon and moved closer to Grady's back, so she could whisper in his ear. "We need to get in that plane."

He nodded, but didn't lower his weapon or take his attention from Barnes.

They were on the edge of the group, a strategic move from Intelligence to make Skylar the farthest position away from the plane. But it played in their favor now. Once Barnes was clear of the bottom step and in custody, they had a clear shot to run up the stairs and try to keep Kristine alive. If she hadn't bled out. If Barnes had even shot her.

There was a low probability it would even work, or that they'd be able to save her. But wasn't life always worth the risk? Sacrifice was noble, when a life was given for someone else. But risking everything on the off chance of saving someone—kind of like what Grady had done with her, basically since they'd met—meant so much more.

I love him.

He felt her shift and glanced over for a second. "Don't move until I give you the order."

She patted his shoulder, so he'd know she understood.

They waited while Barnes descended the stairs. Would he kill himself? Or shoot at the agents and make it so they had to use lethal force? Neither outcome was satisfactory to her. She wanted Barnes to pay for what he'd done. She wanted to go to court and testify about everything she'd seen him do today.

"Put the gun on the floor, Agent Barnes." The lead agent's voice invited no argument. Skylar figured he called the man *Agent* so Barnes might hold on to some latent camaraderie and it might lessen the likelihood he'd try to hurt one of them. Whether it would work or not remained to be seen.

"Agent Barnes."

In answer to the demand, he moved his arm

to his side and began to lower himself to the ground. When he'd placed the weapon on the floor, they surrounded him. His arms were tugged back, and Barnes was cuffed.

Grady led the way to the plane, keeping his body between Skylar and Barnes. Even cuffed, there was no way he was going to let that man even get a look under her ball cap. Let alone get near her. It was a good idea to check the plane, and he was proud of her for thinking of it. That simple suggestion meant she cared about people. Even ones who had caused her harm.

Pride swelled up in him. That he knew her and that she was this kind of woman. One who cared, when others might not. Everything about Skylar pulled him to her, drawing him nearer and nearer to her orbit. And he liked it. Enough to wonder if he could stay here long-term.

There was nothing about their worlds that would mesh. Even with them both being Secret Service agents. How was he going to go about fixing that problem?

Skylar could get posted anywhere in the country—or even overseas—once she graduated from training. The only option open to them would be for Grady to get a transfer. The Secret Service wasn't a place where internal relationships tended to thrive, even if it was allowed.

Their lives were too stressful and hectic for that. But he'd seen it work. In fact, there was a married couple on the president's detail with him at Camp David right now.

If Locke and Alana could make it work, then why couldn't Grady and Skylar?

Lord, that's what I want next. This situation is nearly at a close. I'm ready to come out of... relationship hibernation. He nearly chuckled to himself as he recalled Skylar calling it that. Stringer's suggestion, but she'd called Grady's self-imposed singleness for what it was. Hiding. *I'm done with that, Lord. I want to make a change. One that's going to better my life for years to come.*

Because, after knowing Skylar for even such a short time, he knew he wanted her in it. If Grady let her walk away he would regret it for the rest of his life. Skylar was the only thing that was going to make him happy.

Them. Together. Forever.

Grady couldn't think of a single thing he wanted more than that right now.

His eyes locked with Barnes's, but he didn't let the man get under his skin. Grady had everything he wanted right here with him. No one was going to take it away. Not even a traitor.

Skylar's foot reached the bottom step.

He halted her with a hand on her arm, four

other agents around them. He was going to go first, so he put her behind him in the center of the group. She held her gun like she'd been born to be a Secret Service agent, but Grady's nature was to protect. They ascended the stairs.

He was certain Kristine was dead. Skylar might believe it was possible the woman was alive, but someone like Barnes—if he'd shot her—wouldn't have missed. He'd have shot in order to kill. He climbed to the door of the plane and waited. Prayed Skylar wouldn't be faced with a dead body.

Listened.

He didn't hear anything, so he went in.

Suitcases and duffels had been loaded onto the seats and the floor between. Kristine lay on the floor at the back of the plane, a wound on her forehead. No life in her eyes.

Skylar's breath hitched.

"Nothing we can do for her now." He turned to a duffel close to him and unzipped it. Daniel's logbook sat on top. Underneath, hundred dollar bills had been rolled up, secured with rubber bands. Grady whistled.

"Check this out." Skylar showed him another bag, and pulled out a velvet pouch. She loosened the ties and poured a teaspoon of diamonds into the palm of her hand. "Wow."

"That's some bling," one of the agents said.

"I guess they were headed to Aruba with their retirement stash," she said.

"And a ton of money in the bank," Grady added. "All their ill-gotten gains from years of having Daniel Painter make fakes, and then replacing artifacts worth millions with those fabrications."

Skylar whistled softly and stared at Kristine. "They had to have known someone would find out."

"But no one did, until yesterday. Kristine got away with this for years, partnering with Barnes. Keeping it all from us when it was right under our noses." Grady frowned, not liking any of it. "They probably laughed while they did it, knowing we were completely fooled."

"But you weren't, were you?" Skylar asked. "I mean, did you completely trust the guy?"

Grady shook his head. "There was always something off about him."

"That's your instinct telling you that you didn't completely trust him. Which means some part of you *did* know."

Grady squeezed her shoulder. "Thank you for saying that." Even though he didn't like the fact that Barnes had been a traitor, along with Kristine, the reality was they'd all been swindled by the two of them. "We need to hand the scene off to investigators." Grady pointed to the door.

"Let's get out of here. I'm sure there are better things for us to do."

"Oh, yeah?" She looked interested in what he could mean by that.

"Yeah."

He was ready to take Skylar to a late dinner. Very late. It had been a long, crazy day, but he was too wired to go home. Plus he was hungry. What would she say to some greasy diner food at this time of night? He wanted to start there, and then see how things progressed. To tell her about his feelings, and see what she might have to say in return. There was no guarantee. He couldn't tell the future, so he didn't know how things would turn out. But he was willing to risk getting shot down by her for the chance at something he thought maybe could be great. Probably even fantastic.

Grady followed Skylar out of the plane. She glanced over her shoulder and smiled at him. "Are you going to tell me what it is?"

"Secret." He smiled back. They were finally done. "Because you probably need to get that arm seen to, and you look like you're ready to crash, anyway. It'll keep."

She looked at her watch. "I'm so wired I don't think I could rest even if I wanted to."

Grady opened his mouth to reply, but a commotion by the door got his attention.

Barnes stumbled and went down. Grady watched like it was slow motion as the man twisted and pulled a gun from another agent's ankle holster. He continued rotating, coming around. Squeezed the trigger and started to fire.

Bang. Bang.

Bang.

Skylar.

Grady grabbed her and spun her so his body was between hers and the shooter.

The bullet hit him in the back, slicing through him before it lodged in his chest. All Grady knew was a sharp pain. More shots rang out, and he flinched. But they didn't hit him. It was the sound of Barnes being taken out.

Grady's legs gave out, and he let go of her to tumble backward down the stairs.

TWENTY-ONE

Skylar couldn't sit down. She leaned against the wall of the hospital waiting room. Grady was in surgery. The bullet had ripped through his vest and his lung, but not come out. It could easily have hit her, and very nearly did. In fact, it would've been better for Grady if it had. He wouldn't be in such bad shape now.

Still, in the few hours since he'd collapsed, she hadn't stopped thanking God for the fact that it hadn't also ripped through his heart.

He'd have died instantly.

Saving her.

Skylar swiped at a tear.

Stringer touched her shoulder and handed her a cup of coffee. She'd drunk so much already it was swimming around in her stomach. Despite that, she said, "Thanks," then set the cup on side table close to her.

The Secret Service milling around were as antsy as she was. Director Tanner, who had been shot when Wilson was killed, was out of surgery now. The prognosis was good. He would recover. Skylar prayed they got the same news about Grady.

Soon.

How much longer was it going to take?

Movement by the doorway brought her attention around. But it wasn't hospital staff. "Dad." Her uncle was right behind him. Right behind her uncle was Niles.

Skylar's breath hitched as she ran into her father's open arms. She settled her face against his shoulder while he wound his arms around her.

"Any word on Grady?"

She shook her head, her tears wetting the shoulder of his jacket.

"How are your arm and your head?"

Skylar leaned back. "I don't care."

Her uncle leaned in. "I'll talk to the nurse. Have someone come and look at it so they can give you painkillers."

Before she could argue, he trailed off with Niles beside him. The private security guy gave her a wink before he turned away.

Skylar let her gaze settle on her dad. "How did you know?"

The corner of his mouth curled up. "I've been kept apprised." Without missing a beat, he said, "Your scores at Secret Service training are impressive."

She smiled up at the man who had raised her single-handedly. Taught her to be independent and strong. "Thank you."

"And the young man in surgery?"

She nodded, feeling the emotion well up in her again. Talking would only make her cry. Wilson was dead, Kristine was dead and Barnes had been killed after he shot Grady. They'd had to neutralize the threat, and she hadn't cared one bit. Not when Grady had been lying on her, bleeding out on the stairs of the plane.

She didn't want to feel like a bad person over that, but she was going to have to process the forgiveness part of this. After she knew Grady was going to be okay.

Her uncle came back over, saving her from having to talk about Grady with her father. It was all too new. Right now, they didn't even know if Grady would even make it out of surgery. The damage had been extensive. What if he didn't pull through? What if he did but he couldn't be a Secret Service agent anymore? What if that meant he didn't want to see her because it was her fault?

Sure, most of that worry was the fatigue talking, but there was a kernel of truth in it. The concern was real. He might decide she wasn't worth all this trouble. Or he would friend zone her, and she'd never be able to ask for more because it would risk what they did have.

"There's some deep thought going on in there." He touched her cheek. "I'm praying he pulls through."

Skylar nodded. "Me, too."

About an hour later the doctor came in. He took in all the badges and holstered weapons in the room and said, "Grady Farrow."

The crowd closed in around him. Her father stood on one side of her, and Stringer—who had shown up a few minutes ago to wait with her—set his hand on her shoulder.

"The damage was extensive."

"We already knew that," Skylar said.

The doctor shot her a dark look. "That being said, we were able to repair his lung. The recovery time will be considerable, and I'll need to speak with his superior about the particulars of his prognosis, but he'll be alive to enjoy the rest of his life."

Skylar exhaled, realizing she'd held her breath through all of his words. "Can I see him?"

The doctor looked past her, at Stringer, who nodded.

"Five minutes only. I'll have someone come and get you when he wakes up."

Two hours later, after another cup of coffee,

Skylar washed her hands where she was guided to and then was ushered into his room. Grady's face was pale. Tubes and wires ran from his body to the panel of monitors beside his bed.

"He's awake?" He didn't look awake. She glanced back at the nurse, who nodded.

"In and out, and it's likely he might not remember whatever you tell him." She grinned. "Now might not be the time for heartfelt confessions—unless you want him to forget afterward."

Skylar didn't smile back. She could see how some people might want to say what was on their heart at a time when the recipient would forget. It would feel real, but with none of the fallout.

Skylar wanted the fallout. She wanted honest feelings and answers, so she stuffed down everything she'd been planning to say. It could wait until later.

She leaned against the bed rail and watched. A few seconds later his eyes flickered open, and he groaned.

"Yeah, I don't imagine that feels good." She touched his cheek. "Thank you." She hadn't even planned on saying that, but it wasn't as poignant as the rest of what she'd planned to say. Gratitude didn't expire if you used it too much. "Thank you for saving my life."

She would keep saying it. Every day, if he'd let her.

"Even though it could have cost you *everything.*" He really thought she was worth that? "Even though it didn't, diving in front of that bullet for me cost you a whole lot of something." Time would tell exactly what. And yes, it was what he was trained to do, but he'd had a choice.

He didn't have to do that.

He'd done it because he wanted to.

For her.

Maybe even because he loved her.

That would be good because it turned out she loved him as well.

"Sky…" his voice trailed off.

She leaned her face closer to his. "My mom used to call me Sky. *Mi cielo.*" She paused, remembering. "It's Spanish. It means *my sky.*"

He looked at her, his gaze cloudy. Unfocused.

"Thank you for reminding me of that." She'd tried for years not to remember because it hurt. But remembering was beautiful. Was that why her father had never gotten into a relationship with anyone else?

He blinked and said, "Hi."

Skylar chuckled. "Hi yourself, handsome."

"Love you."

Air hitched in her throat. She'd promised herself she wasn't going to say it if he wouldn't remember. But she could hardly let that go unsaid now.

She leaned close and touched her lips to his cheek, then whispered, "I love you, too, Grady. Very much."

EPILOGUE

San Diego field office—eight weeks later

Skylar lifted her coffee cup. Empty. She pushed back from her desk and glanced over at the agent who'd taken her under his wing since she'd finished Secret Service training. The older man, whose kids were all in college and who grilled a mean steak, lifted his own mug. "Two sugars this time."

"What is Barbara going to say about that?"

Hiller smashed his lips together. "What happens in the office stays in the office."

Skylar chuckled. "That's not how it goes."

He glanced over, one eyebrow up.

Yes, that might just have been the first time since she was sent here that she'd actually laughed. He'd tried valiantly to draw it out of her, just as her father and uncle had. The two of them had sent her funny notes, cards, texts with videos of cats riding remote control cars.

They'd tried really hard—and the first time she'd laughed was because of this.

Skylar wandered to the break room. No, she hadn't seen Grady since that day in the hospital. He'd woken up again and asked for Stringer. Not her. By the time she'd realized he hadn't remembered her telling him that she loved him it'd been late, and her father had persuaded her to go back to her uncle's house and get some rest. She'd left her number with the nurse. In case he wanted to call.

He never had.

She'd filled both cups—*one and a half* sugars for Hiller because Barbara might be a preschool teacher but she scared Skylar way more than he did. She could dish out sideways looks that made Skylar want to squirm. And spill everything that was in her head.

She set the mug on his desk.

"New boss is here."

Skylar turned to the boss's office, which had been vacant for the past week after the supervising agent had suffered a heart attack. She'd been nice but demanding. "I didn't know they were replacing her."

Hiller shrugged. "Something about new blood. But I heard he's a hotshot from DC, got injured in a gunfight. He probably thinks sun and sand means he's going to be able to kick back here and take it easy." He shook his head.

Skylar was already walking toward the office. An agent shot at the White House. That didn't mean it was Grady.

The door was open, and two men stood inside. One tall, the other would be if he wasn't hunched over with one hand on his chest.

He straightened, a smile on his face. "Don't make me laugh. It still hurts." He turned and saw her. Swallowed. His smile died. "Skylar."

Stringer was the agent beside him. "I'll give you guys a minute." Grady's friend stopped beside her as he exited the office. "Don't give him a hard time. He doesn't deserve it after the way you left him."

She opened her mouth to argue but didn't have time to ask what he was talking about before he was too far away. Across at his desk, Hiller had leaned back in his chair with a satisfied look on his face. He gave her a thumbs up. *What was that about?* She turned back to Grady.

"Shut the door please."

She did.

"Do you want to sit?"

Skylar shook her head. "What are you doing here?"

Grady studied her. "Making a mess of things, apparently."

"Grady—"

He held up his hand. "How about I start from

the beginning?" When she nodded, he said, "The prognosis I got…well, there are a limited amount of things I can do now. And none of them are tactical. The director figured that if I was going to sit behind a desk, he'd promote me so I could 'do something useful with my time.'" He smiled. "I wasn't going to argue with that."

"Why here?" It could have sounded short, but it didn't. Her words were full of all the longing she'd felt the past couple of months. All the worry after he hadn't called. All the temptation to pick up the phone. Or find out where he lived, just so she could see if he was okay.

Since she wasn't a stalker, she hadn't done any of those things. She'd waited for him to reach out.

And now he was here.

"I asked Stringer to find out where the Secret Service had placed you. I wanted to come and see you, but I didn't know if you wanted to see me." He smiled and wandered over to her. It was slower than he'd moved before, like he was getting used to having limited mobility. "I've always liked the West Coast, so when I found out there was an open position, I applied for it."

He frowned, and she saw a flash of vulnerability she'd never seen before. "I talked to Hiller. Felt him out about how he thought you'd react if I showed up."

Skylar let him know how she felt about that with a lift of her eyebrow.

He chuckled, then set a hand on his tie.

"The suit looks good on you."

"Thank you."

"Do you want to sit down?"

"I'm not fragile. But I am still healing." He took her hand. "Hiller put two and two together and asked me if I was the reason why you've been moping since you got here."

"He said that?" She was going to talk to him about it.

Grady nodded. "So what do you think?"

"About you being my boss?"

"About me being here. Where you are."

Skylar bit her lip. "Do you remember anything from the hospital?"

"I remember waking up and you not being there." He touched her cheek with his free hand. "I kind of thought you would be."

"I was. Then you asked for Stringer and I left my number, and you never called."

He frowned then. "I never got your number. And I even called your uncle. He didn't pass my message on?"

Skylar sighed. "Maybe we should opt for face-to-face communication from now on."

"Deal. So how about dinner?"

"Is that all you have to offer?"

"No." He pulled her close. "There's a whole lot more to follow. You'll have to stick with me long enough to find out for yourself just how far this goes."

Skylar smiled. "That sounds like a great idea."

"I love you."

"I love you as well." She paused. "I loved you before you took a bullet for me." He needed to know. "But that pretty much sealed it."

Grady leaned in for a sweet kiss.

She said, "How is the Secret Service going to feel about our relationship?"

"There'll be some paperwork, but I have an in with the boss. If I have to pull strings, I will."

She smiled. "I heard that whatever happens in the office stays in the office."

"Good to know."

Grady leaned in and kissed her again, and she felt it. Again.

That promise of forever on his lips.

* * * * *

Dear Reader,

What a fun book to write! I hope you had as much fun reading it. My trip to DC was a special time, and it was wonderful being able to add real-life details to the book. If you get a chance to go, I hope you do. It's a great experience.

Both Skylar and Grady were moving on from past hurts. They weren't doing a great job of moving on, but we're all human and we all try our best in our own ways. Thank God that He doesn't let us fumble around in the dark. He leads us with His Word, and gifts us with people who will help us. People who walk this journey alongside us.

What a blessing!

If you'd like to shoot me a note, you can email me at *lisaphillipsbks@gmail.com*. I always reply to my emails, and I'd love to hear from you.

May God richly bless you,
Lisa

Get 4 FREE REWARDS!

We'll send you 2 FREE Books plus 2 FREE Mystery Gifts.

Love Inspired® books feature contemporary inspirational romances with Christian characters facing the challenges of life and love.

FREE
Value Over
$20

HOME *on the* RANCH

YES! Please send me the **Home on the Ranch Collection** in Larger Print. This collection begins with 3 FREE books and 2 FREE gifts in the first shipment. Along with my 3 free books, I'll also get the next 4 books from the Home on the Ranch Collection, in LARGER PRINT, which I may either return and owe nothing, or keep for the low price of $5.24 U.S./ $5.89 CDN each plus $2.99 for shipping and handling per shipment*. If I decide to continue, about once a month for 8 months I will get 6 or 7 more books, but will only need to pay for 4. That means 2 or 3 books in every shipment will be FREE! If I decide to keep the entire collection, I'll have paid for only 32 books because 19 books are FREE! I understand that accepting the 3 free books and gifts places me under no obligation to buy anything. I can always return a shipment and cancel at any time. My free books and gifts are mine to keep no matter what I decide.

268 HCN 3760 468 HCN 3760

Name   (PLEASE PRINT)

Address   Apt. #

City   State/Prov.   Zip/Postal Code

Signature (if under 18, a parent or guardian must sign)

Mail to the **Reader Service:**

IN U.S.A.: P.O. Box 1341, Buffalo, New York 14240-8531
IN CANADA: P.O. Box 603, Fort Erie, Ontario L2A 5X3

* Terms and prices subject to change without notice. Prices do not include applicable taxes. Sales tax applicable in NY. Canadian residents will be charged applicable taxes. This offer is limited to one order per household. All orders subject to approval. Credit or debit balances in a customer's account(s) may be offset by any other outstanding balance owed by or to the customer. Please allow 3 to 4 weeks for delivery. Offer available while quantities last. Offer not available to Quebec residents.

Your Privacy—The Reader Service is committed to protecting your privacy. Our Privacy Policy is available online at www.ReaderService.com or upon request from the Reader Service.

We make a portion of our mailing list available to reputable third parties that offer products we believe may interest you. If you prefer that we not exchange your name with third parties, or if you wish to clarify or modify your communication preferences, please visit us at www.ReaderService.com/consumerchoice or write to us at Reader Service Preference Service, P.O. Box 9062, Buffalo, NY. 14240-9062. Include your complete name and address.

READERSERVICE.COM

Manage your account online!

- Review your order history
- Manage your payments
- Update your address

*We've designed the
Reader Service website
just for you.*

Enjoy all the features!

- Discover new series available to you, and read excerpts from any series.
- Respond to mailings and special monthly offers.
- Browse the Bonus Bucks catalog and online-only exculsives.
- Share your feedback.

Visit us at:

ReaderService.com

BARRON'S BOOK NOTES

MIGUEL DE CERVANTES'
Don Quixote

BARRON'S BOOK NOTES

MIGUEL DE CERVANTES'
Don Quixote

BY
Joyce Milton

SERIES COORDINATOR
Murray Bromberg
Principal, Wang High School of Queens
Holliswood, New York

BARRON'S EDUCATIONAL SERIES, INC.
Woodbury, New York • London • Toronto • Sydney

ACKNOWLEDGMENTS

Our thanks to Milton Katz and Julius Liebb for their contribution to the *Book Notes* series.

All inquiries should be addressed to:
Barron's Educational Series, Inc.
113 Crossways Park Drive
Woodbury, New York 11797

Library of Congress Catalog Card No. 85-4080

International Standard Book No. 0-8120-3512-7

Library of Congress Cataloging in Publication Data

Milton, Joyce.
   Miguel de Cervantes' Don Quixote.

   (Barron's book notes)
   Bibliography: p. 102
   Summary: A guide to reading "Don Quixote" with a
critical and appreciative mind. Includes background on
the author's life and times, sample tests, term paper
suggestions, and a reading list.
   1. Cervantes Saavedra, Miguel de, 1547–1616. Don
Quixote. [1. Cervantes Saavedra, Miguel de, 1547–1616.
Don Quixote. 2. Spanish literature—History
and criticism] I. Title. II. Series.
PQ6352.M48   1985   863.3 .   85-4080
ISBN 0-8120-3512-7

PRINTED IN THE UNITED STATES OF AMERICA

567   550   987654321

CONTENTS

HOW TO USE THIS BOOK

You have to know how to approach literature in order to get the most out of it. This *Barron's Book Notes* volume follows a plan based on methods used by some of the best students to read a work of literature.

Begin with the guide's section on the author's life and times. As you read, try to form a clear picture of the author's personality, circumstances, and motives for writing the work. This background usually will make it easier for you to hear the author's tone of voice, and follow where the author is heading.

Then go over the rest of the introductory material—such sections as those on the plot, characters, setting, themes, and style of the work. Underline, or write down in your notebook, particular things to watch for, such as contrasts between characters and repeated literary devices. At this point, you may want to develop a system of symbols to use in marking your text as you read. (Of course, you should only mark up a book you own, not one that belongs to another person or a school.) Perhaps you will want to use a different letter for each character's name, a different number for each major theme of the book, a different color for each important symbol or literary device. Be prepared to mark up the pages of your book as you read. Put your marks in the margins so you can find them again easily.

Now comes the moment you've been waiting for—the time to start reading the work of literature. You may want to put aside your *Barron's Book Notes* volume until you've read the work all the way through. Or you may want to alternate, reading the *Book Notes* analysis of each section as soon as you have finished reading the corresponding part of the original. Before you move on, reread crucial passages you don't fully understand. (Don't take this guide's analysis for granted—make up your own mind as to what the work means.)

Once you've finished the whole work of literature, you may want to review it right away, so you can firm up your ideas about what it means. You may want to leaf through the book concentrating on passages you marked in reference to one character or one theme. This is also a good time to reread the *Book Notes* introductory material, which pulls together insights on specific topics.

When it comes time to prepare for a test or to write a paper, you'll already have formed ideas about the work. You'll be able to go back through it, refreshing your memory as to the author's exact words and perspective, so that you can support your opinions with evidence drawn straight from the work. Patterns will emerge, and ideas will fall into place; your essay question or term paper will almost write itself. Give yourself a dry run with one of the sample tests in the guide. These tests present both multiple-choice and essay questions. An accompanying section gives answers to the multiple-choice questions as well as suggestions for writing the essays. If you have to select a term paper topic, you may choose one from the list of suggestions in this book. This guide also provides you with a reading list, to help you when you start research for a term paper, and a selection of provocative comments by critics, to spark your thinking before you write.

THE AUTHOR AND HIS TIMES

Unlike many authors, Miguel de Cervantes Saavedra led a life as full of action and adventure as any plot he ever created for his fictional characters. Even a brief summary of Cervantes' eventful life will give you an idea of where some of the author's inspiration for *Don Quixote* came from.

Cervantes was born in 1547, at a time when Spain was the richest, most powerful nation in Europe. Spaniards had explored and conquered vast territories in the western hemisphere, sending home gold and silver treasures by the shipload. The Spanish king, Charles I (reigned 1516 to 1556) was easily the most powerful man in Europe. Charles I also ruled large sections of Germany and central Europe in his capacity as the Holy Roman Emperor Charles V, and he dreamed of uniting the entire continent under the leadership of Spain and the spiritual authority of the Roman Catholic church. The king was an inspiring figure. His bravery in battle was matched by his cultivated mind and charismatic personality. Under his leadership, Spain seemed on its way to consolidating its position as the most fortunate country in the world.

As a soldier and a writer, Miguel de Cervantes contributed much to his country's greatness. However, he received few rewards for his efforts. Although he was a brave man and an honest one, luck seemed to run against him in everything he tried. Perhaps even more discouraging, he lived long enough to see the promise of Spain's Golden Age begin to tarnish with the onset of economic inflation and the beginnings of a retreat into cultural parochialism.

The Cervantes family was part of the *hidalguia*, the noble class, yet it was dogged by poverty and bad luck. Miguel de Cervantes' father, Roderigo, was a surgeon—an occupation that ranked somewhere below a full-fledged doctor but above a barber. (Barbers were responsible for some kinds of minor surgical procedures in those days.) Surgery was a risky business in the sixteenth century. But for Roderigo's patients it seemed to be riskier than for most. On one occasion the family had to move to another town to escape the complaints of a dissatisfied patient. A few years later, Roderigo Cervantes was thrown into prison because of unpaid debts.

In theory, gentlemen (*hidalgos*) were supposed to be exempt from debtors' prison. However, Cervantes' father could not manage to come up with the document that proved his noble ancestry. Perhaps this was just another example of the family's bad luck—or a matter of red tape and mislaid paperwork. Some biographers have suspected that the Cervantes family was not quite what it claimed to be. A few writers have even argued that family members were *conversos*, Jews who had converted to Christianity to escape persecution. On the other hand, it is entirely possible that Roderigo really was an *hidalgo*. In Spain, noble birth did not necessarily mean financial security, and the Spanish people's fondness for titles unsupported by practical accomplishment was a national weakness that Cervantes would later satirize in his adult writing.

Because of his family's money problems, young Miguel had a rather spotty education. However, he loved to read and dreamed of becoming a poet. In his late teens he managed to study briefly with a famous humanist scholar, Juan Lopez de Hoyos. Cervantes' advanced schooling lasted little more than a year, but it must have been an exciting time. The Spanish Renaissance was in full swing and scholars such as Cervantes' teacher were encouraging students to question established values. Students were rediscovering long-neglected masterpieces of Greek and Roman literature, and at the same time developing a lively interest in the life and language of the common people. Religious studies were no longer the center of every curriculum, and Latin was no longer considered the only language suitable for serious literature. Writers and students were beginning to think that they ought to write in the same language that was used in daily life.

By the end of 1569, Cervantes had left Spain for Rome. Here he made himself fluent in Italian and became familiar with the works of Italian authors, such as Boccaccio, who were writing in their native tongue instead of Latin. We do not know for sure why Cervantes gave up his studies to go to Rome. But police records of the time suggest a possible answer. A young man named Miguel de Cervantes was being sought in connection with a duel in which another student had been wounded. Was this wanted man Miguel de Cervantes the future writer? Most authorities think it was.

After a year or so in Rome, Cervantes joined the army. He soon proved his heroism by fighting in the battle of Lepanto—an important naval battle, in 1571, in which European Christian forces virtually destroyed the Turkish fleet. According to contemporary accounts, Cervantes was ill in bed with a fever when the battle began. The captain of his ship gave him permission to stay belowdecks when the fighting began, but Cervantes insisted on fighting—and at the very spot where the action was heaviest. He fought bravely and was wounded three times. Fortunately, two gunshot wounds he received were not serious. However, the third wound, to Cervantes' left hand, resulted in permanent disfigurement. The hand was saved but was paralyzed from that time on. Throughout his life Cervantes remained very proud of his contribution to the naval victory at Lepanto.

Four years later, in 1575, a ship the soldier Cervantes was traveling on was captured by Turkish pirates. Cervantes was taken to Algiers—then controlled by the Turks—as a slave. It was a common practice in those days for pirates to hold their captives until the families paid a stiff ransom. Because Cervantes carried seemingly important letters, his captor believed he came from a very wealthy family. A ransom of five hundred gold crowns was demanded. Cervantes' chances of ever being rescued looked grim.

Over the next five years, Cervantes made four escape attempts, each more daring than the last. After his third try, he was sentenced to two thousand lashes—a punishment that meant certain death. But it was never carried out, perhaps because he had impressed the ruler (*dey*) of Algiers. Cervantes' fourth escape attempt involved a conspiracy with sixty fellow captives. The plan had an obvious weakness. Too many people were in on the secret, and, sure enough, one of them betrayed Cervantes to the authorities. Finally, in 1580, Cervantes was rescued just before he was to be sent to Constantinople. An emissary from Spain managed to borrow some money from local Christians to add to what the Cervantes family had been able to raise, and, the ransom paid, Cervantes was declared free when already on the ship that was to take him to Constantinople.

After returning to Spain, Cervantes tried to establish himself as a poet, an occupation that was no more profitable then than it is today. He was continually in debt, and his financial problems worsened after his marriage, in 1584, to an eighteen-year-old bride, Catalina. After some time he got a job as an agent of the government commissary, collecting grain to feed the army. The position was a tricky one because the government was often slow in paying suppliers for the grain it took. Cervantes' attempts to be fair got him into trouble more than once. Reasoning that the churches had more than enough grain in storage for their needs, he requisitioned a large share from them. As a result he was excommunicated—ejected from the church.

Throughout all these difficulties, Cervantes had been writing poetry. As it turned out, however, his poems were never quite first rate. He also tried writing plays, but these suffered by comparison to the work of the great Lope de Vega, who was just then introducing a more modern and popular style of dramatic writing. Cervantes did not make his reputation as a writer of the first rank until he turned to prose fiction—a form of literature still not considered entirely respectable by many well-educated people of the time. Cervantes' *La Galatea* (1585), a pastoral romance, was well received. More importantly, the first part of *Don Quixote*, which appeared in early 1605, was an instant success.

Cervantes' triumph did not mean the end of his troubles. He made no royalties from *Don Quixote*, having sold the book outright to the printer for a rather small fee. He also continued to attract trouble through no fault of his own. One such incident, in mid-1605, began when one of his sisters gave shelter to a courtier who had been wounded in a streetfight near the Cervantes' apartment. The man died while under Cervantes' roof and, somehow, the magistrate got the idea that the Cervantes family knew more about the attack than it was telling. Once again, Cervantes was arrested and thrown in jail, where he stayed for some days until the matter was straightened out.

Cervantes was now in his late fifties and suffering from an illness that was probably diabetes. He continued working, however, and in 1613 published a collection of short fiction under the title *Novelas ejemplares* ("Exemplary Novels"). However, the project of writing a sequel to *Don Quixote*—what we now know as Part II of the novel—was taking longer than expected. Cervantes delayed so long that an anonymous writer beat him to the punch by publishing, in 1614, a bogus version of Part II. Writing unauthorized sequels to other people's works was a common practice at the time. The author of this sequel, however, compounded the insult by including belittling comments about Cervantes and about the literary qualities of Part I!

Scholars have speculated a good deal about the

identity of the author of this bogus sequel. Some have even suggested that the author was none other than Lope de Vega—Cervantes' literary rival. There is no genuine evidence to support this idea, intriguing as it may be. Whoever he was, perhaps the anonymous author did the world a favor after all. The appearance of the bogus sequel made Cervantes so angry that he was inspired to finish his own version of Part II.

Cervantes had little opportunity to enjoy the acclaim that greeted the appearance of the authentic *Don Quixote*, Part II. Already in bad health, he completed just one more work and died a year later in April 1616—in the same month as his great contemporary, William Shakespeare.

On the closing page of Part II of his great novel, Cervantes had written "For me alone was Don Quixote born, and I for him. He knew how to act, and I knew how to write." These lines were primarily intended as a rebuke to the author of the bogus sequel to his work. However, they were soon to take on a deeper significance. Although Cervantes' active life had never brought him wealth or worldly success, the adventures of his best-known character, Don Quixote, have gained him immortality.

The character of the Don is known all over the world, and millions who have never read the novel have a vivid mental picture of the would-be knight who sets out to do great deeds and ends up tilting at windmills. The story of Don Quixote has been the subject of at least sixteen operas, including works by the nineteenth-century Italian composer Gaetano Donizetti and the French composer Jules Massenet. There have been ballet versions of *Don*

Quixote, a hit Broadway musical (*Man of La Mancha*), and any number of artists' and sculptors' "portraits" of the imaginary Don.

Ironically, because many of Cervantes' contemporaries on the Spanish literary scene considered *Don Quixote* a popular but basically frivolous book, Cervantes' most ardent fans have been other writers. The list of novelists who have admired and been influenced by Cervantes' masterpiece is practically endless. It begins with the seventeenth- and eighteenth-century English writers Daniel Defoe, Laurence Sterne, and Henry Fielding and continues on through the nineteenth-century Russian novelists Turgenev and Gogol. Among the noted present-day writers said to have been influenced by Cervantes are the American authors Saul Bellow and Walker Percy; the English author Graham Greene, popularly known for his spy thrillers, has even written his own version of the Quixote story.

Cervantes' popularity with other writers—and with those who aspire to become writers—is related to his many technical innovations. He was one of the first novelists to succeed in creating fully developed characters, in writing lively dialogue that sounded convincingly like the speech of real people, and in mixing characters from all classes of society and many ways of life in a single work. However, for writers and artists, as well as for the average reader, the greatest attraction of Cervantes' masterpiece is the character of Don Quixote himself. Cervantes was one of the first to treat in depth the theme of a hero who sets out to reinvent his own identity by sheer force of will. And the theme of the search for identity, in one form or another, has continued to fascinate novelists and their readers ever since.

Given the subsequent popularity of his best-known character, Cervantes' words "For me alone was Don Quixote born" seem especially moving. You might expect, considering Cervantes' own history of bad luck, that he would have filled the pages of his writings with bitterness and gloom. On the contrary, for all its serious overtones, *Don Quixote* is also a funny book. Cervantes, who by his own admission did not "know how to act" in order to succeed in life, did know how to turn the experiences of his own life into the material for a masterpiece that would entertain, and often inspire, millions.

THE NOVEL

The Plot

Don Quixote is a very long novel, but its basic plot is fairly simple. A certain middle-aged gentleman named Alonso Quixano has read so many romantic stories about the knights of the Middle Ages that he goes out of his mind and imagines that he really is a knight. He also imagines that he is in love with a princess named Dulcinea—in reality a local girl who has never paid any attention to him. Changing his name to Don Quixote de la Mancha, he puts on a rusty old suit of armor and sets forth in search of adventure. At a certain inn, which he mistakes for a castle, Don Quixote asks the innkeeper to officially dub him a knight. The innkeeper agrees—just to humor his crazy guest. Later, after mistaking a group of merchants for knights, the Don challenges them to fight and ends up much the worse for wear. A passing neighbor takes him home, where his niece, his housekeeper, and two friends—the local priest and a barber named Nicholas—burn his books in an attempt to shock him back into sanity.

Don Quixote is still determined to seek adventure. He convinces a local workingman, Sancho Panza, to accompany him as his "squire." Don Quixote's mad delusions get him and Sancho into many scrapes. He mistakes a group of windmills for giants. He takes a funeral procession for ghosts. He even "captures" a brass bowl, which he believes is a valuable helmet. Finally, he meets a young man, Cardenio, who has been driven out of his wits by an unhappy love affair. The Don decides that he will become a hermit, like his new friend.

In the meantime, Don Quixote's friends—the priest and the barber—have devised a plan to lure him back home. They get a girl named Dorothea to pretend to be the Princess Micomicona. In this disguise, Dorothea begs Don Quixote to follow her back to her kingdom and kill an ogre who has usurped her late father's throne. The Don, his friends, Cardenio, and Dorothea all travel together until they reach the same inn where the Don was "knighted." Here Cardenio and Dorothea are reunited with their lost loves, Lucinda and Don Ferdinand.

The priest now decides that the only way to get Don Quixote back home is to take him there in a cage. He even manages to convince Don Quixote that the cage is a test of his courage, and that once he passes the test he will be able to marry his imaginary love, the divine Dulcinea. But when Sancho lets Don Quixote out of the cage at a rest stop, the Don gets into more trouble. Finally, he attacks a religious procession because he believes the marchers are kidnappers. After this, the Don at last allows himself to be taken back to his native village.

In Part II of the novel, you discover that six weeks of bed rest have not cured Don Quixote's madness. He and Sancho Panza take to the road again. First, Don Quixote wants to visit his true love, the lady Dulcinea. Sancho knows that Dulcinea is not a lady at all, just a rough farm girl. He also doesn't want Don Quixote to find out that a letter the Don wrote to Dulcinea, mentioned in Part I, was never delivered. So Sancho points out a farm girl who just happens to be riding by and convinces Don Quixote that this is his Dulcinea. Sancho tells his master that a wicked enchanter has cast a magic spell that makes Dulcinea look like a mere peasant girl. The Don believes this.

By now, the adventures that Quixote and Pancho had in Part I have been published. A university student named Sampson Carrasco who has read this book has decided to follow Quixote and Pancho. Sampson supposedly wants only to cure the poor madman, Quixote, of his delusions. In reality he is jealous of the Don's literary fame. Disguising himself as the Knight of the Mirrors, he challenges Don Quixote to single combat. If the Don loses, he will have to give up acting like a knight errant and go home. Through sheer luck, Don Quixote wins the fight.

After several more adventures, the Don and Sancho meet a Duke and Duchess who invite the travelers to be guests at their castle. The Duke and Duchess have also heard of Quixote's adventures in Part I. They think up some elaborate practical jokes to play on this make-believe knight. In one of their jokes, the Duke and Duchess manage to convince Sancho that Dulcinea really is enchanted after all. To release Dulcinea from her spell, Sancho will have to whip himself 3300 times on his bare buttocks! Sancho does his best to postpone this punishment.

Meanwhile, the Don and Sancho travel on to Barcelona. Here Sampson Carrasco catches up with them once again. This time, disguised as the Knight of the Full Moon, he manages to defeat Don Quixote. The Don has to keep his promise and give up knight errantry for an entire year.

During the journey home, Sancho pretends that he has given himself the 3300 blows. The Don cannot understand why Dulcinea does not appear in her true form! Finally, he becomes thoroughly disillusioned and is convinced that he will never see Dulcinea this side of the grave. Arriving home, he announces that he is cured of his madness. He is plain old Alonso Quixano once again. Soon after this, he dies.

The Characters

MAJOR CHARACTERS

Don Quixote (key-HOE-tay *or* key-HOE-tee)

During the course of the story, the main character is transformed several times. First of all, he is Alonso Quixano, a middle-aged gentleman who is foolish but basically kind-hearted. Although you meet Alonso Quixano only briefly, he is very vividly portrayed.

When Alonso Quixano goes crazy, he is deluded into thinking that he is really Don Quixote de La Mancha, a brave and noble knight errant who will set right all the wrongs of the world. Thus, the character of Don Quixote is really just a figment of Alonso Quixano's imagination. At times the characteristics of the real Alonso shine through his alter ego, as when the Don's conscience is stricken by the realization of the trouble he has caused. For the most part, however, the Don Quixote of Part I is a ridiculous character, constantly mistaking windmills for giants and blundering into fights that leave him bruised and battered, but no wiser.

The Don's character in Part I may be summed

up by the nickname Sancho Panza gives him: The Knight of the Sad Countenance. (Some translations say the Knight of the Rueful Figure or the Knight of the Woeful Countenance.) However it is translated, this name tends to sound more serious in English than it does in Spanish. The name "Sir Sad Sack" might give you a better mental picture of the Don's character at this stage of the story. Like the Little Tramp character of Charles Chaplin, Don Quixote has some qualities that inspire pathos, but his actions are basically funny.

The comic adventures of Part I spring mostly from Don Quixote's own delusions. In Part II of the story, other characters, for reasons of their own, play tricks on Don Quixote that blur the distinctions between illusion and reality. The change in Don Quixote at this point is summed up by his new nickname, The Knight of the Lions. The nickname comes from the scene where the Don meets a lion, which is being brought as a gift to the King, and decides to fight it. This time the Don is not having another delusion. The lion is real, but it refuses to fight. Don Quixote still comes out of the episode looking ridiculous, but the source of his humiliation is not his own confusion. He is the victim of fickle reality.

Sancho Panza

Some readers feel that Sancho Panza is an even more complex and interesting figure than Don Quixote. In the beginning of the story, Sancho is the typical country bumpkin. He has some good qualities. For example, he loves animals, especially his dear jackass, Dapple. But Sancho's humor is crude and he seems hopelessly stupid.

Sancho consents to become Don Quixote's squire out of greed. He believes the Don's promises that he will be richly rewarded and will even receive an island of his own to rule over. Perhaps no other character in literature gives you a better example of the triumph of greediness over common sense. You may know people who have let wishful thinking lead them into wild escapades in the hope of getting something for nothing. This is Sancho Panza in a nutshell.

Sancho pays dearly for his foolishness. He is frequently beaten up for things Don Quixote has led him into doing. But even as he catches on to the fact of his master's madness, Sancho becomes truly fond of the Don. (One critic has commented that the bickering between Quixote and Sancho reminded him of the quarrels between a husband and wife.)

During the course of Part II, Sancho Panza even takes on Don Quixote's mad quest as his own. He becomes quixotized. You will have to decide for yourself how seriously you take the change in Sancho's character. Some readers take it quite seriously, indeed. They point out that Sancho's troubles in this section of the story may remind you of the struggle that a non-believer goes through in the course of a search for faith.

Dulcinea

The "real" Dulcinea is Aldonza Lorenzo, a big strapping peasant girl who does not even know that Don Quixote exists. The Dulcinea of the Don's imagination bears no resemblance at all to her real-life model. In the Don's mind, Dulcinea is a princess, a paragon of beauty and virtue.

In Part II, Sancho Panza points out another peasant girl and tries to convince Don Quixote that this is his Dulcinea, changed into a farm girl by an evil wizard's magic spell. Of course, this "enchanted Dulcinea" is very much like the girl who inspired the Don's fantasy in the first place.

Perhaps you know some people who, like Don Quixote, have fallen in love with an imaginary ideal. No real boyfriend or girlfriend could possibly live up to their expectations. We find it easy to recognize this fault in others. We find it harder to see, in our own minds, the dividing line between having high standards and pursuing our own imaginary "Dulcineas."

It is interesting to compare Dulcinea with Altisidora, the fourteen-year-old girl at the Duke's court who develops a crush on Don Quixote. We are told that Altisidora is "not misshapen." However, she is said to have teeth like topazes—a backhanded compliment since topazes are usually yellow. When Don Quixote rejects Altisidora's advances, she becomes mean and spiteful. Later, she says she is not the kind of girl to sacrifice so much as the "dirt under one fingernail" for love. Considering what Altisidora is really like, Don Quixote is probably better off remaining true to his nonexistent Dulcinea.

MINOR CHARACTERS

The Duke and the Duchess

The Duke and the Duchess, though important to the action in Part II, are shallow, thinly drawn characters. Some readers find them basically kind, harmless types, who play jokes on the Don and

Sancho but mean them no real harm. Others are struck by the underlying cruelty of the Duke and Duchess' little games. Some readers consider these characters to be Cervantes' comment on the folly and stupidity of wealthy nobles who pretended to act as artists' patrons—while, in fact, patronizing the artists in the negative sense of the word.

Sampson Carrasco

Sampson (whose name is spelled Samson or Sansón in some translations) is the arrogant student who sets out to "cure" Don Quixote of his madness by dressing as the Knight of the Mirrors and the Knight of the Full Moon. Some readers feel that Sampson personifies the emptiness of intellectual pursuits in the absence of faith. Sampson knows how to imitate a knight, but unlike Don Quixote he will never be more than a poor copy of one.

Maritornes

Maritornes, the deformed servant girl at the inn, plays only a minor role in the story, yet her characterization is memorable. Some readers feel that Cervantes' description of Maritornes' physical ugliness is cruel. Others are impressed by the fact that the author does not seem to condemn the servant girl for sleeping with so many of the male guests at the inn. Maritornes may be physically ugly, but as you see during the discussion of chivalry that she has with Dorothea, the innkeeper, and others, her head is full of beautiful romantic fantasies. Whether Cervantes sees this as pathetic, or as a triumph of imagination over physical lim-

itations, is something you will have to decide for
yourself.

The Priest (Curate) and Nicholas the Barber

Considering their importance to the plot, Don
Quixote's friends the priest and Nicholas the barber are not very completely described. Both follow
professions considered respectable for men of the
hidalgo class. (Barbers in Cervantes' day performed
minor surgery and had a higher status than hair-
cutters do today.) Because the priest and Nicholas,
unlike the Don, are realistic enough to work at
useful professions, we are not surprised that they
want to burn the Don's books and "rescue" him
from his mad quest—by force if necessary. Nicholas is primarily a humorous character. However,
the character of the priest is open to more than
one interpretation. Readers disagree over whether
Cervantes meant some of the priest's actions as a
criticism of the church of his time. Notice, for example, in the section dealing with the adventures
in the Sierra Moreno that some of the priest's views,
including his comments on the escaped galley
slaves, are not very charitable.

Gines de Pasamonte

You meet Gines de Pasamonte twice: First, he is
the meanest and cleverest of the galley slaves freed
by the Don. Far from being ashamed of his crimes,
Gines brags that he will write a book about his
adventures and sell it for a high price. Once he is
liberated, he immediately shows his ingratitude by
stealing Sancho's donkey. In Part II, Gines comes
back to haunt Don Quixote, disguised as the pup-

pet master. The condemned slave has been transformed into a successful entertainer! Rogues such as Gines were well known to readers of Cervantes' time, who followed the adventures of such characters in a popular type of work known as the picaresque tale. Cervantes, however, uses Gines in a more interesting role—to point out that both thieves and artists practice forms of deception.

Dorothea

Of all the young people involved in the various romantic subplots of the novel, Dorothea has the most personality. Although she has been betrayed and deserted by her lover, Dorothea shows courage and determination to seek justice and restore her ruined reputation. She also enjoys playing the role of the Princess Micomicona. Notice, in considering Dorothea's part in the action, that while the men in this story all make themselves ridiculous to some extent when they turn to role-playing, Dorothea—the woman—takes role-playing for granted.

Don Diego de Miranda

Don Diego, also called The Man in Green, is the very sensible traveler who meets Don Quixote in Part II of the novel and cannot quite decide whether the poor knight is mad or sane. Don Diego introduces himself to Quixote and Sancho by giving them a lengthy list of his many virtues—he says he is sober, sensible, and pious. One thing he cannot claim to be is modest. Perhaps Don Diego represents nothing but the ordinary, conventional gentleman—his role that of a straight man to the Don's clever speeches. Or maybe Don Diego is meant to satirize the ideal of the humanist philosophers who upheld the importance of rationality and moderation. Don Diego is so moderate, in fact, that he cannot even decide whether Don Quixote is mad or sane. Readers today may find themselves agreeing with Don Diego's conclusion that Don Quixote is half sane, half crazy; however, it is possible that Cervantes expected his readers to see this as an example of muddle-headed thinking.

Other Elements

SETTING

While *Don Quixote* is not, on the surface at least, much concerned with historical events or social commentary, it does paint a lively picture of the Spain its author knew. By the time Cervantes wrote his masterpiece, the price of Spain's dreams of world domination was already becoming apparent. The Golden Age, as Don Quixote says in the novel, was being overtaken by an Age of Iron.

Although the son of Charles I, Philip II, who ascended the Spanish throne in 1556 and reigned until 1598, was in some ways a strong ruler, he was not the inspiring figure his father had been. People called Philip II the "paperwork king" because he preferred to rule his empire from behind a desk, leaving the leg-work to an army of bureaucrats. Cervantes himself was part of this army, and his experiences as a tax collector and commissary officer gave him little reason to view the bureaucracy with admiration. Philip's military ventures were not always successful either. The so-called Invincible Armada, a large naval fleet assembled in 1588 for an invasion of England (a project for which

Cervantes requisitioned food supplies) was defeated by the English before it even reached an English shore.

In addition, much of the country's enormous wealth had been squandered on expensive foreign wars, with disastrous results for the economy at home. The national treasury was bankrupt. Inflation was out of control.

Culturally, too, Spain was beginning to withdraw from its position as a leader in Europe. The spread of the Protestant Reformation in northern Europe had put the Spanish Roman Catholic Church on the defensive. After 1559, Spanish students were forbidden to study at foreign universities, and the office of the Spanish Inquisition—church officials appointed by the pope—had the power to censor books and search through the general population for heretics.

Today, some historians believe that one of Spain's greatest weaknesses was the existence of such a large class of *hidalgos*, or noblemen. At least one quarter of all Spaniards considered themselves part of this class. Unlike the high aristocracy, however, *hidalgos* were not necessarily independently wealthy. Most were poor but proud. Some *hidalgo* youths, like their fathers before them, sought fame and fortune in military careers.

Miguel de Cervantes, an *hidalgo*, realized all too well that the social class he belonged to was becoming obsolete. Its values were those of a bygone age. Economically, it had no place in the modern world. In the meantime, the richest nobles were becoming richer, and the poor farmers of Spain were staggering under the twin burdens of heavy taxes and high inflation. Don Quixote, the most famous *hidalgo* in all of literature, reflects Cervantes' understanding that the *hidalgos* were already living in the past.

It is often said that *Don Quixote* "killed" chivalry with mockery. The English poet Lord Byron expressed this opinion when he wrote that Cervantes "smiled Spain's chivalry away." In fact, as Cervantes knew very well, the society that had spawned the code of chivalry was already dead. Spain had become a modern nation with a global empire. The country was run by bureaucrats, not by a heroic band of warrior knights. Modern nations could not afford to treat war as basically a sport for gentlemen. They could not afford to support a large percentage of the population who lived in idleness, playing at being lords and ladies. Even the high ideals of chivalry had become obsolete. Unquestioning religious faith, a rarefied vision of romantic love, and a code of behavior based on knightly honor still had nostalgic appeal for many Spaniards. But these wonderful virtues were part of a social system based on a rigid class structure, a sexist view of woman's role, and the persecution of religious minorities.

Cervantes might be compared to the boy in the story "The Emperor's New Clothes" who pointed out that the emperor was really naked. Cervantes did not "kill" chivalry. He merely issued a belated death notice.

THEMES

1. QUIXOTISM

Although *Don Quixote* was written in Spanish, its main character inspired the coining of the English word *quixotism*. Normally, we say an individual is being quixotic when he is in the grip of misguided idealism. The novel's view of quixotism, however, is more complex. Don Quixote's overactive imagination turns windmills into giants and poor farm girls into delicate princesses. Sometimes Don Quixote's delusions make him appear ridiculous. Sometimes they do more harm than good. For example, his inept attempt to save the shepherd boy Andrew from a beating (Part I, Chapter Four) only gets the boy into worse trouble. Yet in many scenes in the story Don Quixote is a sympathetic, even tragic, figure. Does his consistent fidelity to his ideals, however unrealistic, inspire your admiration?

Although everyone agrees that quixotism is the principal theme of *Don Quixote*, there are almost as many different interpretations of this concept as there are readers of the novel.

2. A PARODY OF CHIVALRY

For centuries, the majority of readers considered *Don Quixote* a comic novel, plain and simple. They took literally Cervantes' claim that his purpose in writing *Don Quixote* was to poke fun at the popular chivalric romances. Some readers today agree with this point of view. They maintain that the novel was written to be amusing, and that anyone who tries to find tragic overtones in the story is missing the point.

3. THE NATURE OF FAITH

In the nineteenth century, many readers began to take *Don Quixote* more seriously. These readers noted that in popular belief and in literature, mad persons are often thought to be especially close to God. Insanity can be an expression of divine inspiration. (This belief is even discussed in the novel, in the chapters devoted to the Captive's Tale.) Some readers even wondered whether Don Quixote was not merely pretending to be mad. Such questions have given rise to many different theories about the character of Don Quixote.

One theory is that Don Quixote is a Christian hero, a man who holds fast to his faith in a world that can neither share nor live up to his high standards. Readers who take this view usually emphasize the conservative values of the novel. Although Cervantes may make jokes at the expense of the church hierarchy or the upper classes, these readers say, he never ridicules such basic values as courage, fidelity, and chastity.

Another group of readers has pointed out that the character of Don Quixote is a very accurate psychological portrayal of a revolutionary. Don Quixote, they say, is an example of a man who sets out to transform the world in accordance with his vision. Like the fanaticism of real-life crusaders, religious and political, his can be laughable, even dangerous. Yet his persistence does succeed—for example, in its influence on Sancho Panza. Readers who take this viewpoint are likely to emphasize the elements of the novel which show that the author had been exposed to the thinking of humanist philosophers. They feel that many of his criticisms of the established order, while humorous, have a hidden sting. Cervantes could hardly have been more direct in his satire, they point out, since he was writing under the restraints of censorship.

4. IDEALISM VS. REALISM

Some readers feel that quixotism is a comment on the unresolvable conflict between idealism and realism. Don Quixote's ideals may be admirable, but they are doomed to futility because he is out of touch with the world he lives in. Time has passed him by. Our noble intentions can come to a disastrous end if we do not pay attention to the practical consequences of our actions.

Curiously, there have even been a few readers who accuse Cervantes of writing a dangerous, hateful book. Admirers of chivalry and the society of the Middle Ages sometimes take this point of view. G. K. Chesterton (1874–1936), the British journalist and author of the Father Brown mystery stories, even wrote that by ridiculing the values of chivalry, Cervantes had made it impossible for modern men and women to take them seriously. Cervantes, then, must bear part of the responsibility for the confusion about morals that plagues today's world. Although this is certainly an extreme point of view, it illustrates how a book which many see as pure comedy can rouse other well-educated readers to fury.

5. ILLUSION VS. REALITY

There are many layers of illusion and reality in *Don Quixote*. First, there are the Don's own mad delusions. Later, his friends begin to play tricks on him and disguise themselves in order to get him to give up his quest and return home. In the beginning of the novel, you always know exactly what is real and what is fantasy. By the middle of Part II, however, the distinctions sometimes are blurred. For example, when Don Quixote has a bad dream in the cave of Montesinos, you are no longer certain whether the dream is just another delusion—or whether it is a product of the mind of his sane alter ego, Alonso Quixano. Besides all of these complications in the plot itself, you are constantly reminded that what you are reading is "only a book." The narrator—and his imaginary creation, the historian Cide Hamete—both interrupt the story frequently to comment on the action. And in Part II, even the Don and Sancho are aware that they are only characters in a book—in fact, in two books: Part I of *Don Quixote* and the bogus sequel produced by an anonymous contemporary of Cervantes.

Cervantes was certainly familiar with Aristotle's statement that art was a "mirror of reality." He understood that by using a trick mirror it was possible to purposely distort reality, creating illusions that took on a life of their own. While Don Quixote's unrealistic view of the world is a product of his insanity, the author finds ways to remind you during the course of the book that *he* can alter the reality of his novel just for fun. During the course of the story, the Don and Sancho—who on some levels seem real, despite their many improbable adventures—constantly interact with characters who have obviously just stepped out of the pages of other genres of literature. Although some literal-minded readers consider the appearance of these rather shallow characters to be a flaw in the novel, you should keep in mind that Cervantes introduces them purposely, as just another playful twist on the theme of reality vs. illusion.

STYLE

The language of *Don Quixote* is so rich and exuberant that no summary of the story can possibly do justice to it. You have to read the novel for yourself to see just how much fun the author has with language. For the most part, the prose style of the novel is earthy and direct. At times, however, it rises to heights of eloquence. At other times, the author uses high-flown language to parody other types of literature. Don Quixote's speech at the very beginning of Chapter 20, in Part II, is one example of the way Cervantes uses overly elegant language for the sake of humor. Sancho Panza sleeps right through the Don's flowery speech, only to be awakened by the down-to-earth aroma of frying bacon.

There are also a great many puns and other types of word play in the story. Some of the puns will be lost on readers who do not know Spanish. Fortunately, much of the humor survives the translation of the novel into English. The illiterate Sancho Panza constantly confuses one word with another, mistaking "revoking" for "revolting" and "critics" for "crickets." Another of Sancho's quirks is his tendency to quote folk sayings and proverbs at length. Sometimes the proverbs are appropriate to the occasion. At times, though, Sancho's garbled proverbs are laughable, a form of double talk.

As in the plays of William Shakespeare, there are episodes in *Don Quixote* where the humor descends to what we would consider a dirty joke. One example of this occurs in Part I, when the barber Nicholas borrows an oxtail that the innkeeper uses to hang his comb in to use as a false beard. This sets the stage for some bawdy wisecracks when the landlady later demands that Nicholas give her her "tail" back because her husband needs it. This type of humor, as well as Sancho's occasional jokes about bodily functions and disgusting odors, was taken more or less for granted in the seventeenth century.

Of course, you should keep in mind that in reading *Don Quixote* in an English translation you are not reading the actual language Cervantes wrote. However, the translations most commonly used today—especially those by J. M. Cohen and Walter Starkie—will give you a fairly accurate idea of the tone of Cervantes' prose.

FORM AND STRUCTURE

Don Quixote is a very loosely structured novel. Many readers complain that the story is too repetitive and filled with unnecessary, and sometimes confusing, digressions. Others find it jarring that the two halves of the novel are so different in tone. These complaints are not new. The original readers of the novel raised the same objections—and, indeed, you will find Cervantes' reply to these criticisms incorporated in Part II of the book.

There is a simple explanation for the unusual structure of the novel. Cervantes himself had no idea, when he began writing, of how the Don's adventures would end. Most likely, he originally intended to write a novella, or long short story, ending the Don's quest after his first return home and the burning of his library (now Chapter 8, Part I). When he decided to expand his story, he created the series of seemingly endless, and sometimes repetitive, adventures that make up what we know as Part I of the novel. While it is true that the Don's adventures sometimes seem to go on and on, this is just part of the joke. Lack of structure and repetition were among the characteristics of the chivalric romances that Cervantes had set out to lampoon.

When he began to write Part II of the novel, Cervantes had developed a more subtle conception of his characters, and he changed his approach to structure as well. Most modern readers find Part II more satisfying because the episodes seem less randomly strung together. It is easier to see how each new adventure affects the changing relationship between Quixote and Sancho and leads to the Don's eventual return home. But it is possible to disagree with this judgment. Some readers continue to find Part I funnier and more lively, and it is true that the best-remembered incidents from the story—the Don's attack on the windmills and his battle with the wineskins, for example—occur in the first part of the book.

If you enjoy tightly plotted suspense novels—or the kind of economical writing that makes every word count toward a single resolution or a unified theme—then you may find yourself growing impatient with *Don Quixote*. To put it another way, this is not a novel for people who care a great deal about neatness. *Don Quixote* was written in a spirit of experimentation—in the attempt to break out of established literary molds and to put more of life between the covers of a book than anyone had done before. The readers who enjoy this novel most are usually those who relax and get into the free-wheeling spirit of the individual episodes.

POINT OF VIEW

The shifting points of view in *Don Quixote* underline and emphasize the theme of illusion vs. reality. The story is told by an author, presumably

Cervantes himself, who sometimes interrupts his tale to speak directly to you. In the Prologue to Part I, for example, this author even complains about how much trouble he has had finishing his work. The author claims that he is only retelling a true story related by an Arab historian, Cide Hamete Benengeli. Of course, there is no such person as Benengeli. The author made him up. Benengeli's comments on the story represent another level of unreality that lies between you—the reader—and the adventures of Don Quixote. Sometimes Benengeli's observations point out certain aspects of the novel to you. Sometimes Cervantes even uses Benengeli to make fun of Cervantes the author, as when he has Benengeli complain that the Don's story as written has become too long and tedious.

The Story

PART I

PROLOGUE

In his prologue, the author explains that he has written this book in order to parody "books of chivalry."

NOTE: Books of chivalry were very popular in Cervantes' day. The plots typically concerned a pair of star-crossed lovers, a knight and his fair lady. Often, but not always, such loves were platonic. When the lovers did actually make love, however, they had to suffer a great deal for their sin. Chivalric romances also included elements of magic, myths, and fairy tales, and were written in stilted, absurdly flowery prose. In the story that follows, Cervantes makes fun of all of these characteristics. The chivalric romance best known to Cervantes' readers was *Amadis of Gaul*, which is mentioned many times in *Don Quixote*. You may be more familiar with the story of Tristan and Iseult, or of the various tales of King Arthur and his Knights of the Round Table. However, modern versions of these stories may not give you an accurate conception of the florid, overwrought prose which was enjoyed by readers in the sixteenth and seventeenth centuries.

CHAPTER 1

In the opening chapter of the story you are introduced to a middle-aged gentleman who lives in the district known as La Mancha in southern Spain. Like many of his social class, this gentleman has to stretch his pennies. He eats beef stew and beans and an occasional meal of bacon and eggs. His diet may be plain, but his head is stuffed with rich fantasies. In fact, the gentleman has read so many romances about knights and their adventures that he finally goes completely mad. Imagining that he is living in the bygone days of chivalry, he decides that he himself will become a knight-errant!

The gentleman begins by polishing an old, rickety suit of armor that once belonged to his great-grandfather. Unfortunately, the helmet is broken, but he fixes it with a makeshift visor made of pasteboard. Next, he decides to give his broken-down old horse a high-class name—Rozinante. He also decides to change his own name from Alonso Quixano to Don Quixote de la Mancha.

NOTE: In taking the title "Don," Quixano is promoting himself to a higher grade of the nobility—from gentleman (*hidalgo*) to knight (*caballero*). In the seventeenth century, there were still Spanish noblemen who called themselves knights, just as there are still men in England today who use the knightly title "Sir." However, such knights bore little resemblance to the knights-errant of the Middle Ages—knights who took to the road in search of adventures that would enable them to put their ideals of courage and honor into practice.

In all the stories Don Quixote has read, the knight-errant is always in love with a fair and noble lady. It is love, however hopeless, that inspires the knight to do so many brave deeds. Don Quixote has no sweetheart of his own, but a certain farm girl in the nearby town of Toboso is reputed to be very good-looking. (She, however, has no idea that he even exists.) The Don decides to dedicate his adventures to this girl. And since she, too, will need a more romantic name than her real one, he will call her Dulcinea of El Toboso.

CHAPTERS 2–4

Ready at last, Don Quixote takes to the road on his old nag, Rozinante. His head is full of daydreams. He is going to have such great adventures! He is going to set right the wrongs of the world! Don Quixote has read so many romantic stories that he is already mentally composing a book that will be based on his own magnificent saga.

The first order of business, however, is to find someone who can perform the ceremony that will make Don Quixote a true knight.

Just before nightfall Don Quixote reaches a roadside inn. His feverish brain imagines that the inn is a magnificent castle. He mistakes two prostitutes he meets there for beautiful maidens and the innkeeper for the lord of the castle. Everyone is amused by Don Quixote's flowery speeches and by his odd helmet, which is tied on with ribbons and so cumbersome to remove that he has to keep it on even when he is eating and sleeping. When Don Quixote asks to be knighted, the innkeeper decides to humor him.

Don Quixote prepares for the all-night vigil which the future knight must keep before the ceremony. He sets out his armor on an "altar" in the inn's courtyard. Unfortunately, the altar is really a water trough and when two mule drivers move his things so their mules can have some water, Don Quixote attacks them both. In a hurry to get rid of his crazy guest, the innkeeper stages a mock ceremony and declares Don Quixote a true knight.

It does not take the new knight long to find adventure. He comes upon a rich farmer who is whipping a poor shepherd boy, Andrew, for losing some sheep. Don Quixote makes the farmer promise to stop beating the boy and to pay him the back wages he owes. Then he rides away, very satisfied with his good deed. But the farmer has no intention of keeping his word. As soon as Don

Quixote is out of sight he starts beating the boy again, twice as hard as before.

Next Don Quixote meets six merchants from Toledo. Planting his horse in the middle of the road, he challenges the merchants to agree with him that his Dulcinea is the most beautiful woman in the world. The merchants know they're dealing with a madman and they start to tease him. Show me her picture, one demands, and then I'll decide for myself. Angered by this lack of respect, Don Quixote spurs his horse to a charge, but Rozinante stumbles and Don Quixote falls to the ground. One of the merchants gives the Don a good drubbing with his broken lance.

NOTE: Much of the action in *Don Quixote* is pure slapstick. The Don is always getting involved in pointless, silly battles. If you think that some of these fights would not be out of place in a Three Stooges or Laurel and Hardy comedy, you are absolutely right. This is exactly the spirit in which generations of readers have enjoyed them. Notice, however, that even when Don Quixote is making a fool of himself, there is something strangely moving about his character. He always means to do good. Often, when he tries hardest, he fails completely. But he can also succeed by accident. When Don Quixote mistakes the prostitutes for ladies, they treat him with kindness, almost as if they really were ladies. The innkeeper even behaves like a lord, letting Don Quixote leave the inn without paying for his food and lodging, as if he were an invited guest and not a paying customer.

CHAPTERS 5–7

A poor man from Don Quixote's village finds
the Don on the road, battered and delirious, and
brings him home.

The Don has been missing for three days, and
his niece, Antonia, and his housekeeper are fran-
tic. After putting him to bed, the women consult
his best friends, the local priest and Nicholas the
barber. Together they decide that Don Quixote's
madness has been caused by too much reading.
The solution, therefore, is to burn his library.

Before throwing the books into the fire, the priest
and the barber go through them, making comments on individual titles. Many of their remarks
will mean nothing to you because the books are
no longer read today. But one book, *Galatea*, is an
earlier work by Miguel de Cervantes, the author
of *Don Quixote*! The barber and the priest agree that
this particular book is worth saving. "That Cervantes has been a friend of mine for years," says
the priest. But after the two men leave, the housekeeper burns even the few books they have decided to save.

NOTE: Who is the crazier in this scene? Don
Quixote? Or his friends, who think that books have
evil powers and that by burning them, they can
destroy the ideas the books contain?

When Don Quixote recovers from his wounds
he finds his books gone and the door to his study
walled up. His niece is afraid to tell him what really
happened. Instead, she claims that an evil en-

chanter came riding out of the clouds on a dragon and destroyed his library. The Don believes this.

During the next fifteen days, Don Quixote manages to talk a poor workingman, Sancho Panza, into leaving home to become his squire. The simpleminded Sancho believes Don Quixote's promise that they will have great adventures and win rich prizes. Sancho even believes Quixote's prediction that he will conquer enough land to make his squire governor of a province—or an entire island! Late one night, the two men sneak out of town—Don Quixote on Rozinante and Sancho on his jackass, Dapple.

CHAPTER 8

Don Quixote sees thirty or forty large windmills in the distance and imagines that they are evil giants. He attacks at full speed. Suddenly, the mechanical arm of the windmill he is charging shifts position, dragging the Don and his horse along the ground. Sancho tries to reason with his master. You're having hallucinations, the squire says. But Don Quixote refuses to concede that he was wrong. He claims that the evil enchanter Freston changed the giants into windmills just to embarrass him. Don Quixote's belief that the powerful enchanter Freston is playing tricks on him is another crazy delusion. Remember, however, that this idea did not originate with him. It was his niece Antonia who came up with the idea because she did not want to tell her uncle the truth about the destruction of his library. At times like this Quixote's insanity is hard to separate from his intrinsic goodness. It never occurs to the poor man that his beloved niece would deliberately lie to him. Are white lies, such as Antonia's, ever justified? Or is it always best to be strictly truthful? What significance do you see in the fact that the Don, the most consistently honest person in the novel, is also completely out of his mind? Cervantes seems to be saying here that it is impossible to be truly sane by the world's standards without also being at least a little corrupt. Do you believe this?

NOTE: This is perhaps the most famous of all Don Quixote's adventures. We even use the expression "tilting at windmills" to refer to misdirected and futile idealism. You may be surprised to find that this very well-known episode takes up only a few pages in the novel. Why, then, do you think it is well remembered? One reason is that the image of the skinny, poorly dressed knight attacking a group of enormous windmills has been a favorite subject of painters and illustrators. Perhaps you have seen the well-known print by the nineteenth-century French artist Honoré Daumier that captures this moment of the story. Another reason this episode is remembered so fondly may be that, for once, Quixote is attacking inanimate objects, not human beings. Therefore, you can picture the scene without being tempted to sympathize with his victims.

The next day, Quixote and Sancho meet a Basque (Biscayan) lady on her way to Seville. Don Quixote thinks that the two monks escorting the lady are kidnappers. He attacks one and knocks him to the ground. Sancho Panza then steals the man's clothes, calling them the "spoils of war." Now one of the lady's Basque servants comes to her defense. The chapter ends in mid-fight.

CHAPTERS 9–10

Chapter 9 begins with the author interrupting his tale to deliver an apology and explanation. The old manuscript he's been following, he says, ended right in the middle of the previous chapter. For a while, he feared that he would never be able to tell his readers how the fight came out. But you are in luck! Another tattered manuscript that the author found in a secondhand bookstore picks up the Don's story at just this point. The author tells us that this second manuscript was written by an Arab historian named Cide Hamete Benengeli. From now on, the story will be based on Benengeli's version of the facts.

NOTE: Prejudice Why does Cervantes invent this imaginary historian? He tells us one reason: If his readers doubt the truth of the rest of the story, he says, they should remember that the Arabs and the Spanish are enemies. Besides, he adds, everyone knows that all Arabs are liars. If you don't like this novel, he goes on, blame "this dog of an author, not me." There are always a few readers who feel that Cervantes' comments about Arabs, Jews, and other minorities are evidence of prejudice. Most readers, however, feel sure that the author is actually making fun of bigoted attitudes. Like the other writers of his time, Cervantes often relies on stereotypes—a person's class, sex, and occupation were believed to be reliable guides to character. But at the same time, Cervantes had no use for hypocrisy in any form. Again and again, he portrays prejudice as shallow and self-serving.

You now pick up the action of the Don's fight with the Basque. Don Quixote is wounded: His ear is nearly cut off. He wins the fight, however. In the flush of victory, he gives Sancho a long lecture on the glories of knight-errantry. Sáncho, meanwhile, is wondering how all this foolishness will lead to his becoming ruler of an island. But his master tells him that he has something better than an island, a magic balm (medicine) that will cure all ills.

CHAPTERS 11–14

Don Quixote and Sancho meet a group of goatherds who politely offer to share their simple lunch. This hospitality sets the Don off into another speech. Long ago, he says, mankind lived in innocence. There was no private property and no crime. The goatherds are skeptical. They doubt that such a Golden Age ever existed.

NOTE: In the pastoral romances familiar to Cervantes' readers, shepherds were invariably portrayed unrealistically, as noble innocents who lived in a society free of crime and greed. The goatherds that you meet in this scene are obviously meant as a contrast with these fictitious creatures.

Of course, the Golden Age that Cervantes is describing existed only in the Garden of Eden (or in the realm of the idealized pastoral novel). It has nothing to do with the so-called Golden Age of Spain, an era that was at its height as Cervantes wrote. Nevertheless, the Don's comments in this scene may remind you of the way some people sound when they talk about "the good old days" of their youth. Since Cervantes lived during a time when Spanish power was beginning to decline, he no doubt heard many such conversations.

A young boy enters with news that a local student turned shepherd named Chrysostom has just died. The cause—unrequited love! Sancho and his master attend the funeral, where a friend reads Chrysostom's flowery farewell poem. Its subject is the pain and suffering of loving a woman who does not return that love.

Now Chrysostom's beloved, Marcela, arrives to tell her side of the story. Beauty may be lovable, she says, but it doesn't follow that a beautiful woman can return the love of every man who falls for her. Men say they like women who are modest and chaste. Yet they are always trying to get the women they desire to make an exception for their sakes and give up their modesty. And when a woman turns them down, they resent her.

All the men reluctantly agree that Marcela is right.

NOTE: Again, this incident is a parody of the pastoral romances, a type of literature very popular during Cervantes' time. These tales usually involved the soulful love affair of a shepherd and a shepherdess. But the characters in pastorals bore no resemblance to the simple country folk they were supposed to be. They talked and acted more like the bored sophisticates who enjoyed such stories. Regardless of the original point of the parody, Marcela's complaint still makes sense today. Many young men still see seducing a beautiful young woman as a challenge, a way to demonstrate their machismo. A young woman can not afford to say yes too often if she wants to keep a good reputation. On the other hand, when she says no, she risks seeing her suitor's interest turn to anger.

Cervantes would not have necessarily understood or sympathized with the arguments of women's liberation. However, he had a sharp eye for all sorts of social hypocrisy. As you read notice that the author is often sympathetic to young people in love. However, characters who are in love with the abstract idea of love usually do not fare very well.

Some readers feel that this whole episode is a pointless digression. They see it as an example of the author's bad habit of getting bogged down in long-winded and irrelevant side plots. They find Marcela's speech as tedious and self-serving as Chrysostom's poem. Other readers disagree. They claim that Cervantes is illustrating an important point. In literature and in real life, we are all expected to play certain roles. Marcela wants only to be free and independent. But like Don Quixote, she is out of step with her world. With which group of readers do you agree? Why?

CHAPTERS 15–17

Quixote and his squire camp in a meadow near a group of carriers from the province of Galicia (Yanguas). When Rozinante shows a romantic interest in the carriers' mares, a fight starts. Not surprisingly, Don Quixote and Sancho lose the fight.

NOTE: The carrier, or teamster, was the sixteenth- and seventeenth-century equivalent of the long-haul truck driver. Such men had the reputation of being big, burly, and not likely to tolerate an insult.

The Don and his sidekick return to the inn. There they are placed in an attic bedroom which they are to share with a stranger, another carrier. Once again, Don Quixote is under the impression that he is in a castle. The inn has a poor, ugly servant girl named Maritornes, who has agreed to spend the night in the bed of the stranger. But when she tries to sneak into the attic, Don Quixote wakes up. He has been dreaming of Dulcinea, and he grabs the girl, thinking that she is his beloved. Even when he realizes his error, he thinks the girl must have been coming to visit him. Mistaking her attempts to get away for hysterical disappointment, he tries to explain that he must keep himself pure for Dulcinea. By now, the carrier is awake. Thinking that Don Quixote has stolen his girl, he starts to beat him up. This is the beginning of a free-for-all. The innkeeper arrives to see what the commotion is about and ends up getting drawn into the fight. The police are called. The inn is in total confusion. The only person not confused is Don Quixote, who tells Sancho that they must have wandered into an enchanted castle.

When things finally quiet down, Don Quixote insists on leaving the inn without paying. Knights-errant are too pure to deal with sordid matters like money. He rides off, leaving Sancho to face the innkeeper's wrath. Some local pranksters hanging around the inn courtyard grab the poor squire and toss him roughly in a blanket.

CHAPTERS 18–21

By now Sancho Panza is beginning to become disillusioned. He is especially unhappy when he learns that his master was just outside the inn courtyard throughout his ordeal but did not come to his aid. Don Quixote's excuse is that the enchanter must have cast a magic spell over him. He just couldn't get himself moving!

The knight's next series of adventures leave Sancho even more disgusted: First, Sancho and the Don see two dust clouds in the distance. Quixote is sure that they are caused by two armies, marching to battle. He spins a wild fantasy, making up a saga of the feud between two imaginary kingdoms. He can even envision the knights on both sides. One has a cat on his shield with the motto Meeow (Miau). Another knight has as his symbol the droopy asparagus plant. His motto is "My Fortune Trails." (This might also be translated "my fortune droops"—not a very inspiring motto!) Carried away by his own fantasy, the Don rides off to join the battle. But the "armies" turn out to be two

flocks of sheep. The shepherds pelt the intruders
with stones. Quixote gives Sancho some of his
"magic balm," but the medicine makes the poor
squire vomit violently.

Next, Don Quixote sees a funeral procession
passing on the road. He imagines that the mourners, who are dressed in black or white robes and
carrying flaming torches, are ghosts. Charging the
procession, the Don manages to knock one of the
mourners to the ground, only to discover that his
victim is not a ghost at all but a terrified young
student. Although he regrets having frightened the
young man, it does not occur to Don Quixote that
he may have been at fault. He explains, with twisted
logic, that it was really the mourners' own fault
for looking so much like "something sinister from
the other world" that he, Quixote, was duty bound
to attack them.

Quixote and Sancho then spend a sleepless night
in a meadow, terrified by a loud clanking sound
nearby. In the morning they learn that the noise
was only some large wooden hammers used by
nearby villagers for manufacturing cloth. Finally,
Don Quixote sees a barber (not his friend Nicholas
but another man) carrying a brass basin on his head
to protect himself from the rain. Quixote mistakes
the basin for the "golden helmet of Mambrino"—
a legendary treasure. He frightens the barber into
running away and takes the "helmet" for himself.

NOTE: By this time, Sancho is starting to fight
back. When he wants to keep his master from investigating the horrible clanking noises, he ties Rozinante's hind legs together and tells Quixote that

the horse is immobilized by a magic spell. Sancho Panza is still being portrayed as a buffoon. Although at times he sees through his master's delusions, minutes later he can be totally taken in by them. However, a note of mutual admiration is beginning to creep into the two men's conversations.

CHAPTER 22

Quixote and Sancho Panza meet up with a chain gang of prisoners on their way to serve as galley slaves. The Don is outraged that the king would take away these men's freedom. How can anyone be sure that some of the men are not really innocent? Maybe they are victims of mistaken identity. Or perhaps some horrible misfortune drove them to commit crimes.

One by one, the men give their excuses for being in trouble with the law. The first man claims that his only crime was falling in love. (His jailer explains that he "fell in love" with a basket of linen and stole it.) Another man says his only crime was singing. (It turns out that the only "singing" he has done is to confess to cattle rustling.) A third man is a pimp. (Don Quixote excuses this by observing that a pimp only arranges entertainment for respectable citizens.)

NOTE: Some readers assume this passage represents Cervantes' attempt to defend pimping and are very offended. Others feel that Don Quixote sees nothing wrong with pimps only because he is too naive to understand what they actually do. It is worth reading this passage carefully to make your own decision about what the author had in mind.

The most hardened criminal of all, a rogue named Gines de Pasamonte, refuses to tell his story. He is already writing his autobiography, which he intends to sell for a good price.

NOTE: The idea of a criminal cashing in on his notoriety by writing a book sounds very modern. Nowadays, this happens all the time. Some laws have even been passed to keep criminals from profiting from their misdeeds by selling their stories to magazines and book publishers.

When the guard refuses to free the prisoners, Don Quixote starts a fight. In the confusion the prisoners escape. How do they show their gratitude for being rescued? Gines de Pasamonte promptly steals Sancho Panza's ass, Dapple.

Don Quixote's argument with the guard may remind you of the debate about crime that is still going on today. Should we be tough on criminals to teach them a lesson? Or should we try to discover what makes people commit crimes in order to eliminate the causes of crime? Do people break the law because they are just plain bad? Or are they victims of a bad environment who can be changed by rehabilitation and a chance to live a productive life? Or are they "sick" individuals in need of therapy? (The Don's reasoning is a little different from these modern arguments. He says that any use of force, even by the king, is wrong.) The author purposely makes Don Quixote look foolish by having him take a very extreme and naive position. But you may remember that Cervantes himself was thrown into jail more than once for crimes he did not commit. So perhaps he is in sympathy with Quixote's ideas. What do you think?

CHAPTERS 23–30

This section of the novel concerns Don Quixote's adventures in the Sierra Morena, or Black Mountain.

The Don and Sancho meet up with a strange hermit who acts like a wild man and lives on handouts from the local shepherds. The hermit explains that his real name is Cardenio. He has been driven to his present state by the disloyalty of his former best friend, Don Ferdinand. Originally, Don Ferdinand was in love with the daughter of a rich farmer. He promised to marry the girl. But as soon as she gave in and slept with him, he lost interest in her. Cardenio helped Don Ferdinand escape the trouble he'd caused by inviting him to visit his own hometown. There, Don Ferdinand immediately started a campaign to steal Cardenio's own fiancée, Lucinda.

Don Quixote is impressed with Cardenio's decision to live as a hermit. He decides that he, too, will spend some time in retreat from the world. In the meantime, he sends Sancho Panza to deliver a love letter to Dulcinea, vowing that he has not forgotten her and begging her to wait for him.

Suddenly it dawns on Sancho that "Dulcinea" is none other than the daughter of one of his close neighbors. He knows the girl! "She can pitch the iron bar better than the strongest lad in the village," he says approvingly. "God, what a woman she is! What a pair of lungs . . ." Don Quixote cuts Sancho off angrily. Like many lovers, he is not interested in the true strengths and weaknesses of his sweetheart. He is in love with his own fantasy.

Sancho leaves on his errand, but he gets no farther than the same inn where he had been tossed in the blanket. There he runs into Quixote's friends, the priest and the barber. Sancho now discovers that he has forgotten the letter that his master took so much time writing. The priest and the barber promise to write a replacement letter. In the meantime, they convince Sancho to help them with their plan to trick Don Quixote into returning home with them.

The priest predicts that if Don Quixote doesn't stop acting like a crazy hermit, he will end up being made an Archbishop. This scares Sancho since he is counting on Don Quixote to win fame and fortune for both of them. He doesn't see much profit in a church career.

Sancho returns with the Don's friends to where his master is keeping vigil. On the way they meet Cardenio who now tells the rest of his tale of woe. Don Ferdinand tricked him into leaving town and then got his father to arrange for his (Don Ferdinand's) marriage to Lucinda. Cardenio returned home just in time to find the wedding under way. This is what drove him mad.

No sooner is this story finished than a young girl in boy's clothing comes on the scene. She turns out to be Dorothea, the farmer's daughter whom Don Ferdinand had seduced. But she has good news for Cardenio. Lucinda did not marry Don Ferdinand after all. In the middle of the wedding ceremony, Lucinda fainted. A letter found stuffed into her dress explained that she was secretly pledged to marry Cardenio and was planning to commit suicide if forced to wed Don Ferdinand. Cardenio is overjoyed to hear that Lucinda is not married. In gratitude he promises to help Dorothea get justice from Don Ferdinand. Cardenio will force him to keep his promise and marry the girl he seduced, whether he wants to or not.

NOTE: Cardenio's tale is long, complicated, and full of impossible coincidences. In this sense it may remind you of the plot of a television soap opera. Remember that readers in the seventeenth century were not surrounded by instant entertainment, as you are today. They wanted an author to give them their money's worth, and they were likely to be more tolerant of complicated detours from the main plot. Of course, no one expected such tales to be entirely believable. Improbable coincidences and unlikely cases of mistaken identity were all part of the fun. It is interesting to see that Cervantes uses many of the same devices—coincidence, disguise, and multiple cases of mistaken identification—throughout the novel. Why do these same devices seem more artificial in this section of the story than they do elsewhere? One possible reason is that Don Quixote and Sancho are more fully drawn characters than Dorothea, Cardenio, and Ferdinand.

Before leaving with Cardenio, Dorothea agrees to help the priest and the barber with their plan to trick Don Quixote into coming home. Back at the inn, the priest had disguised himself as a young maiden while the barber put on a false beard so that he could pretend to be the maiden's servant. The men decide, however, that Dorothea will be better cast in the role of the damsel in distress. The barber keeps his disguise but the priest will now pretend that he has just run into Don Quixote by accident.

Dorothea will act the part of the Princess Micomicona. The men are a little worried that a farmer's daughter will not be able to pass herself off as a princess. She tells them not to worry, for she's read plenty of chivalric romances!

"Princess Micomicona" tells Don Quixote that her father, the king, is dead. A giant named Pandafilando has usurped the throne and forced her to flee the country. The Don promises to go back to the princess' kingdom and slay the giant. Of course, the whole story is just a ruse to get Don Quixote on the road to his home village. But you may wonder who really understands Dorothea best. The priest and the barber see only a farmer's daughter, a girl of the lower classes. They're amazed that she can play a princess so convincingly. Don Quixote at least knows a damsel in distress when he sees one. Dorothea is the victim of a selfish young man, not an evil giant. But in real life she is as deserving of help as any princess.

The whole group sets out together. Cardenio and the barber are still in disguise, posing as the princess' servants. The priest will do his best to flatter Don Quixote to make him more cooperative.

At the very end of this section, Sancho sees Gines de Pasamonte, disguised as a gypsy and riding on Dapple. Sancho grabs his donkey and Gines flees. The squire is so happy to have Dapple back again that he weeps tears of joy.

CHAPTER 31

Don Quixote still believes that Sancho Panza has delivered his letter to Dulcinea. Afraid to admit that he lost the letter, Sancho invents ridiculous answers to the Don's questions about Dulcinea and her reactions to the letter. Fortunately, something happens to distract Don Quixote's attention. At a roadside fountain the travelers meet up with Andrew (Andres), the shepherd Don Quixote saved from a whipping in Chapter 4. Andrew tells everyone that his master was so angry at the Don's interference that he took out his rage by beating him all the harder. He has only recently left the hospital. Once again, Don Quixote looks like a fool and a meddler in the eyes of his friends. The story of Andrew illustrates the moral that good intentions alone are not enough. Often, naive and ill-considered interferences only make a bad situation worse. In this case, the Don is sincerely sorry to learn that Andrew had to suffer for his bad judgment. But, do his sincere regrets atone for the mistake? Some readers feel they do. It is inevitable, they say, that some attempts to do good will not succeed. If we worry too much about results we will end up as cynics, who stand by doing nothing while evil takes its course. Other readers disagree. This group sometimes compares the Don's attempts to help Andrew with the visionary program of Marxist revolutionaries or other varieties of political crusaders. It is not enough, these readers say, to have a vision of the perfect society. Unless we are also thoughtful enough to foresee how such visions will work out in practice, we may wind up doing more harm than good. What do you think?

CHAPTERS 32–35

The next day the travelers reach the inn. While Don Quixote is put to bed in a loft room, the others are served dinner by Maritornes, the innkeeper, and his wife. (The innkeeper considers the Don's madness amusing, and since he's been promised that this time his guests will pay for their lodging, he holds no grudge.) During the meal, the innkeeper admits that he, too, is a great fan of books of chivalry. "When I hear tell of those furious and terrible blows that the knights hand out," he confesses, "I long to be doing the same myself." Maritornes adds that she, too, enjoys the "lovely goings on" in these romantic stories. The only thing she can't understand is why the female characters are so coy. How could any woman let a man pine away and die for want of a little affection?

Like many who are addicted to romance novels or soap operas today, Maritornes wants to escape the depressing realities of her own situation. Even while he makes fun of the silly invention of chivalric romances, Cervantes shows in this scene that he understands why some people have a need for escapist entertainment. Notice, however, that while Maritornes is in some ways pathetic, her attitude toward these romantic stories is basically sensible.

She knows that she cannot afford to be as aloof as the heroines of the stories she enjoys. You may find it interesting to compare her attitude with that of Altisidora—a young girl who is more cynical when her fantasy of romantic love fails to work out as planned.

Dorothea remarks that the innkeeper, who literally believes many of the fantastic stories told in these romances, is almost as crazy as Don Quixote. But there is a difference between the two kinds of belief. The innkeeper will never actually try to become a knight-errant because he knows that "it's not the fashion today." Because the innkeeper is content to pay lip service to the high ideals found in his favorite books, the world considers him sane. Since Don Quixote tries to put those ideals into practice, he is considered crazy. What do you think of this definition of craziness? Does it make you sympathize with Don Quixote? Or is the innkeeper right to take such a practical attitude?

Quixote's friend, the priest, remarks that he still thinks that books of chivalry are a bad influence and ought to be burned. To prove him wrong the innkeeper invites him to read a manuscript left behind by a traveler who recently stayed at the inn. Most of the next three chapters of the novel concern the priest's reading of the story.

The story is entitled "The Man Who Was Too Curious For His Own Good." (In some translations it is called "The Tale of Ill-Advised Curiosity" or "The Novel of the Curious Impertinent.") The main characters are two good friends named Anselmo and Lothario. Anselmo has a beautiful wife, Camilla. Unfortunately, he is the type of person who can never let well enough alone. He wants to test Camilla to see if she is really faithful to him. Anselmo, who is going out of town, makes Lothario promise to try to seduce Camilla, just so he can report on her reactions. The plan backfires. Lothario finds himself falling in love with Camilla. Camilla has been a faithful wife so far. But when Anselmo refuses to come home and help her deal with the lovesick Lothario, Camilla decides that her husband doesn't love her. She gives in to Lothario after all.

After Anselmo returns home, Camilla and Lothario resort to all kinds of ruses to keep Anselmo from finding out what is going on. Eventually, however, their guilty consciences catch up with them. Convinced that her maid is going to tell Anselmo the truth, Camilla flees to a convent. Lothario joins the army. Anselmo dies of a broken heart, regretting his foolish curiosity that caused so much trouble. Lothario is killed in battle soon after, and Camilla dies as well.

NOTE: Anselmo presents another contrast to the character of Don Quixote. The Don has an idealistic view of what the world should be like, and if the evidence of his own senses doesn't conform to that view, he simply assumes that an evil enchanter has been deceiving him. Anselmo is just the opposite. He can't take anything on faith—not even the love of his own wife. He needs continual proof in the form of reports from his friend Lothario. By constantly trying to test reality, he ends up changing it. Once again, readers disagree about whether this story serves a purpose in the novel. Some argue that it is out of place and distracting. Others feel that it sheds new light on the character of Don Quixote—and on the nature of quixotism. What is your opinion? If you were editing the novel, would you omit this story about Anselmo?

While the priest is reading downstairs, something strange is going on up in the loft. At one point Sancho Panza interrupts the reading to announce that his master is doing battle with giants. Rushing upstairs, the innkeeper finds that the "giants" are large pigskin sacks filled with wine which have been stored in the loft. Half asleep, the Don has mistaken the winesacks for his enemies and slashed away at them with a knife. When the wine came gushing out he was sure he had drawn blood! For the innkeeper this "battle of the wineskins" makes him lose his patience. He agrees to let Don Quixote stay on only because the priest promises to pay for the damages.

CHAPTERS 36–42

No sooner has the priest finished reading the story of Anselmo than a party of strangers arrives at the inn. The group consists of a lady in white, heavily veiled, and her escort of four men in black masks. It turns out that the lady is Lucinda, Cardenio's fiancée. And one of the masked men is Don Ferdinand. Lucinda, brokenhearted over Cardenio's disappearance, is on her way to enter a convent. Now she and Cardenio rush into each other's arms, happily reunited. Even Don Ferdinand, after being confronted by the rest of the company about his past behavior, has a change of heart. He is impressed by Dorothea's faithfulness to him and decides that he loves her and wants to marry her after all.

Sancho Panza is very disappointed to learn that Dorothea is not really the Princess Micomicona. However, when Sancho tries to break this news to Don Quixote, the Don simply refuses to believe that the "Princess" was not real.

NOTE: Sancho's contradictions Sancho's behavior over the last several chapters has been very inconsistent. At times he seems to believe that the wineskins are human attackers; at other times he seems quite aware that they are not. He listened to Dorothea and her friends at dinner discussing the fact that knight-errantry is no longer in fashion and seemed to understand what they were saying. Yet now he is back to believing that Dorothea was a real princess. Some readers try to find logical explanations for Sancho's contradictory statements. Some have even suggested that Sancho is only trying to humor Don Quixote at this point. However, there is another possibility to consider. In real life, people who are quite sane often subscribe to contradictory beliefs. Some people do this quite consciously. For example, they may accept the biblical story of creation on one level and at the same time accept the scientific truth of evolution. If you read *Don Quixote* as a novel about the quest for faith, then you may see Sancho's changing opinions as an attempt to reconcile the mystical teachings of religion with everyday reality. Of course, a less sympathetic view of Sancho is that he simply believes the last thing he hears. Accord-

ing to this interpretation Sancho is the eternal fol-
lower—ready to be led by any strong personality
who comes along.

Soon another party of travelers arrives at the inn.
They are a young man named Ruy Perez de Viedma
and a Moorish (Arab) lady called Lela Zoraida. This
young man, too, tells an amazing story: Twenty-
two years ago, the young man's father decided to
divide his estate among his three sons. Each brother
chose a different profession. One became a mer-
chant, one a scholar, and the young man himself
decided to make his fortune as a soldier. Unfortunately, his luck was not good. He was captured
and sold into slavery in the North African city of
Algiers. The lady Zoraida happened to live in a
house overlooking the young man's prison yard.
One day she dropped from her window a package
containing some money and a note. The note explained that she was the daughter of a wealthy
family. She wished to become a Christian and would
be willing to escape from Algiers with the young
man if he would promise to marry her. After many
complications, the pair managed to arrange their
flight from the city. But on their way back to Spain,
their ship was attacked by pirates who robbed Zoraida of her fortune.

NOTE: This story, called "The Captive's Tale,"
draws to some extent on Cervantes' experiences as
a captive in Algiers. At one point the young man
even mentions a certain fellow prisoner called
"something de Saavedra." You may find more evi-

dence of the author's attitude toward this period of his life in Chapter 38, which is devoted to a long speech by Don Quixote, comparing the rewards and difficulties of a soldier's career and those of a life devoted to learning. The Don concludes that the soldier, while exposed to much hardship, has the nobler calling. Although Don Quixote is insane, his speech here is rational, even eloquent. You will have to decide for yourself whether you agree with his conclusion.

A third party arrives at the inn, which by now is becoming very crowded. These travelers are an influential judge and his lovely young daughter Clara. The judge eventually recognizes the young man (the captive) as his long lost brother. Another happy reunion follows.

Everyone except Don Quixote retires to bed for a well-earned night's rest. The Don decides that he had better stand guard all night in case the concentration of so many fair ladies in one place encourages a "giant" to attack the inn.

In the middle of the night, the sweet singing of a young mule driver awakens some of the guests.

CHAPTERS 43–46

Clara hears the singing and bursts into tears. She tells Dorothea that the mule driver is really Don Luis, her sixteen-year-old neighbor. Don Luis and Clara are in love, but since there seems to be no hope that his wealthy father will ever let him court her, he has run away from home. He has been following Clara and her father throughout their journey.

In the meantime, Maritornes and the innkeeper's daughter have decided to play a trick on Don Quixote. The daughter calls the knight to her window. The Don has already convinced himself that the daughter is in love with him. However, he protests that he must keep himself chaste for his true love, Dulcinea. Maritornes convinces the Don to put his hand through the window to comfort the disappointed girl. As soon as the Don does this, Maritornes slips a knotted thong over his wrist. The other end of the strap has already been tied to the bedroom door.

The Don is caught. He has been standing on the back of Rozinante to reach the window. Now he has to remain still all night for fear that his horse will bolt and leave him hanging by one arm. He stays this way until dawn when four men on horseback ride into the courtyard. Their arrival distracts Rozinante, and the Don slips from his perch.

NOTE: You may have noticed that this silly trick parodies the romantic tale of the young captive and his Moorish lady, Zoraida. Why has the author placed this episode here? To make fun of the captive's story? To ridicule Don Quixote or Maritornes? Or for some other reason?

The four horsemen announce that they have been sent by Don Luis' father to bring the boy home. This is the first time that the judge, Clara's father, has heard that the mule driver is really his neighbor's son. He is more sympathetic than Clara expected him to be. Eventually the judge convinces Don Ferdinand to help him work things out with Don Luis' father. Don Ferdinand, now reformed, has sympathy for the young man in love with a girl poorer than he. Since he is even more important and influential than Don Luis' father, we assume Don Ferdinand's advice will be listened to.

By now your head may be spinning. Ever since the Don met Cardenio in the Sierra Morena you have met a series of minor characters whose lives are connected in a web of thwarted love and coincidences. Now, suddenly, all their problems are resolved. More surprising still, Don Ferdinand, the cause of much of the trouble in the first place, seems to be completely reformed. It is important to remember that Cervantes did not expect his readers to take these twists of plot very seriously. No doubt he is parodying the improbable but lovely "goings on" which delighted readers such as Maritornes who were addicted to chivalric romances. Do you think that the public has grown more sophisticated in its expectations over the last four centuries?

Now one final traveler arrives at the inn—the wandering barber whose basin Don Quixote stole in Chapter 21. The barber wants his basin back, along with the ass' pack saddle that Sancho is now using on Dapple. Quixote's friend Nicholas the barber thinks it is very funny that the Don has mistaken a brass basin for "Mambrino's Helmet." He goes along with the joke, swearing to the other barber that the basin is really a helmet and the pack saddle the fine trappings of a horse. The wandering barber thinks the whole world has gone crazy.

Soon the argument begins to get out of hand. Four troopers of the Holy Brotherhood arrive and take the wandering barber's side in the quarrel. Then Don Quixote appears and attacks the barber. The troopers attack Don Quixote. In the course of the fracas you learn that the troopers are carrying a warrant for the arrest of the man who helped Gines de Pasamonte and the other galley slaves escape.

CHAPTERS 47–52

The troopers finally decide that Don Quixote is too crazy to be worth arresting.

The other guests prepare to leave the inn in a very happy mood. All their troubles have been resolved, and the various pairs of lovers are happily reunited.

The priest decides that he had better think of a way to get Don Quixote back home before he gets into any more trouble. He builds a crude wooden cage and hires an oxcart and driver to transport it. Don Quixote, still asleep after his hard night's vigil, is locked inside. When he awakens, Nicholas the barber tricks him into believing that he is under a magic spell. The cage is not really a cage at all, he tells Quixote. It is an enchanted vehicle, a final test of the Don's faith. If the Don behaves with courage he will be transported to a triumphant wedding with the "dove of Toboso," the beautiful Dulcinea.

On the road, the priest meets a canon (a learned churchman) and falls into an earnest conversation about the theater. Sancho, meanwhile, is just beginning to sort out his reactions to the crazy goings-on. He finally decides that the cage really is a cage after all. But his attempts to make his master believe this end in total frustration. Finally, Sancho convinces the priest that it isn't sanitary to keep Don Quixote penned up day and night. The priest agrees to open the door of the cage so the Don can relieve himself in the woods.

While Don Quixote is free, a young goatherd joins the group. He tells another sad, romantic tale. This story concerns Leandra, the most beautiful girl in his village. Leandra could have had her pick of young men. The goatherd, Eugenio, was in love with her himself. But she fell in love with a newcomer in town, a handsome but worthless fellow who did nothing but brag about his past deeds. Leandra agreed to elope with this fellow, only to learn too late that he was interested only in stealing her jewelry. Abandoned and disgraced, she was placed in a convent by her father.

Don Quixote is always alert for stories about damsels in distress. He declares that he's going to find the convent and rescue Leandra. Eugenio the goatherd thinks this is ridiculous. In his opinion, Leandra got exactly what she deserved. He is no longer in love with her himself now that he knows how foolish she is. Soon Eugenio and the Don are involved in a scuffle.

As they are fighting, a religious procession appears. Some of the marchers, or penitents, are carrying a statue of the Virgin Mary on their shoulders. Quixote mistakes the statue for a noble lady and the penitents for kidnappers. He charges into the group, hoping to spear one of the kidnappers on the point of his lance. Instead, one of the penitents knocks the Don senseless.

NOTE: The Don and the Virgin Mary This attack on the sacred image of the Virgin Mary is the Don's most outrageous escapade yet. Some readers feel that Cervantes uses this incident to ridicule the Roman Catholic church's adulation of Mary. Others argue with equal conviction that Quixote, the pure Christian, is moved by Mary's suffering. In any case, these readers say, Cervantes' humor is directed only against the superstitious excesses of the cult of Mary. Which view you agree with will depend to some extent on your view of the Don's character: Is he the champion of religious ideals in an unworthy world? Or is he merely an impractical fool—one who is unable to tell the difference between ordinary lies and the kind of lies sanctioned by the church and society?

For a while, everyone thinks that Don Quixote is dead. Sancho even delivers a tearful eulogy over his master's body. Finally, however, the Don comes to. He is so ashamed of himself that he agrees that he had better get back into his cage and be taken straight home.

As you read these last chapters of Part I, pay special attention to the changing attitude of Sancho Panza. In the beginning of this section, Sancho is completely disillusioned. Then he hears a conversation between Don Quixote and the learned canon. Quixote argues forcefully in defense of chivalric romances. However unrealistic these tales may be, he says, books containing them have been published with the approval of the king and the church. They have not been censored. Therefore, if you attack the books, you undermine religion itself. Quixote also defends Sancho's worthiness to become a nobleman. Although Sancho comes from the lower classes, he has done his best to show courage and loyalty. Doesn't the Bible teach that God rewards the good intentions of the humble? Even the canon has to admit that this is so. By the time he returns to his own house, Sancho is more convinced than ever that his master is a true knight-errant. He tells his amazed and skeptical wife that there is nothing more pleasant than to be a knight's loyal squire.

NOTE: Do you agree with Don Quixote that Sancho has behaved nobly? Remember that Sancho has shown courage time and again by staying and fighting at his master's side—even though, unlike the Don, he sees that they are hopelessly outnumbered. What is the true test of nobility? To be truly noble, must we be winners at everything we do? Or is nobility a matter of style, of doing whatever we do gracefully? Or, as the Don suggests, do good intentions count?

PART II

In the dedication to Part II of the novel, Cervantes takes a poke at the ungrateful patrons who have failed to reward him for his literary efforts. He jokes that the Emperor of China has offered to found a school that will use *Don Quixote* to teach Spanish to the Chinese. Yet the author still prefers to stay at home in Spain where his efforts have so far not brought him any great wealth.

In the prologue proper, Cervantes goes on to launch a bitter attack on the author who has dared to publish a counterfeit sequel to Part I of the adventures of *Don Quixote*. Not only has this author tried to capitalize on Cervantes' work, he has written insultingly about Cervantes himself.

From the tone of this prologue you may guess that Part II of *Don Quixote* will not be quite as light-hearted as Part I.

CHAPTERS 1–7

Don Quixote has been back home for a month, convalescing in bed from his adventures in Part I. His friends the priest and the barber pay him a visit to see how he is getting along. They are dismayed to find that the Don, though seemingly more rational, still believes that the knight-errant heroes of his favorite books really exist. He even suggests that the King of Spain would have no trouble defeating the Turks if only he summoned these great heroes to fight under his banner. The Don, his friends conclude, is as mad as ever.

Sancho Panza arrives at the house with very exciting news. A student named Sampson Carrasco has returned home from the university with word that Cide Hamete Benengeli's history of Don Quixote is already being read and enjoyed all over Europe.

NOTE: Here the author is introducing a new twist on the theme of reality vs. fantasy. The Don and

Sancho Panza suddenly realize that they are characters in a book. They can't wait to hear what their readers have had to say about them.

The student, Sampson Carrasco, is delighted to come to Don Quixote's house for dinner and discuss the faults that some readers have found with Part I. In fact, the objections he raises reflect actual criticisms that were made of Cervantes' work by his contemporaries. You may have caught one of the mistakes that Carrasco complains about in the course of your own reading. At one point, after Gines de Pasamonte steals Sancho's donkey—and before it is returned—Cervantes describes Sancho as riding on it. If you have been finding the twists and turns of the plot of this novel a bit hard to follow, you may find it comforting to realize that even Cervantes occasionally lost track of what had happened in his own story.

Sampson Carrasco is described as a young man, excessively proud of his own cleverness, who enjoys making fun of others. (Later on, we are told that he longs to become a poet and is jealous of the success of the literary version of Don Quixote's adventures, Part I.) You may well be suspicious, then, when Sampson seems not to notice that Don Quixote is mad. He even mentions a jousting tournament that will be held in the town of Saragossa and suggests that Don Quixote attend.

Sancho Panza, meanwhile, is having trouble convincing his wife Teresa that he ought to continue as Don Quixote's squire. Sancho still believes that Don Quixote will eventually make him a rich man, the governor of his own island. Teresa Panza is not impressed. She is not even sure she wants to be rich. She is a plain person who feels that by putting on airs she would only be making a fool of herself. Sancho disagrees. The whole world, he argues, is impressed by ready money and fine clothes. Appearance is everything. No one cares what people are really like, as long as they can put up a good front.

In Part I, Sancho was a naive country bumpkin. Here, he is not only cynical but able to defend his opinion with a certain eloquence. Whom do you agree with—Sancho or Teresa?

NOTE: You may recall that in Part I you read that Sancho's wife was named Juana. Once again, Cervantes seems to have gotten confused.

Back at Don Quixote's house, his niece Antonia is desperately trying to convince the Don to give up his plan to leave home once more in search of adventure. The Don refutes every one of his niece's practical arguments. No one is too old, too sick, or too poor to do brave deeds, he insists. Antonia turns to Sampson Carrasco, hoping that as an educated man he will have better luck in talking Don Quixote out of his folly. To her surprise, Sampson does nothing of the kind. On the contrary, he even encourages the Don.

CHAPTERS 8–11

At the beginning of Chapter 8, Don Quixote and Sancho take to the road once again. The Don decides that he will first go to Toboso to see the lovely Dulcinea and renew his vows of loyalty to her. Sancho is panic-stricken. He knows very well that Dulcinea is not a princess and does not live in a magnificent castle. Moreover, he only pretended to deliver the letter to Dulcinea that Don Quixote entrusted to him in Part I. Now he is sure to be found out.

Sancho decides to humor his master. He tells the Don that the wicked enchanter has cast a spell over Dulcinea. The Don will not be able to see her as she really is. Instead, she will look like an ordinary country girl. So too, her fine steed will seem to be a humble she-donkey. Just then, three very ordinary girls riding on donkeys come into sight. Look! says Sancho, here come Dulcinea and her attendants now.

Don Quixote is terribly disappointed. All he sees are three peasant girls. The one who is supposed to be Dulcinea even has garlic on her breath. Tearful and confused, the Don begs Sancho to describe the beautiful Dulcinea that he, the Don, has been tricked out of seeing.

You may have noticed that in this scene the Don's and Sancho's roles have been reversed. It is Sancho who claims to be seeing a vision. Don Quixote, for once, sees reality all too clearly. He only believes that the peasant girl is Dulcinea because he trusts Sancho.

You might wonder why suddenly the Don's vivid imagination has failed him. Some readers think it is because he truly loves Dulcinea—or at least the image of her he has created in his mind. The Don might mistake windmills for giants, but he would never wrong his imaginary love by mistaking a rough country girl for her. Suddenly, he is plain old Alonso Quixano again, heartbroken at being deprived of a glimpse of the girl he longs for. Other readers think that it is Sancho's betrayal that has destroyed Quixote's confidence in his own mad delusions. A few readers have another answer: They suggest that the Don has been acting all along. He only pretends to be insane to teach Sancho and the world a moral lesson. Since the Don knows very well that Sancho is trying to trick him, he gets even by refusing to go along with the ruse. How do you assess this situation?

At the end of this section, a wagon comes into view. The passengers are a strange crew, indeed. The wagon driver is the Devil. With him are Death, an angel, and a jester. In reality these creatures are a band of traveling actors, still wearing the costumes from their last performance. Nevertheless, their appearance would seem to be a perfect occasion for Don Quixote to get involved in another of the knock-down battles you saw so often in Part I. This time, with a little prompting from Sancho, Don Quixote sees that the actors are not worth fighting.

CHAPTERS 12–15

Don Quixote and Sancho next meet up with another knight-errant, The Knight of the Wood, and his squire. This knight boasts of the beauty of his true love, Casildea. He even claims to have bested the great Don Quixote himself in single combat. Naturally, the Don is outraged by this lie. "I am Don Quixote," he announces. And he challenges the other knight to fight.

The next morning, at the appointed time, the knight arrives in a glittering suit of armor, covered with mirrors. He tells the Don that his real name is The Knight of the Mirrors. He makes the Don promise that if he is defeated, he will give up knight-errantry for two years. By pure luck, Don Quixote wins the fight. Sancho, meanwhile, has discovered that the other squire, under his false nose, is really Thomas Cecial, Sancho's neighbor. And the Knight of the Mirrors is Sampson Carrasco! The disguises are a trick invented by Sampson, the priest, and the barber to get Don Quixote to come home.

NOTE: When the knight changes his costume, you might guess that the new costume and name are meant to symbolize something. In this case, it isn't very difficult to figure out the symbolism of the mirror suit. Sampson has made himself the mirror image of Don Quixote. Some readers have called him the "false Quixote." Like the Don, Sampson is an ordinary man dressing up as a knight for what is supposedly a good cause—getting the Don safely back home. The difference is that Sampson is sane and the Don is crazy. Or is it the other way around? Since Don Quixote really believes in fair ladies and evil enchanters, you might say that his behavior is logical. Perhaps Sampson, who knows better, is the foolish one. It all depends on your point of view.

CHAPTERS 16–18

Another traveler happens along. This well-to-do, sensible gentleman is at first known only as "the man in green" because he is wearing a green suit of clothes. At first, the traveler takes Don Quixote for a madman. But when they start to discuss poetry, the Don expresses some very sensible opinions. Amazed, the gentleman concludes that Quixote is only half-mad.

Next, a wagon appears carrying two caged lions, gifts to the King of Spain from the Sultan of Oran. Don Quixote insists that the wagon driver open the cage so that he can fight one of the lions. The terrified driver opens the cage and stands aside. Don Quixote confronts the lion bravely. However, the lion takes one look at Don Quixote and lies down inside its cage, totally uninterested in attacking him.

Don Quixote considers this a great victory. From now on he will call himself Knight of the Lions. Do you think he has proved his courage or just given another example of his foolishness?

NOTE: Readers in seventeenth-century Spain would have surely recognized this scene as a parody of a famous confrontation between a lion and El Cid, Spain's great epic hero. In that story, the lion refuses to fight because it is abashed in the presence of El Cid's courage.

CHAPTERS 19–21

Two students whom the Don and Sancho meet on the road invite them to attend a wedding. The bride and groom are the beautiful Quiteria and Camacho the Rich, a wealthy farmer. Their wedding festivities are interrupted by the arrival of Basilio, a young man who loves Quiteria but has been rejected by her family because he is poor. Basilio announces that he is going to kill himself in grief. He falls on his dagger in front of the horrified wedding guests. Apparently dying, he begs to be granted one last wish. He asks that Quiteria marry him. Since he will be dead in a few minutes anyway, she will be free to marry Camacho as planned. The guests decide to humor him.

Of course, it's all a trick. As soon as Quiteria says "I do," Basilio revives. He had only pretended to stab himself. Quiteria, however, is not sorry, for she had wanted to marry Basilio all along and has been in on the plan. Naturally, though, Camacho and his family are furious. For once, Don Quixote plays peacemaker. He points out that in a way Basilio has done Camacho a good turn. Since Quiteria loves Basilio, her marriage to Camacho would have brought misery to all concerned.

CHAPTERS 22–23

Don Quixote now decides to explore the famous Cave of Montesinos, which is supposed to be enchanted. He has Sancho let him down into the cave on a rope to a ledge about sixty feet below ground. There he falls asleep and has a dream.

In his dream the Don sees himself in a castle where he meets the knight Sir Montesinos himself. Montesinos shows the Don the body of Durandarte, one of the greatest knights-errant in history. Durandarte had been "killed" in combat centuries ago. According to legend, his last wish was that his heart be cut out and given to his beloved, Belerma. In the dream, Don Quixote learns that because of the curse of a wicked enchanter, Durandarte cannot really die. He lies on his mortuary slab, weeping and moaning and begging to be released from the burden of life. Belerma, too, is cursed with immortality. She has turned into a yellow-complexioned old crone who wanders around carrying her knight's heart.

NOTE: Durandarte and Belerma were famous characters of medieval legend, celebrated in poems and ballads. The story of Durandarte's last wish, to have his heart cut out and taken to his beloved, was considered exquisitely romantic. Cervantes may be saying that this rather gory example of the chivalric romance has outlived its usefulness and deserves to be killed off.

At the end of his dream, Don Quixote sees the three peasant girls that Sancho told him were Dulcinea and her two ladies-in-waiting. One of the "ladies" approaches the Don and asks him to lend Dulcinea some money. The Don is stunned by this request. Cadging money from a stranger is totally out of character for the Dulcinea of his imagination. Nevertheless, he hands over what little he has. Shortly after this, Sancho hauls Don Quixote out of the cave and he wakes up.

This episode differs from any of Don Quixote's previous adventures. Even the Don is confused by his dream, since it seems to mock the values of chivalry. Also, for the first time you cannot be sure what is real. Is the dream just another of the Don's delusions? Or is it a "real" dream—one which may shock the Don back in the direction of sanity? How might a psychiatrist interpret it?

The uniqueness of the dream is emphasized in the succeeding chapter when the author tells you that even Cide Hamete Benengeli found this dream hard to believe. If the Don were not so truthful, Cide Hamete would have suspected him of lying, of making the whole story up. For this reason, the dream episode is sometimes called "Don Quixote's lie." A few readers, those who think that the Don is only pretending to be mad, take this suggestion literally. The Don concocts this "dream," they say, to repay Sancho for inventing the story of Dulcinea's enchantment. Another view is that it is Alonso Quixano, Don Quixote's sane alter ego, who dreams this dream. Alonso knows that the real Dulcinea is a peasant girl who would be interested in an old man like himself only for his money. If you had to vote for one of the choices, which would it be? Why? Could you suggest another possibility?

CHAPTERS 24–29

On their way to a roadside inn, the Don and Sancho meet a man driving a mule loaded with weapons. The man tells a strange story: Two aldermen from his village went looking for a lost jackass. Each of them brayed loudly, hoping to lure the ass in his direction. The two friends never recovered the ass (which was later found dead) but they brayed so well that they fooled each other. Soon the rest of the village, having heard of the friends' braying contest, started to make fun of them by braying every time the friends appeared in public. The joke got so out of control that people from other villages started to make fun of the jokesters. The village became known as the braying village. Now, to restore their reputation, the villagers are going out to fight those who mocked them.

You might think that the Don would rush to champion the cause of the braying village. Not at all. In Chapter 27 he intervenes as the fight is about to start. He lectures the villagers sternly, telling them that wars should be fought for important causes, not over silly quarrels. Sancho, however, can't resist showing off his own imitation of a jackass. When he starts braying, the villagers think he is making fun of them and beat him up. They didn't have adhesive bandages in Cervantes' time, but does it seem to you that his characters would have purchased them by the car load?

Inside the inn, the Don meets a traveling entertainer, Master Peter. Master Peter has a pet ape who, for money, is supposed to be able to answer any question put to it. This is an obvious fraud, since the ape only "whispers" the answers in his master's ear. It is Peter who relays them to the audience. Nevertheless, the ape seems to perform impressively. He recognizes Don Quixote and Sancho and gives Sancho "news" of his wife Teresa.

Later, Master Peter gives a puppet show depicting a fight between Spanish knights and the Moors. Don Quixote is so carried away that he draws his sword and attacks the puppets, totally destroying them.

Still later, you learn that Peter the puppet master is really Gines de Pasamonte, the rogue whom Don Quixote freed in the episode of the galley slaves

(Part I, Chapter 22). This is how Master Peter was able to recognize Quixote and Panza and answer their questions. Perhaps Don Quixote was not so mistaken after all in attacking the puppets. Gines, alias Master Peter, really was making fun of him.

NOTE: This is one of the few times in the novel when Cervantes draws comparisons between art or theater and real life. Cervantes seems to be saying that all authors are, at least in part, swindlers. Writers manipulate their characters in order to deceive their readers into mistaking fiction for real life. In what way could the writing of fiction be a kind of lying? Are the readers of novels, like Sancho Panza, partners in their own deception? If not, why not? Notice that Cervantes goes to great lengths, even inventing the imaginary historian Cide Hamete, to convince you that *Don Quixote* is a true story. If someone said this is just carrying artistic lying to another level, what would he mean? Is there evidence that he is trying to set his book apart from the frivolous products of popular culture? Where do you find it?

At the end of this section, the Don and Sancho arrive at a flour mill, where a large waterwheel is being used to turn the grindstone. The Don mistakes the mill for an enchanted castle and tries to reach it by boat. His boat is about to be swept into the waterwheel and smashed when the millers run out to save him. Naturally, the Don mistakes the flour-covered workers for demons. He seems to be as crazy as he was in Part I.

CHAPTERS 30–41

Before you can catch your breath, the next series of adventures begins. Don Quixote and Sancho meet a Duke and Duchess out hunting and accept their invitation to be guests at the Duke's castle. The Duke and Duchess have read Part I of *Don Quixote*, and they arrange to play some very elaborate tricks on Quixote and Sancho, all for their own and their court's amusement. The Duchess decides that Sancho is even funnier than his master, so she convinces the Duke to promise to make Sancho a governor after all.

One trick that the Duke and Duchess play involves getting a servant to dress up as the evil wizard Merlin. This "Merlin" tells Quixote and Sancho that there is only one way that Dulcinea can be transformed back from a peasant girl into a princess: Sancho must promise to give himself 3300 lashes on his own bare buttocks. Of course Sancho is horrified. For one thing, he made up the story of Dulcinea's enchantment himself. For another, he can't see why he should be the one to suffer. Dulcinea is Don Quixote's beloved, not his. The Duchess cleverly persuades Sancho that Dulcinea really is enchanted. She also hints that Sancho will never get an island to rule if he doesn't agree to "save" Dulcinea. After much moaning and groaning, Sancho promises to do what Merlin wants. By the next day, however, he has given himself only five perfunctory spanks. He's still 3295 blows short of his quota.

NOTE: With this incident Sancho becomes thoroughly "quixotized." Through a combination of greed and affection for his master, Sancho has taken on Don Quixote's mad quest as his own. If you've ever been talked into accepting a dare against your own better judgment, perhaps you know how Sancho feels at this point. One compromise has led to another until finally he feels he has no choice but to carry the logic of the enchantment story to its conclusion.

Some readers, however, see a positive moral in Sancho's dilemma. Sancho, they say, represents the miracle of religious faith that inspires people to believe in the existence of God. Sancho's agreeing to whip himself might even be compared with the sufferings of Christ, who died for the sins of mankind. What weaknesses, if any, do you detect in those theories?

A second practical joke played by the Duke and Duchess involves a group of court ladies who dress up as "Countess Trifaldi" and her ladies-in-waiting. They tell Quixote that they have been cursed by an evil giant who has caused them to grow beards. The Don is fooled by the women's false whiskers into believing this, and he gallantly promises to do battle with the giant. But to reach the giant's faraway kingdom, he and Sancho will have to ride on a magical wooden horse that flies through the air. Trembling with fear, the Don and Sancho mount the horse. They are blindfolded, supposedly because the giant does not want them to see where they are going. Of course, the horse, Clavileno, is really a wooden toy stuffed with firecrackers. A servant blows air over the Don and Sancho with a bellows to make them think they are really flying. Then someone sets fire to the horse's tail. The firecrackers explode and Quixote and Sancho are thrown high into the air. After a good laugh at both men's expense, the courtiers convince them that their courage has made the giant relent. The "Countess" and her ladies remove their false beards and pretend to be very grateful.

During the course of these chapters, Sancho loudly expresses his dislike and fear of ladies in waiting—an opinion that is easy to understand if you realize that such ladies traditionally served as chaperones. The staunchly forbidding lady in waiting was a universally recognized figure of fun, much like the stereotypical interfering mother-in-law today.

But what of the Duke and Duchess' behavior? Some readers have pointed out that elaborate practical jokes such as they play were more acceptable in the sixteenth and seventeenth centuries than today. Some noblemen even had trick fountains which spewed water at unsuspecting guests. On the other hand, it is one thing to play jokes on one's equals, another to enjoy teasing a crazy man and his peasant servant. The Duke and Duchess are so far removed from the problems of everyday life that they treat the whole world as their playground. In a way, they are living a fantasy just as the Don is. One difference is that their fantasy is the product of boredom and aimlessness. Perhaps you can think of other differences.

CHAPTERS 42–53

The Duke keeps his promise and makes Sancho the governor of the town of Baratario. Sancho is so gullible that he even believes Baratario is on an island, although it is actually landlocked.

NOTE: *Barato* means cheap in Spanish. Sancho has become the ruler of "Cheapsville."

Sancho has achieved his impossible dream. Much to the surprise of the Duke and his steward, Sancho turns out to be an excellent governor. Presented with a series of tricky legal cases to judge, he bases his decisions on common sense and does very well, indeed.

You, however, may feel that a few of Sancho's decisions are sexist, at least by modern standards. For example, he tells a young girl who longs for more freedom that an honest maid should stay at home "as if she had one leg broken." This advice probably represented the majority male opinion of the time.

On a lighter note, Sancho has problems dealing with an overenthusiastic doctor who is so aware of the health dangers of different types of food that he won't let Sancho eat anything at all. The character of the doctor shows that health food fanatics are not just a modern phenomenon.

The Duchess has written a letter to Teresa Panza, who is amazed and delighted to find that her husband has succeeded after all. However, the Duke has no intention of allowing Sancho to keep his island. When Sancho's governorship starts to turn out too well, the Duke is not pleased; he does not enjoy the thought that a mere peasant can rule as

wisely as a lord. So he stages a mock invasion that
ends Sancho's brief reign.

Don Quixote, meanwhile, has remained at the
Duke's castle where he is having problems with
women. One young lady of the court, fourteen-
year-old Altisidora, has fallen madly in love with
him. When the Don tells Altisidora that he is going
to remain faithful to Dulcinea, Altisidora takes the
rejection angrily. She begins to scheme for revenge.

Another lady, the middle-aged Doña Rodriguez,
presents Don Quixote with a different type of
problem. She comes to the Don's bedroom late at
night and begs him to help her save her daughter's
honor. A young man has seduced the daughter
but refuses to marry her. The Don will have to
fight the young man to force him to do the right
thing.

CHAPTERS 54–57

On his way back to meet Don Quixote at the
Duke's castle, Sancho runs into a Moor named Ricote, a shopkeeper from his own village. Ricote
has been forced to leave the country; however, he
has returned in disguise to recover a buried treasure of gold that he left behind. Sancho does not
have time to help Ricote recover the treasure, but
he promises not to betray his former neighbor to
the authorities.

NOTE: The Moors, descendants of Arabs who
had once ruled much of Spain, were a despised
minority. Between 1609 and 1613, Moriscos—Moors

like Ricote who had adopted Christianity—were expelled from the country.

Cervantes is obviously sympathetic to the Moors. He has Ricote note, ironically, that it is easier for a Moor to live as a good Christian in Algeria than in Europe. On the other hand, Cervantes seems to defend the reasoning behind the expulsion of the Moriscos. Passages like this one lead some readers to believe that Cervantes was basically a conservative—he sympathized with downtrodden individuals but did not challenge the system. Other readers think Cervantes merely outwitted the censors by using irony and humor to soften the impact of his social criticisms. You will have to decide for yourself which view is right.

Back at the castle, the Duke has arranged a tournament so that Don Quixote can defend the honor of Doña Rodriguez's daughter. Unfortunately, the young man the Don was supposed to fight has fled the country. (You are told, in passing, that he wanted to escape having Doña Rodriguez for a mother-in-law.) The Duke gets his servant Tosilos to take the young man's place. Tosilos is coached on how to put up a good show without actually hurting the Don, since the Duke wants only to have some fun at Don Quixote's expense. However, when Tosilos sees Doña Rodriguez' daughter, he calls off the fight at the last minute. He has fallen in love with the girl and wants to marry her. Even though Doña Rodriguez and her daughter know that Tosilos is the wrong young man, they are delighted by this turn of events. In the seventeenth century, a young lady who was no longer a virgin considered herself lucky to find a loving husband.

NOTE: In spite of all the tricks the Duke and Duchess have played on them, Don Quixote and Sancho Panza have fared rather well. Sancho Panza was a good governor. He has even overcome the greedy side of his nature in refusing to betray the Moor Ricote. A letter written by Sancho's wife Teresa has revealed her inner dignity and her touching pride in her husband's success. Don Quixote, meanwhile, really has been able to help Doña Rodriguez, though in a roundabout way. He also shows some restraint in refusing to take advantage of the lovesick Altisidora. The Duke and the Duchess, who think they are so smart and sophisticated, have been exposed as petty, rather foolish people. What are these reversals telling you about Cervantes' philosophy?

CHAPTERS 58–60

Don Quixote and Sancho leave the castle, continuing their journey to the jousting tournament described by Sampson Carrasco at the beginning of Part II.

Don Quixote is hiking through a wood when he gets caught in some threads strung between the trees. A young woman appears and explains that the threads are snares set to trap birds. She and her companions introduce themselves as well-to-do ladies who have retired to this part of the country-side to play at being shepherdesses. The young women and their male companions make a big fuss over Don Quixote. He, in turn, offers to stand in the middle of the road and challenge anyone who comes by to acknowledge the shepherdesses' beauty. Unfortunately for Don Quixote, the first "travelers" to come along are a herd of bulls. They stampede right past the Don and Sancho, leaving both men bruised and breathless.

NOTE: The young ladies playing shepherdesses are acting out the fantasies of the pastoral romances that were still quite popular in Cervantes' time. Their modern equivalent would be a group of wealthy young people going to a town in the Old West to play at being cowboys and frontier dwellers. You might also be reminded of the hippie communes of the 1960s and early 1970s that were founded by young people from the cities who tried, often very self-consciously, to "live off the land."

Moving on, Don Quixote is quite depressed to hear two gentlemen at an inn discussing the unauthorized Part II of *Don Quixote* that has just been published. In fact, it was while writing this chapter of the novel that Cervantes learned that such a sequel, written by another author, had appeared in print. Cervantes took his revenge through the characters in his story. Because the author of the unauthorized Part II supposedly had his characters travel to Saragossa, the "real" Don Quixote—Cervantes' character—decides to prove the sequel false by changing his destination. He and Sancho will go to Barcelona instead.

In the meantime, Don Quixote has another problem. He is upset because Sancho has not yet given himself the 3300 lashes that will free Dulcinea from her magic spell. At night, while the pair are camping out under the stars, the Don creeps up on the sleeping Sancho and tries to deliver the lashes himself. Sancho wakes up and wrestles with his master.

Next, the Don and Sancho meet a band of highway robbers led by a notorious outlaw named Roque Ginart. The knight and his squire are afraid that their end has come. To their surprise, however, Roque turns out to be a gentleman outlaw. Recognizing that the Don is mad, Roque does not rob him. The outlaw treats his other victims with similar courtesy. He takes only from the rich and undeserving, and even then he limits himself to stealing no more than they can afford to lose.

NOTE: Roque Ginart was a real outlaw who operated in eastern Spain during the time Cervantes was writing. You might compare him to the legendary Englishman, Robin Hood. Roque's philosophy of robbing from the rich to give to the poor is a real-life example of "quixotism." Yet Roque does not recognize Don Quixote as a kindred spirit. Why not? One reason might be that Roque knows the score, so to speak. He realizes that in the eyes of the law he is still an outlaw. Unlike Don Quixote, he is in touch with reality. What other differences did you find between the two characters?

CHAPTERS 61–62

The Don and Sancho finally reach Barcelona. Roque has given them a letter of introduction to a gentleman named Don Antonio Moreno who welcomes them as guests in his home. Quixote and Sancho discover that they are now celebrities. The townsfolk recognize them as characters in a famous book. Don Antonio even gives a ball in Quixote's honor.

It does not take Don Quixote and Sancho very long to discover that being famous has as many drawbacks as being poor and unappreciated. The Don wears himself out dancing at the ball. He and Sancho grow weary of being stared at every time they appear in public. Furthermore, the wonders of city life turn out to be greatly overrated. In one scene, Don Antonio shows off a disembodied "talking head." Of course this is just an elaborate parlor trick. The head is made of bronze, and its voice is produced by Don Antonio's nephew, hiding in a room below and shouting through a pipe.

CHAPTERS 63–66

During a visit to a ship docked in the harbor, Don Quixote and Sancho meet a young woman named Anna Felix, who has just escaped from Algeria. Anna Felix turns out to be the daughter of Sancho's Morisco neighbor, Ricote. Anna tells a complicated story about her lover, Don Gaspar, who is still a captive in Algiers. Everyone agrees that if Ricote cannot buy the young man's freedom, Don Quixote will have to rescue him.

Before this can happen, however, Don Quixote
meets his last defeat. While he is enjoying a quiet
walk on the beach, the Don sees a mounted knight
in full armor riding out of the mist. It is the Knight
of the Full Moon. The Don challenges him to acknowledge Dulcinea's beauty. In reply, the knight
offers to fight one-on-one. If the Don wins, the
knight will praise Dulcinea. If the Don loses, he
must give up knight-errantry for a full year. Don
Quixote accepts the challenge. He charges forward
on Rozinante and is promptly knocked to the
ground. Defeated, he must now give up his quest.

Does this knight's request sound familiar? This
is the same trick that Sampson Carrasco tried to
play as the Knight of the Mirrors. You soon learn
that the "Knight of the Full Moon" is indeed the
persistent Sampson. But this time his plan has
worked.

You may find yourself wondering at this point
why Sampson has been so persistent. We learned
one reason at the beginning of Part II when the
author describes Sampson as an arrogant young
man out to prove himself cleverer than any small-
town *hidalgo*. It is tempting to suppose that in
creating the character of Sampson, Cervantes had
in mind the imposter who was arrogant enough to
publish a counterfeit sequel to Part I of his novel.
At the same time, you may have encountered some
real-life counterparts of Sampson. Sampson brings
to life the phrase "Too smart for his own good."
He plays along with behavior he considers crazy
hoping that in the end his superiority will be obvious to all. Instead, he often seems sillier than
poor, mad Don Quixote.

CHAPTERS 67–74

On his way home to keep his promise to the knight, Don Quixote encounters Tosilos, the young man he had almost fought at the Duke's castle. Tosilos tells the Don and Sancho that the Duke did not keep his promise to let him marry Doña Rodriguez' daughter after all. So another of Don Quixote's "successful" adventures has turned out to be a failure.

Arriving at the Duke's castle, Quixote and Sancho find a funeral in progress. Altisidora is lying stretched out on the funeral bier. Two black-robed figures appear, supposedly the judges of Hell personified. They announce that Altisidora has died of unrequited love for Don Quixote. Only Sancho can bring her back to life by allowing himself to be pinched, pricked, and slapped by the Duchess' ladies-in-waiting. The ladies fall upon the protesting Sancho. Just then Altisidora sits up, not dead at all.

Don Quixote never quite realizes that Altisidora's resurrection was an act, invented by the Duke and Sampson. Convinced of Sancho's powers of disenchantment, he offers to pay his squire if he will only give himself the lashes necessary to free Dulcinea from her magic spell. That night, Sancho finally agrees. But he only pretends to whip himself, yelling in pain while beating his lash on the tree trunks nearby.

Don Quixote believes that Sancho has kept his promise. Yet he still has not found Dulcinea. He looks for her everywhere, his depression turning to despair. Don Quixote overhears two young boys talking. One of them says to the other, "Thou shalt never see her while thou hast breath in thy body." The Don begins to think that this message is meant for him. He will see Dulcinea only after he dies.

Don Quixote arrives back at his own house. His niece and his friends are overjoyed to see him safe. But the Don knows that he will soon die. He tells his surprised friends that he is now cured of his madness. Don Quixote of La Mancha no longer exists. He is plain Alonso Quixano once again.

Sancho begs his master not to die. In tears, he reminds him that there are still brave deeds to be done, many wrongs that need to be set right. But Alonso Quixano, now sane, cannot see what this has to do with him. His last act is to write into his will the provision that his niece must promise to marry a man who has no interest in reading books about chivalry. After this, he dies.

NOTE: Some years ago, *Don Quixote* was made into a musical play, *Man of La Mancha*. In this version of the Quixote story, you are led to believe that Sancho will continue the Don's mission after his master's death. Do you think this is what Cervantes had in mind when he wrote this final scene? Has Sancho been infected permanently with the Don's "madness"—with his idealism? Or, does Don Quixote's advice to his niece represent Cervantes' feelings? Is the author saying that the "quixotic" idealism of Don Quixote belongs only in books, and in rather silly, dangerous books at that? These are only two of a broad spectrum of conclusions that thoughtful readers have drawn from the ending of this novel. Deciding upon the meaning of all that has taken place is now *your* quest.

A STEP BEYOND

Tests and Answers

TESTS

Test 1

1. Alonso Quixano is driven mad by   _____
   A. poverty
   B. reading too many books about chivalry
   C. his fantasies about the wicked enchanter Freston

2. Sancho Panza becomes Don Quixote's squire   _____
   because he
   A. thinks he will become ruler of an island
   B. wants to get away from his wife
   C. wants to recover his stolen ass, Dapple

3. The story of Anselmo and Camilla illus-   _____
   trates the
   A. pain of unrequited love
   B. evils of arranged marriages
   C. importance of trusting those we love

4. Don Quixote's *main* reason for freeing the   _____
   galley slaves is that he
   A. believes they are victims of a wicked enchanter
   B. thinks Gines de Pasamonte was unjustly convicted

C. does not believe the king has a right
to take away anyone's liberty

5. Some major themes of *Don Quixote* are _____
   I. illusion vs. reality
   II. the evils of the class structure
   III. the role of idealism in the real world
   A. II & III only   B. I & III only
   C. II & III only

6. Don Quixote's dream in the Cave of Mon- _____
   tesinos is about the
   A. impossibility of romantic love lasting
   forever
   B. curse of immortality
   C. dangers of mistaking fantasy for
   reality

7. Dorothea is able to act the part of the prin- _____
   cess because she
   A. really does come from a noble family
   B. knows what it is like to be a damsel in
   distress
   C. is secretly in love with Don Quixote

8. Altisidora is _____
   A. spiteful and self-centered
   B. just the type to die for love
   C. too young to know her own mind

9. One good definition of quixotism is _____
   A. the belief that one's own ideals are
   superior to everyone else's
   B. misguided idealism
   C. a form of idealism that went out of
   style at the end of the Middle Ages

10. Early in Part II of the novel Don Quixote _____
    learns that

A. the knights-errant he admires are
   fictional characters
B. Dulcinea never existed
C. he himself is a character in a book

11. What was Cervantes' view of religion?

12. How does Sancho Panza change and become "qui-
    xotized" in the course of the novel?

13. Discuss some different forms of humor in *Don Qui-
    xote*.

14. Why is the episode of the Cave of Montesinos some-
    times called "Don Quixote's lie"? How does it differ
    from the adventures that precede it?

15. Discuss the mirror symbolism in *Don Quixote*.

Test 2

1. Don Quixote believes that a knight-errant   _____
   in search of adventure must
     I. abstain from sex
    II. fight only with other knights, never
        with those beneath his station
   III. always sleep in a castle
        A. I & II only   B. II & III only
        C. I & III only

2. Cide Hamete Benengeli was   _____
   A. the author of many chivalric romances
   B. a creation of Cervantes' imagination
   C. a Moor expelled from Spain for
      refusing to convert to Christianity

3. One character who is in part autobiograph-   _____
   ical is

A. Ruy Perez de Viedma   B. Camacho
C. Roque Ginart

4. The episode of the braying villagers shows   _____
   that
   A. the people of seventeenth-century
      Spain could be very intolerant
   B. wars are often fought for petty
      reasons
   C. you should mind your own business,
      not your neighbor's

5. The innkeeper will never try to become a   _____
   knight-errant because he
   A. knows that knights-errant are out of
      style
   B. is a married man
   C. thinks chivalry is boring

6. Why did Cervantes write: "For me alone   _____
   was the great Quixote born, and I alone for
   him"?
   A. Because so many of Quixote's
      adventures are based on Cervantes'
      own experiences
   B. Because *Don Quixote* was the book
      that made Cervantes' fortune
   C. Because he understood his hero far
      better than the author of the
      unauthorized version of Part II

7. One episode that points up the relationship   _____
   between artistry and deception is
   A. the reading of the novel about "The
      Man Who Was Too Curious For His
      Own Good"

   B. the puppet show
   C. Countess Trifaldi's tale

8. Sampson Carrasco disguises himself as the   _____
   A. Knight of the Mirrors
   B. man in green
   C. hermit of the Sierra Moreno

9. When Sancho has become "quixotized" he   _____
   A. becomes less talkative
   B. must beat himself on his own backside
   C. treats Dapple more kindly

10. Don Quixote is "cured" of his madness   _____ when
   A. Altisidora's suffering makes him ashamed of himself
   B. Sancho finally disenchants Dulcinea
   C. he realizes he will never see Dulcinea in this life

11. Why is *Don Quixote* sometimes called the first true novel?

12. Some psychologists have pointed out that people who have to cope with the insane often start behaving as if they were insane themselves. Can you find any instances of this kind of behavior in *Don Quixote*? What function do these incidents serve?

13. How does Cervantes further the theme of illusion vs. reality?

14. Do you think Don Quixote shows true courage in his adventures? Why or why not?

15. What is Cervantes' attitude toward the lower classes?

Be sure to discuss the character of Sancho Panza in your answer.

ANSWERS

Test 1

1. B **2.** A **3.** C **4.** C **5.** B **6.** B
7. B **8.** A **9.** B **10.** C

11. There is no one right answer to this question. You should keep in mind, however, that the majority opinion is that Cervantes attacked only superstition and hypocrisy, not religious values as such. It is easy to find places in the novel where the author pokes fun at the church hierarchy. For example, Quixote's friend, the priest, is a small-minded man who makes himself ridiculous by dressing up in women's clothing. When Don Quixote is behaving like a wild-man hermit, the priest even predicts that the Don will be made an archbishop if he continues to act that way. A few readers think that Cervantes was mocking basic Catholic beliefs. They even compare Dulcinea, a princess only in the Don's imagination, with the Virgin Mary. Whether you agree or not, your answer to this question should discuss the Don's attack on the penitents, and his conversation with the learned canon, both near the end of Part I. These incidents can be interpreted in more than one way.

12. At the beginning of the story, Sancho is a country bumpkin. He knows that Don Quixote mistakes the windmills for giants. Yet Sancho's greed makes him want to believe in the rich rewards his master has promised him. When he does try to fool the Don, by tying Rozinante's legs together, for example, his tricks are crude and obvious. Also, in the scenes at the inn (Part I) you see Sancho torn between belief and disbelief. He is surprised to hear the other guests say that the days of knight-errantry are over. Yet he goes along with the Don's fantasy that the wineskins are giants. In Part II, Sancho plays a very successful trick on Don Quixote, convincing him that a wicked magician has turned Dulcinea into a peasant girl. Sancho pays for this trick when the Duke and Duchess set him up as the butt of their humor. They convince him that Dulcinea really is enchanted and that only when Sancho agrees to flog himself 3300 times will the spell be broken. Sancho has been "quixotized" when he becomes Dulcinea's champion.

13. There is a great deal of physical, slapstick humor in the novel. The Don and Sancho are continually getting beaten up, and these scenes are funny because Quixote believes in a heroic battle while you can see how ridiculous the fights really are. In discussing this form of humor, you might want to consider why the Don's beatings seem less funny in Part II. Is this because you have started to identify with him to some degree? Note that the humor in this section comes from Sancho's trying to *avoid* a beating. Another source of broad humor is Sancho's way of talking. He uses a mixed-up vocabulary, quotes proverbs in laughably inappropriate situations, and deflates other characters' pretensions by his unwitting honesty. The Don's mock-heroic delusions are also a source of humor. An example of this is found in the scene where he concocts a wild tale about opposing armies after watching the dust raised by two flocks of sheep. More subtly, the author mocks himself and teases you, as when he has the imaginary "historian" Cide Hamete complain about how long and tedious the Don's story is becoming.

14. The episode in Montesinos' Cave is out of character with the Don's other visions. Dulcinea, instead of being noble and ethereal, asks to borrow money. The knight Durandarte is a hero who has outlived his time. For the first time, Don Quixote does not know whether to believe what his imagination has shown him. He has become a doubter. Cide Hamete also interrupts the story to suggest that he can't believe the dream either and that perhaps Don Quixote is lying. A few readers take this seriously. They believe that the Don made up this vision to pay Sancho back for pretending that the peasant girl was Dulcinea. Others suggest that the vision is a "real" dream, dreamed by the Don's sane alter ego, Alonso Quixano.

15. The most important use of mirrors as symbols occurs when Sampson Carrasco appears in a suit of armor covered with tiny mirrors. Sampson, who even calls himself "Knight of the Mirrors," is pretending to be a knight only in order to trick Don Quixote into giving up his quest. Sampson's trick "mirrors" the Don's madness. If you have read the novel carefully, you may recall that in the Prologue to Part I, Don Quixote himself is described as the "mirror" of chivalry. Remember, mirrors not only reflect reality, they sometimes distort it. In a sense, literature mirrors real life. And life itself may only be a distorted mirror in which we see the reflections of eternal truths.

Test 2
1. C **2.** B **3.** A **4.** B **5.** A **6.** C
7. B **8.** A **9.** B **10.** C.

11. Although there are many elements of fantasy in *Don Quixote*, the story was realistic for its time. The author introduces a wide variety of characters from different regions of Spain and many walks of life. He comments on problems of his day, such as the expulsion of the

Moriscos or the state of the theater. Perhaps most important, Don Quixote and Sancho are full-bodied characters who change and grow over the course of the story. They cannot be summed up by any one-line moral or disposed of by a convenient happy ending.

12. The priest and the barber Nicholas create the elaborate story of "Princess Micomicona" in order to lure Don Quixote back home. Sampson Carrasco twice dresses up as a knight to trick Don Quixote into giving up his quest. The Duke and Duchess create elaborate illusions just to see how the Don and Sancho will react. Sancho makes up the story of Dulcinea's enchantment so Quixote won't find out that he never delivered the letter to Dulcinea. All of these characters' motives are rational, yet self-serving to some extent. They contribute to the confusion between illusion and reality. Yet, we do not come to love them the way Sancho loves Don Quixote, who is completely crazy.

13. In addition to the story itself, the narrative structure of the novel creates different planes of reality. The history of Don Quixote is supposedly a true story, written by an Arab historian named Cide Hamete Benengeli. This historian is really an invention of the author, who uses the imaginary Cide Hamete as a commentator on the action. The comments of the "author" himself may or may not reflect the actual opinions of Cervantes. In addition, in Part II the Don and Sancho realize that their adventures in Part I have become the subject of a book. They know they are characters in literature.

14. Some readers would argue that despite some exceptions, the Don shows courage throughout the story. Others would argue that true courage cannot grow out of ignorance and delusions. A third point of view is that the nature of the Don's courage changes over the course of the story. In Part I, the Don's courage often seems to be false, just as much of an illusion as the giants he sees around him. For example, when Sancho is being tossed in a blanket by some ruffians, the Don doesn't help. He later blames the wicked enchanter for his inability to come to his squire's aid. In Part II, however, the Don confronts a real lion. He has no way of knowing beforehand that the lion is not going to attack him.

15. Like Shakespeare and other writers of his time, Cervantes used lower-class characters for comic relief. Sancho's crudeness, even his greed, are sources of humor. Yet in Part II, when Sancho is given an "island" to rule, he turns out to be wise and just. It is the Duke and Duchess who seem petty and unfair. Most readers feel that the sheer variety of ordinary people, good and bad, in the novel shows Cervantes' understanding of and sympathy for the common people of Spain. In answering this question, consider not only Sancho's performance as governor but the Don's statements about him—for example, his speech on the nature of nobility at the end of Part I.

Term Paper Ideas and other Topics for Writing

The Novel

1. The French novelist Anatole France wrote: "Woe to him who is not sometimes a Don Quixote, and who never took windmills for giants!" What is your reaction to this statement?

2. Choose one of the following interpretations of *Don Quixote* and discuss:

   A. Don Quixote is a comic character, created purely for our entertainment.

   B. Don Quixote is a Christian hero who lives by his faith despite many trials and temptations.

   C. Don Quixote is an existential hero, who through sheer willpower imposes his moral values on an amoral world.

   D. The character of Don Quixote is an excellent psychological portrait of a revolutionary.

3. What does the novel say about romantic love?

4. The famous novel *Madame Bovary* by the French writer Gustave Flaubert has been called a modern version of *Don Quixote*. You might read Flaubert's novel and discuss why you do or do not think the comparison is valid.

Structure and Style

1. Discuss the differences between Part I and Part II of *Don Quixote*. Which part do you prefer?

2. How does Sancho's fondness for proverbs contribute to the story?

3. There is a great deal of slapstick comedy in *Don Quixote*. Choose one or more scenes and explain how the author uses timing, mistaken identities, and suspense to keep the humor moving forward.

Minor Characters

1. Compare Dulcinea and Altisidora.

2. What is Cervantes' attitude toward Maritornes? Is it cruel or compassionate?

3. Do you think Cervantes created the characters of the

Duke and Duchess to criticize the aristocracy in general and the attitudes of wealthy patrons? Or were these characters merely intended as comic devices?

4. What is the symbolic function of Sampson Carrasco's disguise as the "Knight of the Mirrors"? Why is Carrasco sometimes called the "false Quixote"?

5. Did Cervantes believe that the obsolescence of chivalry was a tragedy? Or did he think its passing was a good thing? Whatever you decide, use evidence from the novel to support your conclusion.

Don Quixote and Sancho

1. Some readers think that Cervantes became aware of the serious implications of Don Quixote's character only after his book was partly written. Can you find any evidence to support this idea?

2. Why does Don Quixote die?

3. In what ways does Don Quixote continue to resemble Alonso Quixano, even in his madness?

4. Why does Don Quixote cry when he sees the peasant girl who is supposed to be his Dulcinea?

5. Find three incidents in the story in which Sancho tries to trick Don Quixote. What are his motives in each incident? How do such incidents show Sancho's developing character?

6. Were you surprised when Sancho turned out to be a wise governor of his island. Why or why not?

Further Reading
CRITICAL WORKS

There have been many English language translations of *Don Quixote*—the first, by Thomas Shelton, appeared in 1612–20. Two excellent recent translations that convey the texture of Cervantes' style are by J. M. Cohen (available in a Penguin paperback edition) and Walter Starkie (available in a Signet paperback). Another notable recent translation is by Samuel Putnam.

Of the numerous good biographies of Cervantes you might enjoy *Cervantes* by Melveena McKenrick (Boston: Little Brown, 1980) and Richard Predmore's life, also titled *Cervantes* (New York: Dodd, Mead, 1973). Most histories of Spanish literature, as well as surveys of world literature, devote chapters to Cervantes. Also, novelists who turn to criticism seem to be attracted to *Don Quixote*. The list below covers just a few of the better-known critical essays and specialized studies.

Allen, John Jay. *Don Quixote: Hero or Fool?* Gainesville, Florida: University of Florida Press, 1969.

Brenan, Gerald. *The Literature of the Spanish People.* London: Cambridge University Press, 1951.

Cervantes: His Life, His Times, His Works. (Created by the editors of Arnoldo Mondadori Editore.) New York: American Heritage Press, 1970. A popular survey, it includes photos of La Mancha and illustrations of seventeenth-century Spanish art.

Chesterton, G. K. *A Handful of Authors.* New York: Sheed & Ward, 1952. The author blames Cervantes for "killing" chivalry.

Close, Anthony. *The Romantic Approach to Don Quixote.* Cambridge: Cambridge University Press, 1977. A survey of nineteenth-century views of Cervantes.

Duran, Manuel. *Cervantes.* Boston: Twayne Publishers, 1974. Includes a good survey of the various critical views of Don Quixote.

Flores, Angel and M. J. Benardete. *Cervantes Across the Centuries*. New York, Gordian Press. Essays by Americo Castro, Miguel de Unamuno, and others.

Krutch, Joseph Wood. *Five Masters*. Bloomington, Indiana: Indiana University Press, 1930, 1961.

Nabokov, Vladimir. *Lectures on Don Quixote*. Edited by Fredson Bowers. New York: Harcourt Brace Jovanovich, 1983. Interesting if at times individualistic criticism by a great writer.

Nelson, Lowry, ed. *Cervantes: A Collection of Critical Essays*. Englewood Cliffs, N.J.: Prentice-Hall, 1969.

Northup, George Tyler. *An Introduction to Spanish Literature*. Chicago: University of Chicago Press, 1925.

Van Doren, Mark. *Don Quixote's Profession*. New York: Columbia University Press, 1958. Van Doren suggests that Don Quixote is an actor who adopts madness as part of his role.

AUTHOR'S OTHER WORKS

In addition to *Don Quixote*, Cervantes wrote poetry, other novels, novellas, and dozens of plays (many of which have been lost). Major works include

La Galatea, a pastoral romance (1585)
Exemplary Novels, a collection of novellas (1613)
Voyage to Parnassus, a long poem (1614)
Eight Plays and Eight New Interludes (1615)
The Travels of Persiles and Sigismunda, a novel (published posthumously in 1617)

If you want to go beyond *Don Quixote*, you would probably do best to begin with Walter Starkie's translation of the *Exemplary Novels*. The translation is called *The Deceitful Marriage and Other Exemplary Tales* (New York: New American Library, 1963).

The standard edition of Cervantes' complete works in Spanish was compiled by R. Schevill and A. Bonilla y San Martín. The 19 volumes of the *Obras completas* were published between 1914 and 1941.

Glossary

Alonso Fernandez de Avellaneda The pen name of the author of the spurious sequel to Part I of *Don Quixote*.

Amadís of Gaul The most famous chivalric romance in the Spanish language. The adventures of Amadís and his lady love Oriana take place in Wales, the setting of the legends of King Arthur.

Arcadia Originally a district in ancient Greece, the home of the god Pan. By Cervantes' time Arcadia was known as a mythical land of happy shepherds and shepherdesses, the setting of many of the pastoral romances.

Bachelor A title accorded to university students who had completed a certain portion of their studies.

Biscayan (Basque) In Cervantes' time the people of the Basque country had a reputation for being plain-spoken, honest, and a bit humorless.

"Here Tyrians and Trojans all were silent" The opening line of Book Two of Virgil's *Aeneid*. A good example of Cervantes' use of classical references for humorous contrast, this heroic line introduces the ridiculous episode of the puppet show in Part II, Chapter 26.

Hippogriff A winged horse with the head of an eagle.

The Holy Brotherhood A kind of lodge whose members were sworn to keep the highways safe from bandits.

The Holy Office The official name of the Inquisition, a group of officials appointed by the Pope to stamp out heresy. In the beginning, the Spanish arm of the Inquisition concentrated on punishing converted Jews and Moslems who practiced their former religions in secret. Later, its duties included censorship.

Knight-errant A knight who has taken to the road in search of adventure.

La Mancha An arid, thinly populated region of central Spain. The people of La Mancha (known as Manchegans) were considered backward and unsophisticated, so the concept of a knight-errant calling himself Don Quixote de La Mancha was something of a joke.

Lazarillo de Tormes The title and main character of the most famous of the picaresque novels—tales of lower-class rogues who lived by their wits. Gines de Pasamonte compares himself to Lazarillo.

Mambrino's Helmet The legend of King Mambrino and his helmet can be found in *Orlando Furioso* by Ariosto.

Maravedi A copper coin worth very little.

Melisendra (also spelled Melisande or Melusina) The heroine of perhaps the best-known French chivalric romance. The heroine of Gines de Pasamonte's puppet show does not necessarily bear any resemblance to the original heroine.

Moor A North African Muslim. The Moors conquered Spain in the eighth century and held most of it until the thirteenth century. The last Moorish stronghold in Spain was conquered at the end of the fifteenth century.

Morisco A Moor who converted to Christianity. Spain's Moriscos were descendants of the Moorish invaders who had conquered Spain. By Cervantes' time they were a despised minority.

Mr. Merryman This nickname, which the Don gives to Sancho, recalls the custom of referring to a knight's companions in arms as "merry men."

Orlando Furioso A chivalric romance (dealing with the Medieval hero Roland) written in the form of an epic poem. The Italian author, Ludovico Ariosto, was known for his sophisticated wit. A number of incidents in *Don Quixote*, including the adventure in the Sierra Moreno, parody episodes in this famous poem, which appeared in 1532.

Rhadamanthus Along with Minos, two of the mythological judges of hell.

Roland One of Charlemagne's commanders and, according to legend, a hero of the Christian forces that in the eighth century defended Europe against Moorish invaders (in fact, Roland fought the Basques). His exploits are recounted in the French *Chanson de Roland* (Song of Roland) and the Italian *Orlando Furioso* (Roland is Furious).

Santiago and close! A Spanish battle cry. Santiago was Saint James, the patron saint of Spain. "Close" was an exhortation to close in on enemy lines.

"Sleeves are good even after Easter" A Spanish proverb meaning "better late than never."

Tirant lo Blanch (Tirante the White) The title of a romance written in the Catalán language. It was said to be one of Cervantes' favorite books. See the comments made about it in Part I, Chapter 7.

The Critics

> There is no one so stupid as to praise *Don Quixote*.
> —Lope de Vega, Cervantes'
> contemporary and rival

This harsh judgment of *Don Quixote* was unusual, even for its times. Nevertheless, it reflects the general tendency of the early readers of *Don*

Quixote to see the novel as a comic entertainment, unworthy of serious criticism. A few critics today still insist that *Don Quixote* should be read for its humor alone.

In the nineteenth century, the majority opinion on the novel swung to the opposite extreme. Readers found the novel almost unbearably sad and poignant. Typical of this reaction was the comment of the critic John Ruskin, who said: "*Don Quixote* always affected me throughout to tears, not laughter. It was always throughout real chivalry to me: . . . and because all true chivalry is thus by implication accused of madness and involved in shame that I find the book so deadly."

George Tyler Northup in his *Introduction to Spanish Literature* (1925) summarizes the twentieth-century view of the Cervantes masterpiece:

> The vast majority of critics have considered *Don Quixote* the greatest novel ever written. What are the qualities which give it this pre-eminence? Other novels show more carefully constructed plots, greater perfection of technique, characters more perfectly drawn, a deeper philosophy, a style more polished. These very limitations contribute to its universality. It appeals to both the cultured and the uncultured. It was addressed to no narrow group. . . . What makes it appeal to all countries, to all ages, and to all classes is that it taps the well-springs of human nature, and human nature is the same everywhere.

The Spanish philosopher José Ortega y Gasset, in *Meditations on Don Quixote* (1914), discussed Quixote as a Christ-like figure:

> The figure of Don Quixote, set in the middle of the work like an antenna which picks up all the allusions, has attracted exclusive attention, to the detriment of the rest of the book, and, consequently,

to the character himself. . . . in a certain way, Don
Quixote is the sad parody of a more divine and
serene Christ: he is a Gothic Christ, torn by modern
anguish; a ridiculous Christ of our own neighbor-
hood, created by a sorrowful imagination which has
lost its innocence and its will and is striving to re-
place them.

Gerald Brenan stresses the influence of Erasmus
and other Renaissance thinkers on Cervantes and
sees *Don Quixote* as the portrait of a revolutionary:

Its subject is militant—which is as much to say revolutionary—faith. It explains the psychology of the
believing and half-believing man with a subtlety and
penetration not approached by any other writer. If
one wanted a modern equivalent, one could rename
it the adventures of the [Communist] party man and
his fellow traveller. And where do its sympathies
lie? The revolutionary is the hero of the book, yet
its author has not only made him mad, but casts
doubt on the purity of his motives. . . . [Neverthe-
less,] With all his failings, Don Quixote towers above
the other characters as the one great and noble man
in the book.

The noted American critic Joseph Wood Krutch,
in *Five Masters* (1930), calls attention to the novel's
realism, which makes it an honorable progenitor
of the modern novel:

But he [Cervantes], on the other hand, could not
but be aware that *Don Quixote* violated the literary
canons of his age. Outwardly it was nearer to the
picaresque romance than to anything else—it was
strung upon a thread of comic misadventures and
it not only dealt realistically with the common people but carried such realism further than it had ever
been carried before—yet it touched upon high things
which had no place among the vulgarities of the
picaresque romance and it seemed to strive for that
synthesis of the comedy and tragedy of life which

we recognize as the distinguishing mark of the modern novel. . . .

The following are two recent views of *Don Quixote*.

Both parts of *Don Quixote* form a veritable encyclopedia of cruelty. From that viewpoint it is one of the most bitter and barbarous books ever penned. And its cruelty is artistic. The extraordinary commentators who talk through their academic caps or birettas of the humorous and humane mellowly Christian atmosphere of the book, or a happy world where 'all is sweetened by the humanities of love and good fellowship,' and particularly those who talk of a certain 'kindly duchess' who 'entertains the Don' in the second Part—these gushing experts have probably been reading some other book or are looking through some rosy gauze at the brutal world of Cervantes' novel.

> Vladimir Nabokov, *Lectures on Don Quixote*, 1983

Don Quixote may have failed at the herculean task of rebuilding his society: he managed at the very least to establish in his own mind, and perhaps also in the mind of his readers, the legitimacy of dreams and protest. It is undeniably true that we would seek in vain for a precise conclusion, a moral to the fable. The fact that many messages, often contradictory, have been found, seems to prove that we can approach Cervantes' meaning only 'through a glass, darkly.' Lord Byron thought that Cervantes' novel had sounded the death knell for the Spanish heroic spirit and therefore had accelerated the political decadence of Spain. The authors of the modern musical comedy, *Man of La Mancha*, on the contrary, believe that the enthusiasm and idealism of the knight are infectious: Sancho and Dulcinea, somehow, will continue the struggle and the quest.

> Manuel Duran, *Cervantes*, 1974

NOTES

NOTES

NOTES